MW01128398

KING'S RANSOM

A DARK BRATVA ROMANCE (RUTHLESS DOMS)

JANE HENRY

J. HENRY ROMANCE PUBLICATIONS

KING'S RANSOM: A Dark Bratva Romance (Ruthless Doms)

By: Jane Henry

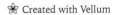

SYNOPSIS

USA Today bestselling author Jane Henry delves deep into the Russian underworld, with a high-stakes, heart-rending story of betrayal, atonement, and a hard-won happily-ever-after

He'll make me call him daddy.

Demand my obedience.

Drive me to my knees.

I've been in love with Stefan Morozov for as long as I can remember.

He's fearless. Powerful. A vicious leader of the Bratva underworld.

And he barely notices my existence.

That is, until the day I see something I shouldn't.

The day the man I love makes me his prisoner.

The day my love turns to hate...

FOREWORD

Please note: although this novel is fictional and deliberately dark in tone, many of the details included in this book are drawn from real life: namely, the large influx of Afghani refugees to Russia and the dangers they face. While researching this book, I was inspired by the bravery and perseverance of these refugees despite overwhelming odds. It's my hope that I managed to address the very real and heartbreaking circumstances behind my fictional world with care and respect. Thank you for taking this journey with me.

Jane

Chapter 1

Stefan

IT'S BEEN TOO LONG since we've encountered conflict. Too long since we've had a skirmish or a battle. We've had nothing but peace, and though I appreciate these moments of quiet, I know Bratva life well. I don't trust the quiet.

I walk the grounds of our compound observing everything. Everyone. Who's home for the night, who isn't, if anything's out of place. As *pakhan,* I'm father to all and ever vigilant. Trusting no one, I'm always alert for the hint of anything that might put my men, my brothers, my son in danger.

Something's wrong. Like the quiet before a storm, the still air tonight holds the promise of uncertainty.

Amaliya called me a pessimist. She said I saw a threat in the very moving of the clouds in the sky. But Amaliya is now dead. I'm arguably more guarded than before she was killed.

There are rhythms and cadences, what others might call ups and downs, in Bratva life. It's not so much highs and lows, but silences. Any musician will tell you that the quiet places in a composition often have the greatest impact.

So when we hit the lulls, the quiet moments, I'm more alert than ever. I hardly sleep.

For well over thirty years I've been Bratva. I was inducted as a full-fledged member before I graduated high school. We don't induct teenagers into Bratva life anymore, now demanding fluency in Russian, signature ink, and jail time sentences served before we even consider new membership. We've upped the stakes. I'm glad we have. Teenaged boys need to earn their spurs before they dedicate themselves to the Bratva.

I'd killed a man before I'd even lost my virginity. And I swore to fucking God that wouldn't be my son, and it wouldn't be the boys *I* brought into Bratva life. And I've kept my word. Though I still recruit and welcome younger men into our brotherhood, I demand a high school diploma and life experience before I'll even consider a new applicant.

Christ. I'm getting too old for this shit. At least that's what I tell myself. I'm barely over fifty, having had Nicolai in my early twenties, but being Bratva since adolescence ages a man.

I sigh, scrub a hand across my brow, and make a mental note to have the landscaping team trim back the bushes by the main entrance. They obscure my vision.

I can't shake this feeling I have. My instincts say shit's about to go down, and soon. I think of calling Nicolai to check on him but stop myself when I swipe the phone on. He's a full-grown adult with a child and a pregnant wife, and I don't need to be waking him to check ghosts. Soon enough, he'll be giving me hell about getting old and senile. I don't need to start now.

So tonight, I make more than one round of our compound. I check every lock, every window. I sweep the beam of my flashlight in every corner of our interrogation room, though we haven't used it in months. I swear that when I turn away from the ominous darkness, the screams of the men that we've interrogated echo behind me.

We should move this room. It's not hidden well enough.

I even walk back to my office and scan security footage. I see nothing, and almost get up to leave, when a shadow crosses my vision. Someone's awake, moving. I turn back to the screen. It's one from my private home.

I squint at the image. It's a shadow of a woman. I look more closely and breathe out a sigh of relief.

It's only Taara. Of course.

When Taara's mother could no longer fill the task as housekeeper and personal assistant, I hired Taara. I like keeping non-Bratva employees within the same family when possible, and Taara is the most attentive assistant one could have.

My worries forgotten momentarily, I sit back in my chair and watch her. It soothes me, and for a moment, I forget my troubles. She's in the kitchen, wiping down the counters, but she must have some type of music playing in the background, for the girl is dancing like no-one's watching. She knows I have cameras trained on every inch of our property, but I think she either forgets sometimes or no longer cares.

I watch in rapt fascination as she sways her hips and skips to a beat I can't hear. And hell, it's the most beautiful thing I've ever seen.

Born a Russian refugee, Afghani blood runs in her veins. With her exotic dark skin and thick, straight black hair she reminds me of a foreign princess. It's easy enough to imagine her swathed in magenta, her head covered in a traditional *chador*.

If she were mine, I'd dress her in a burka. I'd cover every inch of her stunning beauty.

My phone rings, shaking me out of my reverie. I don't know what the fuck is wrong with me, letting my mind wander like that. Taara is young enough to be my daughter, *and* she's my employee. I heave a sigh.

It's been way too long since I've had a woman warm my bed. I'll have to do something about that before I make a decision I fucking regret.

I glance at the image of Taara one more time as I answer my phone.

"Yes?"

"It's me."

Nicolai. He never calls me this late. He should be at home with his expectant wife. I scowl at the screen.

"Nicolai." My gut instinct tells me this is the call that brings the cadence of Bratva life back into full swing. "What is it?"

"Tonight, Marissa went shopping with Laina. The plan was for them to stay at a local hotel, as we're several hours away from home."

I wait for the other shoe to drop.

"They were attacked in the parking lot."

"Jesus." I'm on my feet, willing myself to be patient, to hear the rest of the story before I act. "Are they alright?"

"Yes. They had three men on them, and what their assailant didn't realize was that *I* was one of them."

Of course. He's training one of our youngest new recruits. I wait to hear more details.

"I insisted we take the man back to our compound. I've got him in the car with me now, and I'll take him to the interrogation room, but I don't need a fucking interrogation room for me to tell you who he is."

His voice is hard, the tone he gets before he's about to make a ruthless, irrevocable decision. I hear a muffled voice in the background, a hard *thump,* then silence.

"You know who he is then."

I watch Taara spin and swirl on the screen in front of me in rhythmic circles. So pretty. So innocent. In such contrast to the violent world outside her door.

"I do. He's one of the fucking traitors that worked with Myron."

"*Christ.*" Myron, Marissa's father, would have been Nicolai's father-in-law. Several years back, he sold his daughter into slavery to pay off a debt. Nicolai systematically tracked down every fucking traitor who worked with Myron and eliminated them so none would pose a possible threat to his wife. Or so he thought.

"I was under the impression you got all of them."

"So did I. I wouldn't have settled until I did. But he's said enough that it's obvious. He's said *way* too much."

"Are Marissa and Laina taken care of?"

"Yeah. I secured Marissa and Laina. Now I'm heading home with this motherfucker."

Home. That's here.

I swallow hard. I don't want another man's blood on my son's hand. Not again. "I'll be waiting. I'll deal with him for you."

Taara puts the broom away, then comes back to the kitchen with a rag, wiping down the counters and appliances. I didn't know she did this at night, but it makes sense. She keeps my home impeccable.

I don't like having this conversation with Nicolai while Taara is right there. Though she can't hear me, and isn't privy to our conversation, it feels wrong. I want to keep her safe, and well insulated against any threat that could harm her.

"No. I know why you're offering, but I can't allow it. If I'm to take over as *pakhan*, you need to allow me to do this." He takes in a deep breath, and I feel a sense of pride rise in me at my son's words, despite my desire to keep his hands clean of this. "And anyway, this is my battle to fight."

When the time comes, he'll be ready to assume the role of *pakhan*.

I nod even though he can't see me. "Where are you?"

"On the road, and I'll be home in a few hours, but once I arrive, I'd like you to give me time with him before you join me."

I automatically nod again. He wants to be sure no one else is implicated before he kills him.

Neither of us will sleep tonight.

"Let me know."

I hang up the phone, staring unseeingly at the dancing girl on the monitor. I don't want her to suspect anything's awry. I'll go back to my home and spend the next hour doing what I normally do, my evening ritual. I'll let her think I've gone to bed.

Then I'll join my son and witness the execution.

Chapter 2

Taara

I WAIT for Stefan until the wee hours of the morning. I've cleaned every room, and left the fire burning in the hearth. Though it's warm in Atlanta in springtime, the evenings sometimes get a little cold, and Stefan likes to relax by the fire.

I always wait up for him.

He works hard, often staying up until late in the night to make sure that the men under his care are well taken care of. That whatever job or task of the day well finished. Like a father, he looks out for his brood of men of the brotherhood with steadfast care and concern until everyone's settled for the night. And when all has finally been put to rest, he pours himself a shot of vodka, sits in front of his fireplace, and drinks it in silence before bed. He never wavers in this ritual.

I wonder what he thinks about then.

He's had the same nightly ritual since I've started working for him, though I suspect he's done it even longer than that. I never knew what he did at night when I was a little girl. I just remember him bringing me sweets or books when he traveled, and taking very good care of me and my mother.

Tonight, I watch him from the top landing where my bedroom lies. I don't interrupt him. I don't speak to him. I don't let him know I'm even here.

Stefan doesn't know how I feel about him, and it's better this way.

Hell, *I* didn't know how I felt about him until about a year ago. And to be honest? I think I've been in denial about it.

My mother fled to Russia as an Afghani refugee when I was just a child. I don't remember anything about our trip to Russia. All I know is that when I came to this country, I spoke English with a Russian accent, even though I look as if I don't have a drop of Russian blood in me. Not now, though. That was years ago. Few would ever suspect my roots.

I don't know who my father was. My mother told me so little. But given her obsession with the men of the Russian Bratva, I suspect that my roots aren't purebred Afghani.

In Russia, my mother fell in love with a man of the brotherhood. And when he moved to America, she followed. She never pursued him, though. Theirs as not a love story but a tragedy, as her love for him remained unrequited. Destined to fulfill the Bratva mission to marry strong, he wed someone else. I don't know who and never will, now that my mother's left to wisps of memory and broken thoughts, her mind consumed by Alzheimer's, in one of Atlanta's most prominent assisted living facilities.

Stefan saw to that.

It's reason number one why I love him.

As she was one of the most dedicated staff to his brotherhood, when my mother became too frail to work, and too mentally ill to care for herself, he ensured she was well taken care of. As for me, he kept me on as paid staff. I graduated college last year, the youngest in my class, but I didn't pursue the arts as I'd thought. I assumed the role of caretaker for Stefan's home, a job that fills me with immense pride.

The Atlanta brotherhood owns a sprawling estate, dotted with multiple small houses, apartments scattered about like flowers in a garden. Various members of the brotherhood are single, but some begin married life here at the compound. Stefan's son Nicolai and his wife Marissa have. They had one child together, and Marissa's expecting another baby now. I love the way Stefan takes care of his family with such steadfast devotion.

Reason number two why I love him.

Honestly? I could tally these all night long.

I don't lie to myself. Stefan does evil, wicked things. I know he does. I've seen some with my own eyes, though he's tried to hide them. The man commands a brotherhood of ruthless, fearless soldiers. Though they keep the details of the work they do hidden, I'm no fool. I know they skirt the law and outright flaunt it regularly.

But I refuse to believe a man with eyes that blue, that impassioned, that a man who takes such tender care of my mother, could ever be anything but redeemed in the end.

Tonight, I watch as he pours two shots. I observe silently from my position on the landing and admire him from afar. And I allow my mind to wander, to fantasize about what it would be like to sit on that couch beside him. To share a drink. We wouldn't even have to talk. Just sitting beside him would be enough.

From where I'm crouched, I can see his muscled legs stretched out before him, his feet clad in thick black boots. The jeans he wears are faded, but well mended. I see to that. My eyes travel up the length of his body, to his trim waist and torso, enhanced by the black t-shirt he wears. He folds his arms on his chest, and his muscles bulge. Strong and built, he keeps his body in top form. I've seen Stefan outlift the younger men in his brother-hood. He's got tinges of silver in his hair and beard, but his eyes are that of a much younger man. Kind. Probing. Brilliant.

Though he maintains a fatherly air with all of them, there's good reason he keeps himself in such impeccable shape. Not one of them would cross him.

Last year, when we got my mom situated in her new facility, one of the orderlies decided to give me a hard time about going in to see her. Fortunately, Stefan was with me. One look at him, adorned with signature Bratva ink, and muscles for *days,* and the jerk forgot how to speak.

"There a problem here?" Stefan had asked in his deep, rumble of a voice.

"No, sir."

Only there was a problem because *I* had forgotten how to speak, too.

But I got my act together and thanked him.

Maybe my mother would scold me for loving a man old enough to be my father. But I've never been one attracted to younger, less seasoned men. To be honest? I've never been attracted to any other man but the one brooding in front of the fireplace before me.

I want his bed to be prepared for him when he finally turns in tonight, so I creep away as quietly as I can and go to his room. I inhale deeply as I enter his personal space, because it smells like him in here. Strong and masculine and fearless, bold like a wind-swept prairie or snow-capped mountain. My senses come alive with vivid visceral awareness.

I'll admit, I've got it bad. I've got it *so bad*.

I swallow and stand here, inhaling and exhaling, while I look about his room.

Stefan is a moderately tidy man, but I enjoy when he leaves things about, so I have an excuse to clean up after him. There's a scattered pair of boots by the door, a jacket shrugged off, and coins and bills strewn on his bedside table. Quickly, efficiently, I place the coins in a little basket alongside the bills that I fold, then I straighten his shoes and place them by the door. Next, I go to the bed and smooth out the covers. I fluff his pillows and turn down one corner of the sleek black duvet.

I close my eyes, resting my hand on his bed, indulging in one brief second of fantasy before I leave.

I'd slip into "something a little more comfortable" before

he came to bed. Maybe a pale ivory nightie would complement the dark skin I inherited from my mother. I'd sweep my long, thick black hair into a braid, and climb into bed beside him. I sigh. My fantasy only *borders* the sexual. Just imagining lying beside his strong, strapping body, massaging the tension from his shoulders, and inhaling his scent before bed has me heady with awareness and longing.

I would die if he ever knew what I fantasize about. I would shrivel up and literally *die*. Change my name and go into witness protection or something.

He would maybe think I were some sort of stalker, but I swear I'm not. There's a major difference between admirer and stalker, and I know where I stand.

"Taara?"

I jump when I hear Stefan's rumbling voice from the doorway behind me.

"Oh! I didn't hear you coming," I say nervously. I turn to face him. He stands in the doorway, leaning one hip against the frame with his arms crossed on his chest. Piercing blue eyes meet mine, but they're kind and a little curious, and so tired I want to take his hand and lead him to bed myself.

Was I sniffing his sheets? Stroking them lovingly?

God.

He only smiles at me, those blue eyes crinkling around the edges making my heart flutter in my chest.

"You're a good girl," he says gently. "I appreciate that you take the time to prepare my room for me." His voice is deep and husky with exhaustion, but I feel it right down to my very toes.

"Of course, sir," I say to him, bowing my head. My cheeks heat as I make my way to the doorway, closer to *him*, but he grabs my arm when I draw near. I freeze. "Sir?"

Is he angry with me? Did I somehow break a rule?

But when I look at him, he releases my arm.

"There's no need to run away," he says, his brow furrowed. I swallow hard, my heart racing so hard and fast I'm dizzy. "I've been meaning to ask you, how your mother's doing?"

"She's about the same, sir," I say. My voice sounds so soft and quiet following his. "I saw her yesterday. She misses the food of her homeland, but she gets confused. In one sentence, she's asking for *bolani* and the next she's begging for *solyanka*."

He smiles. She hasn't had bolani, the traditional stuffed bread from her home country, in decades, but the common Russian soup she's had more recently.

"In any event, she has no use for the chicken pot pie and burgers they serve at the facility." I smile and feel my cheeks flush deeper, suddenly afraid that I might sound ungrateful. His brotherhood pays for her care, and it's not cheap. "The food is delicious, though. They feed her well. She just misses some things she's had for years."

"I see," he says. "Do you remember Tomas from Boston?"

I nod, a little confused why he's bringing him up. "I know who he is, though I don't believe I've met him."

"He and his wife Caroline will be visiting tomorrow. His wife is a chef and cooks the most delicious traditional Russian food you'll ever eat. I'll have her bring your mother some dishes while she's here."

My heart squeezes and to my embarrassment, my eyes water. "Thank you."

But he's already turning away from me. "Think nothing of it." He's walking toward the bathroom. "Now go to bed, Taara."

His back is to me. I'm dismissed. I feel as if I've been doused with cold water. But it's after midnight, and I don't think my stern Russian master has any patience left for a silly girl like me. Or perhaps there's something on his mind. If there was, I could—*no*.

"Good night," I whisper, as I leave.

I never sleep well, and tonight's no exception. I toss and turn, but don't question whether or not something's amiss. It's normal for me to have disrupted sleep. I spin things in my mind, my fears about my mother's wellbeing, whether or not I spoke out of turn to Stefan.

As usual, I sleep fitfully, until finally I wake in the early hours of the morning, somewhere deep in the shadows between midnight and sunrise. I yawn, roll over, and sigh. I might as well get up and start making Stefan's breakfast.

But I blink in the darkness when I think I hear a door open and shut. Did I imagine that?

I always get up before Stefan and spend some of the morning in the solitude of the garden. I've been taking pictures of the blooming spring flowers, and making a collage of the photos at morning, midday, and dusk. I have a full week's worth catalogued.

I sit up in bed and pad to the doorway. I open it, listening. The fire has died out. I must've imagined the noise. Quiet reigns over the grounds as I step outside, dressed still in my pajamas and holding my phone switched onto camera. I frown when I turn the door handle. It's unlocked. Stefan *never* leaves the doors unlocked.

I quietly shut the door behind me and make my way to the garden. It's so early, it's hard to see my way, but I know this path by heart by now. I go to the arched walkway at the foot of the garden, surrounded by bushes and shrubbery and trees, all in early spring bloom. I use the camera on my phone, as it takes excellent shots, and I aim it to take a photo when I hear voices approaching.

I freeze, panicked.

They're coming closer.

Oh, *God*. I'm not alone.

I don't know who it is, but the men who live here are dangerous, and I don't want to be seen. And as the voices draw closer, I can hear them, angry and hushed, and someone is whimpering.

Oh *God*.

Just in time, I fall to the ground and scurry behind a shade of bushes. I hope no one can see me. Thankfully, it seems the men are otherwise preoccupied.

I peak through the greenery, shocked to see Stefan and his son Nicolai dragging a man between them. They don't speak, and I can't make out their expressions in the darkness, but the way they're holding the man between them scares me. He's gagged and bound. A prisoner, then.

My breath catches in my throat when the man trips and neither of them stop. They're yanking him along like he's a worthless bag of garbage. Good Lord, I'm terrified. I'm shaking, my belly swirling with nausea.

I don't need to know who he is. I don't need to know what he did.

Stefan and Nicolai are Bratva.

They're going to hurt this man.

Maybe even kill him.

At first, I think they're taking him to the compound, when they turn abruptly and head *straight toward me.*

On hands and knees, I scramble as quietly away from them as I can, but I can still hear them. I will die if they see me. What if they think I'm spying? But the further I go trying to get away, the closer they come. I finally give up, falling to my knees behind the cover of thick shrubbery.

Oh God, *oh God.* I don't know where to go or what to do. I'm shaking, trying to keep as inconspicuous as I can. Clouds shift, and moonlight catches the man's face. His eyes are swollen, his face bloodied. He's already been beaten. They're bringing him here for another reason. I'm shaking so badly I'm frozen in place.

"I don't want our brothers involved in this," Stefan says tightly. "We have his confession. We have him on record admitting he collaborated with Myron. We know he tried to harm Marissa."

Myron. Marissa.

Oh, *God.*

Marissa is Nicolai's wife. She was sold into slavery by her traitorous father Myron. Their story has become legend among the staff. Nicolai gave up everything to hunt down the men who had her, to punish those who stole her, and bought her for his own. He joined another brotherhood under an alias. Nicolai now owes his allegiance to both the Atlanta Bratva and the Boston group. With Stefan's help, they killed her father and every single traitor who was loyal to Myron.

Except, apparently, this one.

Stefan takes out a keyring and inserts a key into a lock. I don't know the area beyond the garden well. Where are they taking him? They open the door and drag the man in behind them. I stare when they shut the door. Have they locked it?

Like the fool that I am, I wait a moment, then scurry toward the door and try the door. It's locked, of course. Why would I even want to go in? I have no doubt I don't want to see what they'll do next, but I can't turn away, like a moth toward flame. That's my Stefan down there and I want to be sure he's okay. But I know there's more to it than that. He's the brutal, fearless *pakhan*. I've never seen him so angry, and though it terrifies me, I'm enthralled.

My gaze falls on a small window. The basement light is on, and I can see everything from where I am. I fall to the ground and creep over on my hands and knees, just in time to see Nicolai force the man into a kneeling position. I stare, unable to move.

I can't hear anything they're saying, but I watch as Stefan paces the room. Nicolai holds the man by the hair and bares his neck. I cringe, my stomach tightening, as the man's mouth drops open. I can imagine his whimpers and pleas.

Stefan steps to the side so I can no longer see his face from where I am.

He issues a short command to Nicolai. Nicolai nods.

I should shield my vision. Although I know the Bratva do wicked things, I've never actually witnessed it with my own eyes. And if I see them… I will myself to go, but I'm frozen in place. I can't even blink or swallow. It's like I'm petrified right here in this position.

I stare at the doorway as Stefan steps toward it, as if to block it. His arms are on his chest and he's watching Nicolai. He nods to him and Nicolai cocks his pistol. The man begins to cry and though I can't hear what he says, I can imagine him swearing his innocence. Though I don't know the story, I suspect he lies. If Stefan has ordered his death, he's no innocent. If these two are going to execute him, there's good reason, I *know* it.

The man sobs. I'm shaking so badly I can't still the trembling in my limbs. The man faces his last moments on earth, probably begging for his life, and even though I know he likely deserves to die, I can't bear to hear it. I cover my ears, not bothering to swipe away the tears that stream down my cheeks. I hate this. I hate knowing Stefan is complicit. I hate seeing this with my own eyes.

Nicolai pulls the trigger. I flinch, expecting an explosive sound, but the shot is almost silent. Despite the fact that they're on their own property, they've chosen to hide this, to use a silencer.

The man's screaming immediately stops. His body falls

to the ground with an ominous, sickening thud. I cover my mouth to stifle the scream that rises within me as Nicolai shoots another round of bullets, each one making the man's body flinch and shudder and crimson blood stain the tattered clothing.

Bile burns the back of my throat, and my stomach clenches with fear and nausea.

I cover my face. I wish I hadn't seen any of this. I want to run away and eradicate this from my mind. This was a terrible, terrible mistake. I'm going to be sick. My hands are wet, and I don't know why, but I quickly forget my predicament when a strong hand comes to my neck. I scream in utter terror when I'm lifted straight up off the ground and into the air. I flail, trying to get away, and can't see who holds me.

"Well, what do we have here?" says a familiar voice. I crane my neck and can barely make out the form of Rafael, Nicolai's best friend. The massive giant of a man plops me down on the ground in front of him, fixes me with a ferocious stare, and pulls out his phone. "Don't you fucking move."

The next minute, he's talking into his phone. "Got you a present, boss."

Chapter 3

Stefan

I HEAR a scuffle outside when my phone rings, but I'm distracted, watching a body on the ground in front of me twitch in the throes of death. It's not a sight one gets used to.

I answer on the first ring. Rafael. He tells me he has a present for me.

"You have a present for me? What the hell are you talking about?"

"Caught someone spying outside the window to the interrogation room."

"Who the fuck was it? We're still down here." It matters. Another brother is a problem easily fixed, someone else another thing altogether.

"I don't know her name. It's that girl that cleans your house?" There's a question in his voice.

Jesus *motherfucking* Christ.

No.

Taara?

Nicolai meets my eyes. He's doing clean-up now, the body already removed, mop in hand. This room is specifically designed for easy clean-up and disposal. Normally, we'd call help to come and do with this sort of work, but we don't want to involve more men from the brotherhood than necessary. That said, we'll tell them all that happened so everyone's abreast of what's gone on.

"What is it?" Nicolai asks, mopping sweat off his brow with the back of his sleeve when the door to the room opens. Rafael enters, dragging in a furious, terrified, disheveled Taara.

Nicolai groans out loud. "You've *got* to be fucking kidding me." He straightens up, glaring at Taara, and I swear to God even though he's my son and I feel about the same as he does, it's all I can do not to deck him for looking at her like that.

"Thought we'd only have one death on our hands tonight," he mutters, wiping his hands on a rag like he's a mechanic who's just finished an oil change. He shakes his head, and Taara starts crying.

"God! Oh my God!" Tears stream down her beautiful face, but she can't wipe them away because Rafael holds her wrists by her side. "I'm so sorry. I didn't mean to see anything. It's… I can't… I'm going to—"

Then she turns to the side, bends over, and literally retches all over the floor.

Nicolai shakes his head. "Mother*fucker.*"

I can't believe she came out here, that she saw this. My hands shake, and I can't decide if I want to turn her over my knee for spying on us, or hold her to me and tell her it's okay. That yeah, she just witnessed brutal, cold-blooded murder, but she'll be alright. That everything will be alright. Instead, I just shake my head and jerk my chin to Rafael.

I want Rafael's hands the fuck off of her.

"Give her to me."

He shoves her in my direction, and I catch her before she falls, her beautiful black hair brushing my arms. I swallow hard. She's in huge trouble, and this isn't going to be easy.

"We can't let her go, boss," Rafael says. "You know how I feel about innocent lives, but she's seen too much."

"I agree," Nicolai says. He's throwing sawdust all over the floor for clean-up, and he won't meet my eyes. "We always abide by the rules."

Why do they think I'm not going to abide by the code of law that binds me to the brotherhood? Do they actually suspect I won't? Then I realize I'm holding the girl to my chest, one hand on her lower back and the other cradling the base of her head, comforting her. I release her, spin her around, and cuff her wrists with my hands.

"Taara's worked for us since she was a child," I say. I look her up and down. She sure as fuck isn't a child anymore.

"Doesn't matter," Nicolai counters. "We don't bend the rules for fucking anyone." Part of me is proud of his insistence on abiding by the Bratva code. He'll make a good *pakhan* someday.

But this is Taara.

"I agree," Rafael says, his eyes on me. "But I know you're partial to the girl. You don't have to do it. I will."

I wish to fucking God I hadn't trained these two so well.

Taara trembles and shakes her head. "I won't say anything to anyone. Oh, God, I promise. I won't! Never." She's sobbing freely now. "Just let me go. You don't want more blood on your hands, do you?"

"Sweetheart, you have no idea how much blood I have on my hands," I tell her. She doesn't. She doesn't have a fucking clue. "Suffice it to say, a little more won't matter."

I have no intention of killing her, but I want her to know how serious this is.

She only cries harder.

I give her a rough shake. "Stop that," I order. "I don't want you throwing up again."

But it isn't just that. I hate how weak I feel, watching a woman like her cry. Taara is an innocent in this.

"What the hell were you doing spying on us?" I say, shaking her between my hands until her teeth rattle, because I'm pissed that she made herself complicit in this. She's put herself in danger... even if that dangers because of me. My men saw her. She deserves to be killed, though her crime is simply being in the wrong place at the wrong time. But if she told the authorities what she'd witnessed, at best, my son's life would be ruined. His child practically fatherless. His wife little more than a single mother, raising their kids while her husband served life in prison. At worst, he'd face the death penalty.

My anger rises, and I shake her again. "Why weren't you in the house? Were you spying?" I want to hurt her.

"I found this," Rafael says, showing me her phone. "And it was on *camera*. She was fucking taking *pictures*."

Nicolai curses and takes a step toward us, the look in his eyes menacing. He knows as well as I do what's at stake. Involuntarily, I pull her to me and shield her from him, moving my own body in front of her.

"Stop," I order Nicolai. "And listen."

His brows shoot up in surprise. He opens his mouth to protest, then closes it and bows his head. He may disagree with my methods or logic, but I'm still his *pakhan*.

"We're not making a hasty decision with her," I tell them. "I want to hear what she has to say." I turn to Taara. "Explain yourself."

She doesn't hesitate. "I come out in the early morning to take photos," she says. "I didn't know you were here until I heard you. Then I'll admit, I did come over here to see what you were doing, but I didn't *mean* to spy. And I'd never, *never* tell anyone *anything*."

"Enough!" Nicolai fumes at her. I feel my nostrils flare and my chest expand with the sharp intake of breath I take to steady myself. My son is a good man, but in this moment he's overwrought.

"Son of a bitch," I mutter. "I don't know what the fuck to do with her."

Rafael cocks his head to the side. "We know what the code declares we need to do."

I do. But I also know I'm *pakhan*. I'm capable of breaking that code if I think I have justifiable reason, and I fucking do.

"I'm not killing her," I state with finality. "No way will I end the life of a woman as dedicated to serving our brotherhood as Taara." She sobs quietly, closing her eyes as if to accept her fate. "And both of you would do the same. I know you would."

Their silence confirms this.

"Fine, then," Rafael says. "We can punish her well and good and send her to another Bratva group." A muscle ticks in his jaw and he flexes his muscles. She cowers against me, likely knowing that punishment at our hands would be swift and severe.

Nicolai still glares, muttering under his breath. "We could send her away to Boston. Tomas would keep her prisoner. I trust him."

But no, I'm not doing that either.

I turn over the options in my mind like a dealer distributing cards. I discard the ones I don't like before I make a decision.

"You will leave Taara to me," I finally say. "I will deal with her. I will see to it she doesn't speak to anyone, and I will be sure she faces punishment for what she's done."

"I didn't mean to, Stefan," she whispers. "I promise."

"When did you know we had a prisoner with us?" I ask her, my tone razor sharp. It angers me that she put me in this position, and have a hard time believing that she's innocent. Why didn't she leave well enough alone?

In Bratva life, you learn that betrayal runs deep, that few are to be trusted, and that appearances aren't always what they seem. For all I know, she's a spy hired by a rival, and she lies.

She looks away and bites her lip, a dead giveaway to guilt. Without another word, I yank her out in front of me and slam my palm against the fullest part of her ass. "Answer me."

She yelps out loud, then her eyes go wide and fearful.

"After I came outside," she whispers. "I just came to take some pictures of the flowers. I swear I didn't take any of you."

"She lies, sir," Rafael says, shaking his head and swiping through her phone. "There are several of you and Nicolai both."

Son of a *bitch*.

Her thick obsidian hair is wrapped around my fingers, and I pull so hard she comes up on her toes to escape the pain. I hate that she betrayed me. It's hard enough knowing I have few friends in this world, that enemies press in on all sides, but when someone I trust betrays me, it's a twisted knife wound straight to the heart. I've learned to dull the pain, but this one burns.

"No!" she screams on a sob when I yank her by the hair again, pulling her toward me.

"I will have the truth if I need to whip it out of you," I hiss. "I despise a spy."

"I'm not a spy," she sobs. "I promise. Oh, God, you have to believe me. Stefan," she chokes. "It was an accident."

I nod my head to Rafael and hold Taara tightly. "Get the restraints." I look toward Nicolai. "You finish the clean-up. We'll summon our men once she's been dealt with."

"Do you need any other tools, sir?" Rafael asks. His narrowed eyes are focused on her though he's speaking to me. He would do anything I asked of him, including extracting the truth from her himself if I wanted.

But no. I'll deal with her personally.

"Fetch me a cane."

"Of course," he says with a frown, giving her a stern look. He likely thinks a spanking is taking things far too easy on her, but I don't give a fuck what he thinks. I have questions that need answers, and I won't mindlessly take another human life. Not tonight. Not yet. And if my suspicions are right, a woman like Taara will cave when punished.

Rafael returns with a thin, supple rod in one hand, and a pair of shining silver handcuffs in the other.

"Thank you," I tell him, as casually as if he just fetched me a cup of coffee. I slide the cane into my back pocket and open the metal rings with my free hand.

I almost lose my resolve when her tear-stained eyes meet mine. "Stefan, please," she begs in a small voice that breaks.

I've heard pleas before. I've been betrayed by those I thought I could trust. And if she's innocent, a punishment meant to extract the truth won't have a lasting effect. She may never forgive me, but it's a risk I'm willing to take.

I don't respond but lift her arms up to a post that's so high over her head I pull her to her tiptoes. We have rings fitted for just this purpose, though our prisoners usually face a worse fate than she does.

I can still see every single captive we've ever held here. I can still hear every scream, every plea. It's unnerving the way a man's deep voice becomes shrill and feminine under duress, or hoarse with begging. We reserve the more severe methods of extracting truth from our most hardened adversaries. Old-fashioned means of inflicting pain works most effectively for those on the cusp of caving. Taara won't need severe methods.

In this room, I've been both witness and executioner. I've meted out pain and ordered others to do so, though it's never been someone so young, so fragile, so fucking beautiful. But I haven't made it to my level of power by quaking in the face of duty.

I snap the rings on her wrists and take one stolen moment to admire the beautiful sight before me. Her vivacious, curvy form still clad in thin cotton shorts dotted with daisies, so ironically innocent, and a tiny ivory tank top against stunning dark skin the color of cream-laced coffee. She has a birthmark on her upper left thigh peeking out just below the hem of her shorts. I never noticed how long and slender her fingers were until I saw them gripped on the bar to support herself. In another life, she could have been a pianist or a sculptor with hands like that.

Standing behind her, I tap the cane on the palm of my hand. Even the lightest touch on my toughened skin ignites a flare of pain. I imagine painting her body with stripes from the cane in foreplay, bringing her to the edge of orgasm until she begged daddy to let her come.

Whoa.

Christ.

Where the ever-loving fuck did that thought come from?

I can't entertain that thought tonight. Hell, not ever. She's young enough to be my fucking daughter, and worse, I'm about to punish her for betrayal.

I snap the cane on my palm again to school my own thoughts and temptations. To remind myself of my purpose.

The slim tool concentrates all impact on such a small surface area, it hurts like hell, making it very effective for certain methods of interrogation and punishment. In kink circles, it's considered one of the most severe tools for impact play. The cane has a deep history as a successful tool for punishment across Europe and Asia.

We have other, far harsher methods of punishment and interrogation at our disposal, and I'm experienced in yielding every one of them.

I take my position behind her. Rafael stands with his arms crossed on his chest, watching, and Nicolai, now finished with his job, stands beside him with the same stern, immovable expression on his face. I hold his gaze for a moment, then he nods. As *pakhan*, I don't need permission from either of them, but I don't want to punish Taara. Still, knowing they stand behind me in solidarity makes it easier to follow through.

I turn back to Taara, rear back, and snap the slender rod

against her ass. Though it has little impact, I know the pain level is intense. She flinches, howls, and squirms in the restraints, but she can't get away.

I pause. "Tell us why you were here."

"I told you!" she says, a note of anger in her voice now. "I came out here to take pictures."

I nod. "Yes, but I want the real reason. So, you didn't know we were out here when you came?"

Silence.

I snap the cane on her again.

"*Ow!*"

"Answer me."

She says nothing for a full minute. Steeling myself, I lift the rod and bring it down with deliberate, steady strokes. I know how to wield this implement, each line of pain building on the next. It would be more effective on bare skin, but the shorts she wears are so thin I doubt they provide much of a barrier, and there's no fucking way I'm baring this girl in front of Rafael and Nicolai. After the sixth stroke of the cane, she screams.

"Okay. Okay! Oh, God, stop. Please, Stefan." She's breathing heavily, panting, and a bead of sweat runs down her nose. It falls off her chin and splashes on the concrete floor.

I pause, the cane tucked under my arm when I cross my arms on my chest. Christ, my cock's a rod of steel. I hate that I've gotten a hard-on punishing her like this. I don't want this to be sexual. We aren't alone and this is no foreplay, but it's undeniably erotic having her under my control before my men.

I ignore the deep desire to punish her and keep my tone aloof and stern. "Let's hear it."

"I—I did know you were here. But I was just curious. I never intended on actually witnessing anything. I had no idea what you were going to do. Just listen!"

"I've got all night," I say with forced nonchalance, my teeth clenched. I hate that she's put me in this position, and I'm eager to mete out the rest of the punishment she's earned for doing this, for putting me in this position, for risking her very fucking *life* by being here.

"I came out to take pictures of the flowers. It's true, I swear! Swipe through my pictures and you'll see."

I nod to Rafael, who does just that. He nods as he scrolls through the images on her phone. "Before the one of you and Nicolai, there are mostly flower pictures." He pauses, then surprises me when he smiles. "Though there are a few here you might want to see yourself."

"Nooo," Taara whispers. "*Shit.*" She whispers, then she closes her eyes and one lone tear rolls down her cheek.

What the hell is this? Why is he amused and why does she look so pained?

"Hand me the phone." I reach for it with my palm facing up, and Taara starts to flail in her restraints.

"Stefan," she says, a note of real panic rising in her voice. "No! Oh, please don't look, please sir, I beg you." But her pleading only solidifies my decision to see what Rafael did. What is she hiding?

The first few pictures are, as he said, of me and Nicolai, but they're blurred and at an odd angle. Several more before that are all flowers, confirming what she's told us, but when I continue to swipe, I feel my brows rise heavenward.

Why does she have so many pictures of me on her phone?

I'm dozing by the fire in one, smiling at someone in the distance in another, and a third is an older shot of me in my younger years.

It's unnerving. I've gone from thinking of her as no more than an employee, to believing she was an enemy, to now wondering what her intentions are.

"Seems you have more to answer for than I thought," I say, taking up my position once more. I hate that she's done this. She should be safely tucked away in her bedroom, away from all of this, apart from me. I'm tempted to dismiss her, but she's seen too much. She knows too much.

"Why the hell did you take pictures of me and Nicolai?"

"By accident! I swear!"

She's lying. The pictures of me on her phone are not accidental.

I let the cane fly.

She sobs and twists in her restraints but can't get away from the harsh strokes.

"Look! Look at them!" she screams.

I pause. "Look at what?"

"The other pictures. I take good pictures. Why the hell would I take such a bad picture of you and Nicolai? My camera was open and on and I must've accidentally taken some. Delete them!" She sniffs. "I don't want them. And I won't tell anyone."

"How do we know that to be true?"

She doesn't answer at first.

I cane her again.

She screams and writhes. "Because I'm loyal to the brotherhood! Because I believe if any of you kill someone, it's justified, and you had good reason." She sobs. "Because I'd rather die than betray you!"

I turn to Rafael and shake my head. "Destroy her phone," I order.

"No! Oh, God. Please don't!" she begs. "I'll lose all my pictures. You can't just—"

But I'm out of patience. "Quiet!" I snap, emphasizing my command with a sharp cut of the cane. She flinches, then falls into silence and hangs her head.

"Destroy her phone," I repeat to Rafael. "Be sure no pictures are stored remotely. I am not convinced of her innocence or her guilt, so she'll remain in my custody."

Rafael drops her phone to the ground before digging his heel through the glass. She flinches but doesn't speak. He lifts his foot and brings it down again and again, until all that remains are bits of shattered glass and metal.

"Nicolai, call a meeting," I tell him. "I want everyone here within the hour. It is best if we keep everyone apprised of what's happened so there are no questions, and no one suspects foul play."

Though there are times I need to keep certain decisions hidden, and initially wondered if what happened in this room tonight was one of those times, I value transparency in the brotherhood. I want my men to know they can trust me. We also found out information in our interrogation that has a direct impact on all of us, and it's time I made them aware. Though I make the final decisions, I prefer hearing input from those who are loyal to me.

Nicolai nods and takes his leave.

"Rafael, Tomas and Caroline arrive at the airport at nine o'clock. I planned on fetching them myself, but since I'll be otherwise occupied, I'll ask that you go and arrange to bring them back here."

"Yes, sir." I wait until Nicolai and Rafael leave before I turn back to her.

A part of me longs to end her punishment now, to draw her to my chest and soothe her tears. To forgive her.

But another part of me longs to give her the spanking of her life, to shock her into fear of me, for she's put herself in harm's way and *I will not allow that.*

I take in a deep breath and stand behind her once more.

"You will tell me the truth, now, Taara. All of it."

"I did, sir," she sniffs.

"Why did you have pictures of me on your phone?"

If she's working with an enemy, she's had more private access to me and my home than anyone else on my payroll. When she doesn't answer, I lift the cane and give her half a dozen firm, measured strokes, one on top of the other. Slower than the previous smacks. Harder. I ignore her cries and wincing while I administer a spanking she'll feel for fucking days. If she's betrayed us, she's earned this. And if she hasn't, I'd rather her have to lay on her belly for a week than endanger her life.

"Let's try this again. Why did you have pictures of me on your phone?"

"I told you, it was an accident—ow!"

She pauses in her lie when I cane her mid-sentence. She knows I'm not speaking of the ones she took accidentally.

"The truth, Taara. Not the pictures you took tonight. The ones of *me*. Are you working with my enemy?"

She doesn't respond at first. The blood pumps hot in my veins, and I have to take several deep breaths to steady my anger. I step toward her and yank her head back with a fist at the nape of her neck.

"You tell me the truth, Taara."

She clamps her mouth shut.

With a shuddering sigh, she lifts her head, her eyes closed tightly.

"Taara, I need the truth," I say, my voice gentler as I look at this beautiful woman in distress, sweat pouring down her face in rivulets, mingled with her tears. She's been good to me, so good to me. Perhaps she hasn't betrayed us after all. And then it dawns on me, a possibility that didn't even occur to me until just now.

Is she... no, she can't be...

But it would explain so much.

Is Taara infatuated with me? Does she have a schoolgirl crush?

Could that be why she won't tell me? Is she embarrassed?

Fuck.

I step in front of her and look down. She stands a full head below me. Though her eyes are still closed tightly, they flutter open when I grasp her chin, slippery from tears, and lift her gaze to mine.

"Are you embarrassed to tell me why you have pictures of me on your phone?" I ask quietly.

Her eyes search mine, hopeful and full of something I can't quite put my finger on, perhaps because she isn't sure how she feels herself. I imagine she's run the gamut of emotion tonight, and if what I suspect is true...

I decide to try a different tactic. Brushing her damp hair from her forehead, I gentle my voice once more. "If you tell me the truth, Taara, I'll end this punishment and we won't need to speak of this again. Can you trust me enough to tell me the truth?"

She holds my gaze for long seconds before she finally nods.

"I like looking at pictures of you," she whispers. "I promise, Stefan, that I had no ill intentions. Never. But..." she tries to break eye contact, but a sharp yank of her chin brings her gaze back to mine. She swallows hard. "I had... I had a crush on you." Then her voice hardens, and she meets my gaze unblinking. "But no more."

I release her, unsure of what to think or how to react. But I know this session is over.

I put the cane away and remove her restraints. She's crying quietly, and I wonder if she'll turn to me for consolation. But when she's free from restraints, I merely cuff her wrists in front of her again.

I watch her reaction carefully. She pulls as far away from me as she can, her eyes cast down and head hung low. When I tug her cuffed wrists toward the door, she walks with me, wincing with each step that she takes. It only takes minutes to reach our house. I marvel at how quickly things changed. Just a few hours ago, she was preparing my bedroom for me to sleep for the night, and now...

I shake my head. I'm not sure what happens next.

I open the door to the house and place her unceremoniously inside before I close the door with an air of finality.

My relationship with Taara—that of boss and paid staff—has forever changed. I'm not sure if I believe her. I'm not sure what will happen next. But until I do, she'll remain my prisoner.

Chapter 4

Taara

HOW COULD I have ever thought I loved this man? How? I was so naïve. Foolhardy. I thought he knew compassion and kindness.

But not this man.

This is a side of Stefan I didn't know existed.

He dragged me around like a prisoner. He *beat* me. I can't believe how much that rod he used on me hurt, so much more than I ever expected. I felt I'd die under the onslaught, and I was so grateful when he finally stopped. I can feel every stripe on my skin, every flare of heat, and I know that if I remove my clothes I'll be welted.

How could he have done that to me?

I was so stupid for getting involved, for not staying where it was safe.

I saw a man killed tonight, and Stefan believes I spied.

I didn't mean to.

But I won't beg him again.

I hate him. I don't care if he beats me again, I won't beg. I have too much pride.

Every single step back to the house hurts. I'm aching with the pain of the beating he gave me, and when I think of the fact that others witnessed this, I want to *die*. Not only did he punish me, he did so in front of others, who all believe that I'm a liar and a traitor. I hate that. I hate it so much.

Honesty matters to me. Especially when it comes to Stefan.

I want to climb in my bed and nurse my wounds. To bring the covers over my head and cry into them.

I want to weep for the loss of the man I loved, because this man is one that I'll never love again.

"Sit on the sofa," he says, pointing to the couch with a scowl.

I plop onto it, not meeting his eyes, trying not to wince when pain radiates along my ass.

He sits heavily in the armchair facing the sofa, his back to the empty, lifeless fireplace, and sighs.

"I didn't want to do that," he says, and my heart gives a terrible squeeze in my chest. I could take his harshness. I could even take the pain. But remorse and disappointment from Stefan? Never.

"You're the *pakhan*," I respond bitterly. "You could have done anything you wanted."

Something flickers across his expression and he stays

silent a moment, finally breaking eye contact and looking away. "If only that were true, Taara."

"You command an army of men," I tell him. "I know what your role is. I know who you are. You could have chosen to believe me, but you didn't." I'm so angry with him I'm shaking. "You could have—"

"Enough!" He raps out in a command so hard I freeze as he gets to his feet. I forgot how tall he is, how large and intimidating, until he towers over me. "I could have had you killed? Yes. I could have had you tortured? Absolutely. I could have ended your life and put your body in a shallow grave next to the man we killed tonight?" I shiver involuntarily at the memory of the bloodied, lifeless body. "Without question. You witnessed my son kill a man in cold blood, and that puts us at risk."

"I realize that," I say through clenched teeth. "But accidents happen."

"Accidents, Taara?" He shakes his head and releases a mirthless laugh. "You call that an accident?"

"Yes, Stefan," I insist. "*An accident.*"

"Oh, no, you do not," he says, and for a moment the look in his eyes is so ferocious, I fear another punishment, and instinctively sink further into the cushions of the couch. "Accidents are things that happen we have no control over. Things we don't choose. Dropping a vase. Forgetting a doctor's appointment. Witnessing an execution is no accident but a grave mistake."

When he reaches me, he lifts me by the elbows until I'm standing in front of him.

"You, little girl, made a choice. A stupid, foolish choice, but a choice nonetheless."

A lump rises in my throat at his admonition. I swallow hard. I have dreamt about being this close to him. I've even imagined what it would be like having him call me that, *little girl.* I've let my mind wander and dream, and in my fantasy world, it was so, *so* much nicer than this.

I'm humiliated and hurt to my very core.

I thought I loved this man, but I know better now. I loved a man who doesn't exist. He isn't the one standing here in front of me.

"You're right," I say, aware of the note of steel in my voice when I speak to him. "I made a mistake."

What he doesn't know is that my mistake was far more serious than stumbling onto an execution.

My mistake was falling in love with him.

But when I admit my error, for the first time tonight, his gaze softens, and he shakes his head. "I wish you hadn't done that," he says softly, right before his phone rings. Still holding my gaze, he answers it. Seeing him answer his phone reminds me of what I lost, and I swallow a lump in my throat. I wish he'd fired me. I would leave and never look back.

"Yeah." He listens, then nods. "We'll be waiting." He sighs and turns to me. "You'll come with me and listen while I explain to my men why I spared your life. If you do anything other than obey me fully, I promise you, you'll regret it." But there's more resignation than threat in his tone. Still, I have no intention of disobeying.

He has several meeting places on the compound, and one is right here in this house. I'm thankful we don't have to walk outside again. It's lighter out now, but chilly in the morning, and it hurts to walk. He leads me to the library and has me sit on a chair directly beside him while we wait.

The men arrive, one at a time. I mull over what I should be doing right now, instead of what I am. I'd be showered and dressed by now, and in the kitchen making his breakfast. I'd brew his coffee—Italian roast with cream, no sugar—and pour him a cup when he came down to read the news. I'd cook him an omelet and toast and fetch him a glass of fresh orange juice. Just as he likes it.

But my thoughts are soon cut short when men begin to arrive. First, Nicolai and a few of his closest friends. I don't look at them. They witnessed my humiliation, and it's their fault I'm here.

Assholes.

Other men come in, but I keep my gaze trained away from them. Instead, I stare at my hands, at my long fingers and tapered nails, focusing in a scar in between my thumb and forefinger. I remember how I got that scar.

I'd taken a casserole out of the oven for Stefan, and placed it on the counter, not realizing the counter was freezing cold and wet. The casserole dish shattered, glass tearing into my hand. Stefan had just arrived from home and witnessed the injury.

I've played that memory over and over and over in my mind. How he took my hand in his and inspected the wound. How he washed it out with the most tender, vigilant care. How he lectured me sternly about kitchen safety and bandaged my injury himself. His concern gave me a sense of comfort unlike anything I'd ever felt before, so much so I even once contemplated injuring myself again just to get his attention.

When I think on this, I realize Stefan is not a bad man. He might do bad things from time to time, but he—*No.*

I stop my train of thought.

No.

I know who he is now. I was fooled before, thinking that he had any good in him at all. I can't let myself go there again.

Soon, the room is filled with the men loyal to Stefan. It's a smaller group than he commands, though, and I suspect he's summoned his inner circle. Even so, I feel as if the walls are closing in, as if I'm about to be on trial and my fate already sealed, and when I remember how he punished me, a lump forms in my throat. I don't want to be here in this state of ignominy and shame, but worse, scorned by the man I once thought I loved.

Stefan stands and points for me to stay seated where I am. Yeah, no worries there. If I could crawl under the floor, I would.

"Thank you for coming, brothers," he says. I don't look at him. I don't want to see his vivid blue eyes trained on me. I can hardly bear to hear his voice. But when the door opens, I see a pair of black leather boots and dark brown ballet flats in my peripheral vision, I hazard a glance up just in time to see a man come into the room with a woman, followed by Rafael. It was hard enough sitting here in front of the brotherhood. But sitting here in front of a woman is far worse.

To my chagrin, she meets my eyes when I look to her and smiles at me. I start when I see the harsh scar that runs along one cheek, but quickly look away from her.

Stefan pumps the man's hand and leans in to kiss the

woman's cheek. He doesn't flinch at the scar but kisses her right there. I watch in rapt fascination as she grins at him, takes both of his arms, and kisses his cheek.

"Welcome," he says with a smile. Then, in a lower voice, "It seems just yesterday I officiated at your wedding. And now I hear you have a brood of mini Russians?"

The woman laughs, filling the room with the beautiful sound, and they speak easily for a few moments.

"I'm sorry you have to begin your visit here with a meeting," he says. "If you'd like to leave us, Marissa might be awake and looking for company. I know it's early. Or we can see to getting you to your room while I borrow your husband for a little while."

"If you wouldn't mind, Stefan, I'd love to spend a little time with the other woman you have here? This is Taara, no? I've heard so many good things of her from Marissa and would love to get to know her a little better."

From Marissa? Marissa, Nicolai's wife, the woman he avenged with the murder committed this morning. She's said good things about me?

Stefan's smile fades, and his voice hardens. "She's here for questioning, Caroline."

I watch Caroline's brows draw together. "Oh," she says sadly. "Does your brotherhood typically question women in a room full of men?" She tips her head to the side, and I'm struck with how sharp she is. This woman misses nothing. Though she speaks pleasantly, in a soft, respectful voice, she knows how to play her cards well, appealing to his innate sense of justice and traditional values. She speaks to him as if she's asked for a cup of tea, and not a chance to rescue me from my predicament.

Why me?

Stefan smiles, but the smile doesn't reach his eyes. "We do, Caroline. If necessary."

Her voice firms just a touch. "And is it necessary, Stefan?"

"Caroline," her husband warns, and he reaches for her hand, but Stefan holds up a hand to stop him.

"As your wife, she's privy to much, Tomas," Stefan says. "And I have no qualms about being honest." Stefan strokes his chin. "Perhaps Taara doesn't need to be here for this particular meeting, but if she goes with you, she may have no freedom. She's under my watch."

"You have my word. She's cuffed, no?"

Stefan nods.

"Good. Then let the two of us have some time together while you men do your work, and I promise that I won't let her get away." She flashes him a captivating grin.

But either Stefan doesn't trust her, or he doesn't trust me, because he sends three of his youngest recruits to join us in the small study adjacent to the meeting room.

I'm curious. What is it that she wishes to ask me? I'm grateful for the momentary reprieve, though. I hated the eyes of everyone in that room on me. Caroline holds me firmly by the arm and marches me ahead of her, and it takes me by surprise. She leads me into the room as if I'm her child caught in the act of disobedience, and I realize that she's not someone to be trifled with.

Still, there's kindness in her gaze.

We reach the small room and she gestures for me to sit. I

do so clumsily. "Did you enjoy your flight?" I ask, not knowing what else to do or say.

"I did, thank you," she says. "Tomas insists on business class these days, and I have to admit, I don't mind it." She winks at me.

"I wouldn't either," I say with a smile, but I'm uneasy. I don't know what she wants or what will happen to me. We sit, and it's awkward because I'm still wearing cuffs. This would almost seem normal otherwise.

Thankfully, she doesn't waste any time.

"You're probably wondering why I brought you in here, Taara. Why I said I had something to ask you about?"

I nod in silence, and she smiles at me. Reaching to my knee, she squeezes. "I saw you in that room full of men, and I know how these men operate. I knew that they wouldn't hesitate to interrogate you with their barbaric methods. But I'm a good judge of character," she says. "And I wanted to prove to myself that my instinct is correct."

I swallow hard. "And what instinct is that?" I ask, my voice choked. To my horror, my eyes fill with tears. I'm so distraught, the slightest show of kindness undoes me. Does she believe me innocent? Does she even know what I'm accused of?

She holds my gaze, unblinking. "That you mean the brotherhood no harm."

I blink, and one lone tear rolls down my cheek. "Of course I don't. These men are like family to me. Why doesn't Stefan know that?" I feel like I'm choking on my own words. How does he not know how much he means to me? Meant.

She waves her hand at the doorway between the rooms and rolls her eyes, and I miss her touch on my knee. It was oddly reassuring, even though I hardly know her. "They're all the same," she says. "He's the head of the Bratva and has an image to uphold. My husband is the same. But if I know Stefan, and I daresay I do, he doesn't want to hurt you."

I scoff. "Well, you're wrong. He already did," I say like a sullen child. *The jerk.*

Her brows rise. "Did he?"

"He—" It sounds almost embarrassing to say it out loud. "He tied me up and *punished* me in front of his men. I swear I'm welted."

"*Ohhh,*" she says, nodding, and it look as if relief washes over her features. "Yes, I could see him doing *that.*"

She isn't horrified?

"How can you act like it's no big deal?"

Her eyes grow steely and she shakes her head at me like a disapproving older sister. "You misunderstand me. I'm not mitigating what you've gone through." She pauses, as if thinking about what to say before she continues. "I don't know if you know my history, do you?"

I shake my head. I don't.

She sighs, but holds my gaze, her voice unwavering as she speaks. "After my parents died, I was left to the care of my brother, brigadier of the San Diego Bratva. I was born into Bratva life. My brother was a terrible guardian and allowed wicked things to happen to me."

I must look horrified, for she waves her hand at me.

"This isn't about me. It's about the Bratva. So listen. Tomas married me as a form of repayment. An arranged marriage, in which I had no say. So now having grown up in one group and lived in another, I will tell you this. I know firsthand the real evil the men of my brother's group were capable of. And I know that Tomas and Stefan have principles my brother never did. *All* of them defy the law. They live by a code of conduct that's unbreakable. And they rule with heavy hands, without question, but the ways some of these men truly do hurt others—"

I wait quietly, trying to take this all in.

She continues, still holding my gaze. "Well, let's put it this way. My brother's Bratva was cruel, and it's because of them I have this scar." She points to her cheek. "And though Tomas and Stefan are capable of wicked things, and I will not pretend otherwise, they live by a code of conduct the truly wicked men of the Bratva do *not*." She looks away, past my shoulder, as if lost in her thoughts. "Someday, perhaps Marissa can tell you her story as well, and you will see."

But I'm not that easily convinced. I won't dismiss what Stefan's done that easily either. Perhaps it's not okay to justify evil simply because there's a spectrum of cruelty. Does the knowledge that he could've hurt me worse than he did make what happened acceptable?

No.

"It doesn't matter," I say. "I meant no harm, and he punished me. He doesn't trust me." My voice breaks at the end and I stop talking because I don't want to cry. The way he's treated me hurts worse than the caning he gave me.

I don't look up when she reaches for my hand, but the tone of her voice catches my attention.

"Tarra, *look* at me."

I snap my head up and do what she says, because her voice brooks no argument. I swallow hard at her fierce but honest gaze. She's quiet for long moments as she peers so intently in my eyes, I feel as if she sees my very soul. It would be unnerving if I wasn't so desperate for her to see the truth. After another moment, she blinks, and her eyes grow wide.

"There's more to this story than first appears," she whispers in surprise. "You have feelings for him, don't you? You might even love him. I can see it in your eyes. The hurt and betrayal run far deeper than they should if you were a mere employee."

"No," I whisper, but it's a lie I can't say. I lose my resolve and cover my face with my hands, cuffs and all. It hurts worse hearing her say it.

"Your reaction is answer enough," she murmurs, her voice gentling. "Taara, please. Look at me."

I have no choice but to do what she says. Gathering both my hands in hers, she squeezes.

"Look in my eyes and tell me that you mean the Bratva no harm."

I don't bother to wipe the tears that stream down my face as I hold her gaze and tell her with as much sincerity as I can muster, "I would never betray the brotherhood. Never. I saw Stefan and Nicolai kill a man last night, and my first thought was 'if Stefan orchestrated this, this was well deserved.'"

"Smart girl," she says. "Stefan never orders execution lightly." She nods. "I believe you. And this hurts worse for you because you have feelings for Stefan?"

If she's to be an ally, there's no point in hiding the truth anymore. So, with a sigh, I nod. "I've known him for years. He's ignorant of how I feel, but before tonight, I thought he was a good man. Now that I know better, I—"

But she shakes her head so sharply, I stop mid-sentence.

"Do not allow his treatment of you tonight to color what you know to be true."

I shake my head. "How could I not?"

She sighs. "Taara, listen to me. Stefan is a loyal man. You witnessed his son perform an execution. If you told the authorities, Stefan's son would be put into jail. Did that not occur to you?"

None of this occurred to me. Still, I'm hardly in the position for feeling sympathy for those two right now.

She continues. "I'm sure given his concern for Nicolai, he assumed the worst about why you were there and what you could potentially do to hurt his son."

"That might make logical sense, but it doesn't make what he did right."

She waves a hand impatiently at me. "Stop talking about right and wrong. You're framing all of this in average terms, but we live by a different code."

We. Not *them.*

Has what happened tonight made me one of them?

I bite back the snarky reply that's on the tip of my

tongue, because it would be utterly foolish of me to deny the opportunity to form an ally in this.

"So, he caught you," she says without emotion, simply stating facts. "He punished you or interrogated you." The sympathy I imagined she felt has fled. What the hell?

I swallow hard, embarrassed to discuss this with her. "He did."

"And now you're likely his prisoner, and he won't allow you out of his sight."

"Yes."

She nods, mulling this over with her chin in her hand for a moment, before she turns to me. "Taara, there's something you should know."

"Yes?"

"The women of the Bratva stand together. *Always.* But we do so in a way that strengthens all of us—our entire extended family. We do not seek to change who they are, what they stand for, or what they do. But we *can* join in solidarity together as one, for those times when we need to withstand the tempest, as it were."

I swallow hard and don't reply. I don't know where she's going with this.

"So, this is what I'm going to do. I'm going to tell you how to handle Stefan. I'm going to assure him of your innocence. And I'm going to promise you that you aren't alone."

Her phone rings, and we both jump. She glances at the screen, muttering, "I'm sorry, that's my husband."

She answers the phone.

"Hello?" She listens for a minute, nodding, then smiles. "Very well. Yes, of course. I would be happy to." She hangs up the phone and smiles at me.

"In the midst of all this, Tomas asked me to make traditional Russian food to bring to Stefan's former housekeeper. An interesting request, considering the circumstances, but if there's anything you should know about Stefan, it's that he takes care of his own."

I blink. He remembered. Even after I did what I did, he remembered my mother.

Oh, Stefan. What the hell are you doing to me?

I don't respond to her, because I can't bring myself to tell her it's my mother she'll be cooking for.

"And that's something else you should know, Taara. Being tied to a man of the Bratva is not for the faint of heart. These men are ruthless, heavy-handed, domineering. They can be brutal. But if you win his heart, he will devote himself to you with a deep, abiding love unlike anything you could ever imagine."

If I win his heart? Is she out of her *mind*?

"Show him your loyalty, Taara. Prove your fidelity to the Bratva, and you will not regret it."

Chapter 5

Stefan

I LET Taara go with reluctance. I want her under my watchful eye, but I also know that if she spends some time with Caroline, it will give me the ability to speak freely to my men, more so than if she were present. So instead, I opt for allowing her to be supervised by my men and Caroline. I am curious what Caroline wishes to say to her, but I trust Tomas. And if Tomas trusts her, so do I.

They go to an adjacent room, and I focus on the men before me. Nicolai stands with his arms crossed on his chest, eyes bloodshot from lack of sleep and stress. I give him a discreet nod, confirmation that we are together in this. Rafael stands beside him in a similar position, and Tomas sits beside me, one leg crossed over the other. Nicolai and Tomas are like brothers.

I look around at my men, the inner circle of the Bratva

that I command. We've risen in stature, together with Tomas, as two of the most powerful brotherhoods in all of America, and for good reason. We've upheld the code of Bratva life since day one, every decision and action we take with the one purpose in mind: to solidify our connections and rise as masters of the underworld. We have connections in every political sphere, law enforcement, the military, throughout the country with the most influential leaders of our time.

The Bratva itself was founded as a quasi-military operation after the fall of Stalin, when brothers-at-arms united forces. What began as a grassroots movement developed into one of the most powerful organized crime rings in the world, branches extending from mother Russia to America. As one of the most experienced members of the Bratva, I've seen my brothers both rise and fall. There are those committed to advancing their own purposes, bent on gaining power, prestige, and money, that eventually succumb to the temptations that press in on all sides when putting their own selfish needs and desires above others. Then there are others—like Tomas, and Demyan in Moscow, committed to strengthening the brotherhood. Fiercely loyal, they unite with others dedicated to that task. These are the brotherhoods that thrive.

Tomas and Nicolai are two such men. However, this is my son whose safety is at risk, the man whose very life can be destroyed by the woman in the other room. It's essential I tell my side of the story while bearing this in mind, and also balancing the need for transparency with the authority I wield as *pakhan*. It's a double-edge sword.

I'm grateful Tomas is here. He had come just to pay a visit, but his timing works in my favor. I've consulted him about what happened last night, and he will help inform my men today. But first, a minor order of business.

"There's an older woman under my care in a nursing facility," I tell Tomas. "She misses traditional Russian food. Do you think Caroline would mind helping us with that?"

"Certainly," he says. "No one cooks the food from our homeland like my wife," he says with pride.

"Thank you, I'll give you the details to pass on to Caroline."

"Of course," Tomas says with a nod. Tomas is younger than I am by a good deal, and it was I who helped facilitate his marriage to Caroline. He is like a son to me and gives me the same loyalty and devotion Nicolai does. If I ask a favor, he will always try to honor it.

"Thank you," I tell him. "I've heard recently that she dislikes the food where she is. Though it's only a trivial complaint, I promised I would ask Caroline to prepare some traditional Russian foods for her."

Nicolai watches me curiously while Tomas calls Caroline. Nicolai knows the only former housekeeper we had on staff is Taara's mother. I ignore his look. Just because Taara is now under our surveillance doesn't negate my end of the bargain. And perhaps this small gesture will make Taara more compliant.

"We aren't here long, but Caroline would be happy to," Tomas says. "All set. Sounds like the girls are getting along fine, too."

I nod. "Thank you."

I turn to face the room. "Now I'd like to take a moment to address you all. Thank you for coming here despite this early hour. It was imperative for me to relay the events of last night without you hearing them from a secondary party, which is why I called you today."

My men sit at attention, stern and formidable, their flinty gazes and rigid posture reminiscent of Russian military, and for good reason. The huge majority, with the few exceptions we've recruited in America, have served our home country.

"Last night, we were told that one of the men that betrayed Marissa Kosolov was still alive." A low murmur of disbelief goes up, but none of them speak. They all know Marissa well, and they know her story, how she was sold into slavery by her father, a former friend of mine. How my own son was left for dead and fought his way back to claim Marissa as his own. How he and I systematically sought revenge for every single goddamn man who betrayed us by joining with Myron in Marissa's abduction.

"As you'll recall, Myron's men were the ones that ordered my son killed. Some of them even put their hands on him." I can't keep the fury out of my voice even now, many years later.

Nicolai speaks up. "Not to mention, they orchestrated the abduction and abuse of my wife."

The air crackles with electric energy. In Bratva life, there is no betrayal deeper, no treachery more worthy of swift and certain punishment.

"I thought they'd all been killed," one of my men in the back asks. "No?"

"We thought the same," I explain. "But we were wrong. Unfortunately, this man decided to attack Marissa, and he spoke of his loyalty to her father. Fortunately, Nicolai was nearby, and prevented any further injury to his wife."

To my daughter-in-law. I'm fucking glad the man who attacked her lies in a grave.

"Tell me you killed him," someone from the back says, and the whole room murmurs its approval of this sentiment.

"We did," Nicolai says. "Last night, he was executed in the interrogation room. Rafael and I disposed of his body."

"To which brotherhood did he belong?" My men are rightfully angry at this breach, and it pleases me they are as eager to out those who pose a threat against Marissa and Nicolai as I am.

Tomas raises a hand. "I am sorry to say, I've looked at footage. He was a member of my group. We had no idea whatsoever that he was still loyal to Myron and posed a threat in any way to Marissa or Nicolai. We thought, as did all of you, that those involved with Marissa's abduction had already been rid of."

Nicolai nods. He knows Tomas well, and believes that if Tomas knew of this brother's betrayal, he would have pulled the trigger himself.

I inhale. And now I need to tell them the other part of the story, why Taara is now in my possession. I'm not looking forward to their response.

"But there's a complication, and I want full disclosure

with all of you," I say to the group. "A woman who works for me, Taara Khan, witnessed the execution."

Several around us curse. "And she, too, has paid the ultimate price?" I don't see who asked the question. Someone at the back.

"She's been taken prisoner by me for surveillance," I say. "I am not convinced Taara is a threat to any of us."

No one responds. The silence in the room is nearly deafening. Even Nicolai doesn't meet my eyes.

"Sir, she can pose a threat to your son," Simon, one of my *brodyaga* says. "Are you sure that's the best way to handle it?"

"No," I say. "I'm not sure. I'm keeping an eye on her for now. She's been loyal to me her entire life." I don't tell them that she's young, and I've known her since she was a child. I'm not sure why I feel such a strong need to protect her. My concern should be for my son above all. "And if it comes down to ending her life for the good of the Bratva, I will not hesitate."

"But what if it's too late?" Brogdan, one of the most dedicated members of my brotherhood, asks. He's tall and formidable, one of our strike force.

"I will not allow it to come to that."

Again, silence. I can feel their judgment, though. They do not believe I've made the correct choice, and their judgment rankles.

"I did what I thought best," I say, my temper rising. "I will not kill an innocent girl who's been loyal to me for so long so easily."

Nicolai uncrosses his arm and steps in front of me, glaring at everyone in front of us. "And need I remind you that my father is *pakhan*. He does not ask for anyone's permission to make his choices. My father has led us unselfishly, and all of you owe him not only your allegiance but your obedience." Silence descends on the room at his stern lecture. "And if anyone has the right to question his judgment, it would be me. But I do not. I have nothing but complicit faith in the decisions he makes."

"As do I," Rafael says, coming to stand next to Nicolai.

"And I." Tomas gets to his feet.

"And I." One by one, my brothers stand before me, the only sounds in the room one man after another getting to his feet. I swallow hard. Though I'm honored by Nicolai's steadfast defense of me, the weight of responsibility to make the right decision weighs heavily.

"I will not fail you, brothers. You have my word. I will keep Taara under my care and ensure she threatens none of us. And now that we've brought you up to date, it's imperative we discuss the next order of business." Tomas looks to me, and I nod, giving him permission to tell them what he needs to. He warned me before we began that he had more information that would impact me, and we decided it best he save time and tell me in front of all of us. I have nothing to hide from my brothers.

"As I said earlier, the man who betrayed Stefan and Nicolai belonged to the Boston Bratva. But it's come to my attention that his betrayal went a lot deeper than his connections with Myron."

We all listen in silence.

"He has heavy ties in Russia. Not with the sister group

some of you know well, the group led by Demyan Federov, but with the rival group."

The skin on the back of my neck prickles with awareness. Though there are numerous Russian Bratva groups, we deal with the two most prominent often. One is run by Demyan, a good man Nicolai and Rafael know well, as they've all worked together at one time or another. I've met him a few times when he's visited America and found him not only to be hard-working, but a man of integrity. Since they are our sister group, we deal with them frequently and trust them.

But the second group, the Thieves, is rival to the Moscow contingent, and responsible for great devastation. Along with other members of American Bratva, the Thieves are responsible for the largest human trafficking ring in America, and some of our members, as well as some of our members' wives, have had dealings with them. They're known for being underhanded, vicious, and cruel, and my dislike for the group is far more personal.

The Thieves are responsible for the death of my Amaliya.

I watch Rafael visibly bristle as well. It is because of the Thieves that Rafael and his wife Laina, once known as Olena in another place and time, relocated to our group in America. Amaliya was Olena's mother.

"The Thieves?" I ask Tomas.

"Fucking Thieves," Rafael mutters, clenching his fists.

"The very same," Tomas says to me, before returning to address the group again. "As you know, when Nicolai joined the Boston group with dual enrollment, I made a promise our group would no longer have any dealings with the trafficking rings. I've adhered to that promise. But many of you also know that the Thieves have *not*. Trafficking still comprises the majority of their business. The biggest concern is that this one insidious traitor is only representative of a larger group," Tomas says. "Before his demise, he promised this group would see an uprising. That we didn't know how deeply the forces against us ran."

A low murmur ripples through the group. The respectable members of the Bratva know that we aren't brother against brother but united in an unbreakable bond, tied to one another by a code of conduct.

"How does this affect us?" one of my men asks. It's a good question. The men all look to Tomas, but it is Nicolai who speaks next.

"Last night, during the interrogation, it came to light that the Thieves intend on taking over as American Bratva. They want to eliminate our group. This much we can surmise from what our interrogation revealed."

"Taking over?" Simon asks. "Eliminating? How?"

Nicolai shakes his head. "We aren't sure, since those who run the group and ultimately make the decisions clearly keep their agenda hidden, but it's obvious to us that at the very least, they intend on increasing the volume of trafficking they do, and once their trade gains power, of potentially wiping out every rival Bratva group in America."

We sit in silence for a minute. This type of insidious uprising among fellow Bratva is unheard of, but given the downward spiral of some of the leadership in recent years, it doesn't surprise me. Myron's betrayal of his daughter was, sadly, only one of many such despicable actions.

Tomas speaks next. "My sources tell me the Thieves plan on relying heavily on Afghani refugees and immigrants. The women are beautiful, and with few connections, difficult to trace."

I imagine Taara, my beautiful prisoner, sold to one of the men at auction, and my fists clench by my sides.

"So, what will we do?" someone asks. "We have to stand against them, even if it means we go to war."

But my mind is already turning over the possibilities. I stroke my chin. As *pakhan*, I am called to make sacrifices. I have, over and over again, but this time… as they continue to talk, my plan grows, until I finally speak up to get their attention.

"I have an idea," I say, aware of how Nicolai's eyes follow me. "You say the plan comes from upper leadership, Tomas?"

Tomas nods. "My sources say that those lower in rank know of no plans, and my investigations confirm this. Most of the Bratva men prefer we remain either neutral or allies."

"Then if we found a way to out those who are plotting to overtake us, we stop the root of the problem before it gains traction, yes?"

Tomas nods. Nicolai's eyes narrow on me. He's already suspecting something risky, and he isn't wrong.

"Yes," Tomas says.

The more I think about it, the more I'm convinced this is the correct choice of action. If my plan goes off without a hitch, Taara will have a chance to prove her loyalty to me, and ultimately redeem herself, and I will be able to put an end to the dangers that threaten my brothers.

"Tomas. Nicolai. You will have lunch with me, and we will discuss what I have in mind. Afterward, we will reconvene to discuss." I nod to Tomas. "Bring Taara and Caroline to me."

Chapter 6

Taara

"Stefan wishes to see you." One of the men watching over us puts his phone away after answering it, addressing both me and Caroline. It almost felt normal there for a little while, the two of us visiting like sisters. I'm surprised to see it's been several hours, and it's now nearly early afternoon. I almost forgot I was prisoner to Stefan.

I've never had a sister, or a sibling of any kind, and I've been turning over what Caroline said to me.

The women of the Bratva stand together.

"Oh?" Caroline asks. She finishes the remainder of the tea in her cup before placing it on a saucer, clearly in no rush. I do the same, then follow her lead when she gets to her feet. "Does he wish to see both of us?"

The guy, clean-shaven and young, nods. He looks like

they recruited him straight out of high school. "Both of you."

Caroline smiles at me. "Very well then. Let's go."

I grit my teeth when the guards flank either side of me, though they allow Caroline to walk unencumbered.

"Am I really this much of a threat I need these guys watching me?" I say, not bothering to temper my voice. "Honestly, Caroline, his arm's as big as my thigh. I couldn't possibly hurt anyone. I can barely open a jar of pickles without asking Stefan for help."

Caroline smiles sadly. "It isn't your physical threat they wish to prevent, Taara."

I sigh. I know why I pose a threat, and it angers me that they don't believe I won't betray them.

"Remember," she whispers in my ear. "Prove your loyalty and this all goes away."

"In here," one says, gesturing to one of the doorways that leads to the dining room. I follow, my stomach gnawing with hunger when I smell something savory and pungent wafting in the air. My unease resurfaces when I see Tomas, Nicolai, and Stefan all sitting at the table. Large, muscled, tattooed, and stern, they're a formidable trio. They stop talking and look up when we enter the room.

Tomas smiles broadly and gestures for Caroline to come to him. She crosses the room with her head held high, regal and powerful. I want to be like her someday. Fearless and undaunted by her exacting husband, dedicated to loyalty for both her fellow sisters of the Bratva as well the brotherhood. Unencumbered with a past that haunts her.

But before I can even begin to think of such things, I need to convince Stefan I am not a threat. I'm not sure I'm a "woman of the Bratva" as Caroline says. *Yet.*

Tomas stands, folds his napkin and places it on the table, then pulls a chair out for Caroline. Stefan pulls a chair out beside him as well, but instead of his gesture being chivalrous, it's a sharp command. "Sit," he barks. "And do not speak unless you are spoken to first." I hate that she's a welcome guest and I'm the prisoner shrouded in shame.

The tone of his voice stings, re-opening the wounds he inflicted earlier with his cruelty. I swallow hard, vacillating between the desire to either cry or tell him to fuck the hell off. Caroline has told me what I need to do. Every action I take will be to serve that purpose. So, when he points, I sit. I keep my hands obediently tucked onto my lap and don't speak, even when large tureens of soup are placed on the table beside baskets of fresh, fragrant bread.

Caroline helps herself to a large bowl of soup and a roll, then looks questioningly to Stefan and me while she butters her bread.

"You may eat," he says to me with a frown. He takes a set of keys out and unfastens my cuffs but warns me. "You stay right here under my watch, and you may continue to have your cuffs off for the remainder of this meal."

"I hardly see her daring to do something stupid in front of all of you," Caroline says pleasantly. "Stefan, though I'm not a member of your Bratva, I promise you my allegiance. Do you trust me?"

Tomas watches her through narrowed eyes, and Stefan sighs. "You aren't the one I distrust, Caroline."

"Then listen to me. I'm a good judge of character. I think it's one of my finer traits, to be honest." She smiles. "And I'm telling you that Taara not only doesn't pose a threat to you but has the potential of being one of your biggest allies."

I could hug her.

"While I appreciate your vote of confidence, Taara will have to prove that with her actions," Stefan responds.

I stifle myself from letting out an angry breath just in time and bite my cheeks. The insides of my cheeks will bleed before I let my tongue get the better of me. I merely nod to her to thank her.

Show him your loyalty.

I cannot forget what she said after that, the promise that spoke to a need in me so strong, I'm near desperate.

If you win his heart, he will devote himself to you…

It's the stuff fantasy is made of, ethereal and whimsical, but hell, I'm not going to deny the fact that *I want that.* Even after what I witness, heaven help me.

I see the way Tomas looks at Caroline, with such tenderness and devotion I know she is his treasure. He would raze an army singlehandedly for her. Nicolai, too. There are no laws he will not break, no adversary he fears when it comes to protecting his Marissa. When in the presence of others, he never takes a hand off of her, resting one on the small of her back or her neck. He lost her once and will not lose her again. These are the men of the brotherhood, fiercely loyal, brutally protec-

68

tive, like modern-day Knights of the Round Table. United as one, devoted to both their brothers and women.

Betray them and earn a lifelong enemy. Earn their trust, and you become one of their own.

I've known this. I've seen this. I've longed for just this, and Caroline's talk has led me to believe my hoping was not in vain.

But I am not one of their own. Not in their eyes. And it is up to me to change that.

Stefan ladles soup into a bowl and places it in front of me, then lifts a roll, still steaming hot, and breaks it open. I watch in rapt fascination, his large fingers spreading the roll open and slathering it with butter before placing it next to me. I blink in surprise. I thought he prepared his own food, but this is for me. "Eat," he orders, and I realize I was staring. "You still may not speak unless given permission."

I meet Caroline's eyes, and she gives me a nearly imperceptible nod. She told me to prove my loyalty to him and obeying him is a good first step.

I lift my spoon and quickly begin eating the soup. It's delicious, a traditional Russian soup made with thin, angel hair pasta, hearty chunks of potatoes, vibrant red peppers and carrots, all in a savory chicken broth that warms me through. I keep my head down, listening to the conversation as I eat. I don't realize what they're speaking of until I hear the word *Afghani*. I open my mouth to speak, when a sharp shake of Caroline's head warns me just in time.

"That's despicable," Caroline says, shaking her head

before ladling more soup into her bowl. "Is it really that complicated stopping such behavior?"

"Of course it is," Tomas says to her shortly. "Those who rise in power often risk anything and everything to gain control. Without knowing how deeply the plot to overthrow us runs, we can only see the tip of the iceberg. If we don't delve into deep waters, we run the risk of utter destruction." He scoffs. "Cowards are those that only face superficial dangers."

Cowardice is anathema to the men of the Bratva. They despise it.

"Yes, I know," she says softly, and I don't understand why her gaze suddenly becomes sympathetic before she looks away from me. She knows something I don't.

"So, it seems the only option, then," Stefan begins, "is to investigate ourselves."

"I agree," Nicolai says. He takes a long pull from a frothy beer stein. "And I'm ready and willing to go with you."

Stefan shakes his head. "Absolutely not," he says. "I will go alone. Me and Taara, of course."

Caroline watches me and doesn't say a word. I blink.

Wait, what?

Tomas nods. "We have a connection on the auction ship. You can find out what you need to know from him in your travels. If I tell him ahead of time you're coming, you can meet discreetly aboard the ship, then report back after you get to Russia."

Auction ship? *Russia*?

I want to ask so many questions I don't even know where to begin, but I'm not allowed to speak. It's probably just as well anyway, as I need to listen to every word they say.

"I think the first order of business is upon us," Stefan says. "The next ship leaves this evening, yes?"

Tomas nods.

Stefan continues. "Then Taara and I will fly to Boston and board that ship. I will find out what I can in the short time we'll be aboard and take my findings to Russia. With the aid of the Moscow contingent, we will find out what we can about who poses a threat to us."

"It's risky, brother," Tomas says. "The Thieves will stop at nothing to get what they want."

"I know," Stefan says coldly, as if his dealing with them is somehow personal. I wonder if it is.

"Very risky," Nicolai says. "You should let me go instead."

"The hell you will," Stefan scoffs. "You have a family here that needs you. My going will be perfect, because you will take on my duties as *pakhan* in my absence, and given that you'll be my successor, it's an opportune time." To my surprise, he turns to me next. "And I want Taara to eventually earn her freedom. She can prove her loyalty to me by playing her role in this."

What does that mean? Still, hope flares in my chest. I don't even know what he's asking of me, but he's casually mentioned exactly what I want. I need to know more.

I open my mouth to speak, then close it abruptly.

"You have permission to ask questions," Stefan says, and I don't miss the weariness in his tone.

"My… role in this? What is that? I'm confused."

I don't miss the way Caroline's jaw ticks, or the way she drums her fingers on the table.

"We will board the auction ship this evening, you under the guise of being my partner. Slave, as it were. I will give you a story," Stefan says, finishing off his drink. "The identity you will assume. And explain in detail what I expect."

My food suddenly feels like a rock in my stomach. "Oh?" I whisper.

"Please, Stefan. Be careful," Caroline begs. "This is no easy task you ask of her."

"We ask no easy task of any of our women," Tomas reminds her, squeezing her knee. "A woman connected to the Bratva knows this. Don't you, sweetheart?"

She sighs. "Yes. But Taara is innocent," Caroline insists, her eyes boring into her husband's. The woman has more pluck than I do. He's terrifying.

"Then let her prove it," he responds.

Oh, *shit*. What are they talking about? What does she know that I don't? I swallow hard. But he said there was a chance for me to prove my loyalty…

I make up my mind then. I sit up straighter. I made a mistake last night, a grave one that's put me in this position. But I want to prove my loyalty. I want this ignominy behind me. I hate being his prisoner. I will do what it takes to earn my freedom.

I eat the rest of my meal while listening to them, trying to piece together the plans, and when we're done, Stefan rises and takes me by the elbow. I follow. Caroline stops me at the door, though, and kisses my cheek. She looks at me with sisterly concern, her brows furrowed, lips turned down at the edges. She's worried for me. Hell, I love that. Someone actually cares.

"Be brave, Taara," she whispers in my ear. "And all will come right in the end. And when it comes right, you'll come see me, won't you?"

Be brave? Oh, God.

"Sure," I say, though I can't imagine anything good coming out of this.

Then she's gone, and all I'm left with is my captor and my thoughts. He's leading me out of the dining room by the elbow, and I barely register where I'm going. We're going back to his house.

Stefan is issuing rapid commands in Russian to people who trot by his side. I gather some of what he says and their response.

Wait. What? We're leaving already?

"Yes, sir. Right away, sir." His staff takes commands in stride. Stefan's face is impassive, and he doesn't make eye contact with me, just holds me in his firm grip so I can't get away.

"Prepare her a bag," he says to one. "Be sure to pack whatever womanly things she needs." He casts an angry glance at me. "You are to follow me in silence and ask no questions until further notice."

Great. Here we go again.

And then it dawns on me. If he's taking me to Russia, how will I see how my mother is? How long will we be gone?

"Stefan—" I begin, but in response he swings me out in front of him and slaps my ass so hard I stumble. Tears fill my eyes.

He's still a jerk.

"I said you may not speak," he says, his voice tight with anger.

"My mother—" I begin, unable to stifle the questions that plague me. "Sir!"

"Enough," he snaps, then to my surprise he stops where he is and drags me out in front of him. "Do you have any idea how much danger you are in? Any idea at all? Do you *know* what we're up against here? *Christ!*"

What the hell?

I blink at him and shake my head. I suppose I don't.

He continues, his blue eyes alight, gripping me so tightly it hurts. "Every one of the men in the room with me today wanted you dead. We don't give second chances here. You have *one,* Taara. And this is it." He releases me and continues marching me by his side. I skip to keep up with his strides as I mull over what he's said. But then maybe he softens or something, for a moment later, he shakes his head. "But some day, I will bring you back to your mother."

Some day? What does that mean?

"After you change into suitable clothing, you will sit by the door," he says, pointing to a window seat. "Keep your hands where I can see them and do not speak until I give you permission." He hands me a pair of black leggings and a red top. They belong to me, so I assume someone fetched them from my room.

With a sigh, I dress in the little bathroom on the first floor while he stands outside the door, then I go to the window seat. I love this place, right here where the light filters in through the large bay window. I often sit here with a book, bathing in the sunlight. But today, it feels very different. I watch him go to his office and retrieve a few things before he heads back to me. His staff wheels luggage on the landing, their rapid packing happening before my very eyes. It seems only minutes later when they come downstairs, wheelie bags in hand. Something catches my eye outside the window. I turn to see a long, sleek black car pulling up out front.

This is it. We're going. I won't get a chance to say goodbye to my mother. I'm leaving her here in Atlanta and going with Stefan as his... I don't even know. Prisoner? What did he say?

Slave?

I hear familiar footsteps on the stairs and look up to see Stefan trotting down. "Come with me," he says, before he grabs my hand and drags me to the door.

I have so many questions. So very many questions. I hope that when we finally find ourselves alone, he'll allow me to ask them.

When we're alone.

It scares me to think about being alone with him again. Just one day ago, it would have been my biggest fantasy come true, but now... now he terrifies me.

When we get outside, he opens the door to our car and

gestures for me to go in, but I must be going too slowly because he practically lifts me and shoves me into the car. I stumble into the dark interior and land softly in a plush, velour seat. He stands just outside the door to the car, speaking to Nicolai and Tomas.

"You will lead well in my absence," Stefan says to Nicolai. "I trust you."

Nicolai nods, and then men embrace briefly, before Stefan joins me in the back of the car.

I don't speak. I don't ask the questions that gnaw at me. I have to be patient. We drive in silence, and my heart aches. I had plans to visit my mother this weekend, and now... What if she has a moment of clarity and she wonders where I went to? Why I left her? But those thoughts flee when I look at Stefan.

His blue eyes no longer hold the anger they did just moments ago. Instead, he looks contemplative.

"I wonder," he says softly, almost as if to himself. "How you will handle this."

Yeah, I'm kinda curious myself, especially since I have no idea what "this" even is.

"Am I allowed to speak now?"

He nods. "Now that we're no longer in the presence of my men, you may."

I take in a deep breath. "Thank you," I say. "But how will I handle *what*? I have no idea where we're going or what we'll be doing."

Be brave, Taara.

He sighs, but to my surprise, actually fills me in. "The

man we killed last night was only one of a group of men banded together to form an uprising," he explains. "Their purpose is to boost the human trafficking ring run by rival Bratva in America and to overtake their rivals. Namely, us."

I blink in surprise. Human trafficking ring? Wow.

"Okay," I say cautiously. "And how exactly does that impact us?"

Leaning forward, he places his forearms on his knees and looks at me with those blue, blue eyes that pierce my very soul. God, how I want to see tenderness in his look again. Just for one moment, an ounce of compassion. It would fuel me for whatever we face next. "Taara, do you wish to vindicate yourself, not only to me but the entire brotherhood?"

"Of course."

"Do you further wish to prevent the abduction and sale of fellow Afghani refugees?"

"Me? You want my help?" I ask in a little voice.

His gaze doesn't waver as he explains. "The men we pursue are doing just that. Their wish is to steal the refugees from Russia and sell them here in America. Since you're Afghani, it will be an easy matter to pretend you are one of them, bought by me. And having you as my slave will make it easier for me to fill my role."

"I see," I say, which is a lie, because I have no fucking idea what he's talking about. This makes no sense to me at all. "For how long?"

He shakes his head. "I have no idea, but you'll remain my prisoner until you've proven your innocence. Until every member of my group and others knows that you do not pose a threat."

I shake my head. This sounds impossible, and I dislike not having more concrete guidelines. What exactly will "proving my innocence" entail? But I fall into silence next to him. I can't control any of this. And though the thought of what he proposes terrifies me, I have a chance to do what Caroline told me to.

"I don't really understand what I'm going to be doing," I tell him.

"You will behave as my slave," he says. "We will board the auction ship and you, as my slave, will do exactly as I say. We will take the ship to harbor, then board a plane to Russia. In Russia, we will meet with our sisterhood Bratva group, and once there we will oust the men who plan on bringing the refugees to America."

"This sounds dangerous," I whisper. I wish I hadn't eaten lunch. I'm afraid I might lose it.

He looks at me curiously and tips his head to the side. "Of course, it is," he says softly. "But you will not do this alone."

I scoff. "Right. I get to have you, the man I once—"

I stop. I can't believe I almost said something that would betray my old feelings toward him. I amend what I was going to say.

"You, the man who's been nothing but a total jerk to me, as my protector. Lovely." I know it's a risky thing to say. He's already punished me, and I have no doubt he'd do so again if given the chance. But I'm angry and hurt and honestly? Fucking *terrified*.

I brace myself for his anger. The Stefan I've seen in the past few hours is nothing like the man I thought I loved. He's so much harsher. Cruel, even.

"Taara." The gentleness in his tone surprises me so much, I whip my head back to look at him. "It was a mistake following me."

I swallow hard. "I know that now. I'd have to be a fool not to have realized that."

He shakes his head. "My men want you dead," he says in a choked voice. I blink in surprise. Is he upset by this turn of events? In front of the others, I saw no such regret. "I *have* to prove your innocence."

"Do you?" I ask. "And do you have to order me into silence and smack my ass and drag me around like a child?"

His brows draw down and he's once again the formidable, fearless leader of the Bratva.

"If I have to? Yes. And much more, Taara. So much more."

I look out the window. I don't want to talk to him anymore. I imagine I hear the regret in his voice. I imagine I even hear his remorse. But I won't let myself even hope for more than eventual freedom.

I sigh. I will do what he says. Even if it kills me.

Do I have a choice?

Chapter 7

Stefan

We take my private jet to Boston. Taara sleeps beside me, and I'm glad she does. She might not even realize that her head falls onto my shoulder in slumber. The girl always looks a little tired, so it actually pleases me to see her resting beside me like this. And for one moment, I imagine she isn't my captive, but my woman, and we aren't going undercover and into the face of danger, but on a trip together. Just me and her.

We land after the sun's set, and when I shake her shoulder, she wakes with a start and a little scream. It saddens me that she's afraid. I wish our circumstances were so much more different than they are.

But I have a job to do, and I will not falter.

"You're fine," I say sharply, though what I want to do is gather her close to me and assure her she's safe. I can't, though. We are about to board a ship under the guise of being master and slave, and I need her to know her role here.

I watch her pretty, pouty lips turn downward while she schools her features. She hates me now. She should, but a part of me wishes this didn't have to be the case. I liked the way she looked at me before, all sweet and eager to please. And though I love a good, feisty woman with spunk, her hatred of me is wholly different.

I turn her to face me. "We board the ship tonight. Remember who you are."

It seems being woken has made her grumpy, for she frowns at me. I shake my head and remove the collar and chain I brought with me from my pocket. "You will pose as my slave."

"I don't know what that means. I didn't even know people still *had* slaves. I seem to recall we abolished slavery back in, say, Lincoln's time."

"This is a different type of slavery," I say, not liking the petulant tone of her voice one bit.

Her eyes grow wide. "Waaaait... ok, wait a minute. You mean... you mean *sexual* slavery, right?" I don't respond, but my silence is answer enough. "Are you out of your *mind*?"

"Taara," I warn. "Curb your attitude. We will join the others aboard the ship and find our room. Tomas handled the details, and he said he'd make sure we had the largest room possible. You will get some sleep shortly, but you must maintain your role in the meantime." I scowl. "So, knock it off."

We exit the plane and walk to the car that already waits for us. I stand her in front of me. Even disheveled and exhausted, she looks so beautiful to me with her dark black hair and petite, curvy, feminine body. In a move I hope I don't regret, I brush her black hair off her forehead and tuck a stray lock behind her ear. Her deep brown eyes open wide, her full, beautiful lips parting. I long to bend and capture her mouth with mine, to kiss her until she moans and melts beneath me. To show her how much she means to me, even now. That my cruelty to her is of necessity and not desire. I'd so much rather treat her with tenderness.

Without explanation, I unclasp the collar and fasten it around her neck. She blinks and looks down, then lifts her eyes back to me.

"What is this?" she whispers, her brows drawing together in anger. Her moods shift so quickly, I can hardly keep up.

"A reminder to you of your subservience to me, and a declaration to anyone who looks at you that you are mine."

A shadow crosses her features, unmistakable pain she can't hide. I wonder what saddens her in this moment. I imagine there are many things, but I can't allow those to be my concern.

"We will speak more freely once in the privacy of our room, but until then, you are to walk beside me and keep your head bowed. Speak to no one and remember your place."

She nods. "Yes, sir."

I'm pleasantly surprised by how easily she assumes her position by my side, humble and meek. Our driver takes our bags and I ease her into the car.

"We're only a few minutes away from your port," he says to me.

I'd have preferred a night alone with her, just one night to ease her into this next stage of the plan, but we have no time. We drive in silence, and she shivers. Without thinking, I draw her closer to me, focusing on my new role:

She is my slave now and I her master, so in these roles it's not out of the ordinary for me to care for her.

"Come here," I murmur, tucking her against me. "It's colder here than in Atlanta, isn't it?"

She shivers again, her body rigid beside me. "Yes, sir."

And right then, with her pressed up to my side, I don't regret any of this. Not what's happened tonight. Not having taken her. Not even her pretending to be my slave. For having her in my arms is worth it all.

But as soon as the thought comes to me, I dismiss it. I can't allow myself to grow sympathetic. It isn't like me. And masters must be firm and unyielding.

"Are you—" she pauses and bites her lip but stops. "I am to only call you master?" she asks in a whisper so low I hardly hear her. "Do they know your name?"

Ah. She wonders if I'll need to change my identity at all.

"Yes," I say to her. "Though the others call me Stefan, you may only refer to me as master." It's answer enough. I will not hide my true identity, because there's no need to. *Pakhan* of any brotherhood is allowed to take a slave, and many have done so. It will be easier to maintain my role as Stefan, *pakhan* of the Atlanta brotherhood, than feign any other identity.

We arrive at the port, and I watch as Taara's eyes grow wide when she takes in the magnificent ship in the harbor.

"Oh, *wow*," she whispers. "That's *beautiful*."

And it is. A luxury cruise ship, our destination is lit with vibrant purple and yellow lights, lending it an almost majestic air.

"Have you ever been aboard a ship?" I ask her.

She shakes her head. It seems tonight is a night of many firsts for her.

"The quarters are rather cramped, but this ship has a reputation as one of the finest." I say this as if it makes any fucking difference, like we're on vacation, and that's such bullshit. I look away from her, not able to meet her eyes.

Still, we only have one day here before we head to Russia, so we need to make the most of it. I wish we weren't so rushed, moving from one place to the next so rapidly. But we will do what we have to.

She follows like a good little girl as we board the ship. And as soon as we enter, we can see why this is no ordinary cruise ship.

The entry room is teeming with people. Many of the men wear suits, the women wearing skimpy sheaths or nothing at all. Taara's lovely wide eyes take everything in in silence, from the crush of guests to their unusual attire. It's soon clear she's far from the only girl collared.

What she doesn't know is that some of these men came alone, many having recently acquired their new partners. They've completed their auction, and we arrive just in time to witness the new couples interacting. I honestly am not sure what we'll see when we board, all I know is that I should be able to find a clue regarding the Thieves trade.

And I get Taara alone. That could either prove helpful or lethal.

"There's a guest reception tonight in the lounge," the woman greeting us tells us. She's tall and thin, her blonde hair tucked into a clip at the back of her head, wearing simple pearl earrings and a black dress. She looks like a stewardess. It's hard to imagine she knows exactly what happens aboard these ships. Working here, she'd have to.

"Please join us and get to know your fellow passengers a bit better."

It's the last fucking thing I want to do, but it's foolish to ignore an opportunity to find out what I'm looking for.

Thankfully, Taara walks by my side and says nothing at all, obediently following me like the good little girl she is. A bellhop brings our bags to a room at the far end of the hall, and we follow in silence. But when we open the door, I don't see the large room I was told Tomas booked for us, but instead a tiny room little larger than a closet.

"What the hell is this?" I ask. "This isn't the room I requested."

The bellhop frowns. "So sorry, sir." He glances at a piece

of paper in his hand. "This is the one we were told you wished for?"

I frown, looking at the interior. There's *one* tiny bed, one little bathroom, and a large window overlooking the sea. I didn't want to be in such tight quarters with Taara, not so soon.

"Transfer me to the bigger room I requested, please," I say, keeping my temper in check with effort. I'm trying to stay patient, but this is bullshit.

"I'll—see what I can do, sir." And then he's gone, and I'm standing there awkwardly with Taara.

She looks about the room. "So much for the biggest room they had," She mutters. "Though this does have a sort of *quaint* appeal."

"You like this room?" The girl baffles me.

She shrugs. "I wouldn't say *like*. I mean, it would be nice to have a little space…" her voice wanders off and she bites her lip. "I mean—yes, sir," she says.

The bellhop is back in the doorway.

"I checked, sir, and unfortunately this is the only room we have left."

I curse under my breath. "Very well."

"But for your troubles, we'll be sure to grant you a bottle of champagne on the house. That will arrive shortly. Please let us know if there's anything else we can do for you." And then we're alone, just the two of us, in this tiny space. As master and slave.

But I'm tired. So very tired.

"Sit, Taara," I tell her. I see our luggage by the door. They've had it brought here ahead of us. When she does what I say, I get up and quickly unpack the luggage. Her clothing is simple and elegant, alongside some silky, sexy little numbers. *Christ*. She'll have to wear the sexy things aboard this ship. If anyone looks at her, if anyone touches her...

I'm suddenly glad we don't have the large room. She'll need to learn to get accustomed to being practically fucking attached to me.

When I finish unpacking, I cast a glance her way. She's sitting with her hands in her lap, looking about the room. Her bottom lip captured between her teeth, her eyes wide and curious.

"I do know a little bit about master and slave, Stefan," she says, then her cheeks color. "I'm sorry, I—"

"You may call me Stefan in private," I allow. "And what do you know?"

She shrugs a shoulder. "I don't know how *accurate* it is, for I've only read fiction, but..." her voice trails off. "Well, let's just say it's intriguing."

"Intriguing is a good word," I say, putting the luggage away. "What else do you know?"

She sighs. "A slave obeys her master. A slave's number one job is to ensure that she serves her master's every wish, with no thought to her own." A short pause, then she continues. "And a—a slave trusts her master to care for her every need."

I nod. "That was more than a little. Now go freshen up before we go to the guest reception and we'll begin our task." With a nod, she gets up and goes to the tiny bathroom. When she's out of my sight, I drop my face in my hands.

I don't know what will happen to us next. But I do know that if I'm honest? I'm not devastated about being Taara's master and having her by my side as my slave. The knowledge that I'm going to fucking enjoy this may be the very thing I fear the most in any of this.

Chapter 8

Taara

IT FEELS like I'm in a sort of dream.

Nightmare?

Dream.

Something in between, I guess. It's hardly utopia here. I'm his slave, and he my master, but hell, there are worse things than being alone with Stefan.

God, I still have feelings for him. How could I? How could I not hate the man? But the truth is, a downturn of his lips, a shake of his head, a stern click of his tongue, and I'm ready and eager to obey him. When he smiles at me, my heart dances, my hope rises, and I know, I *know* I should be more cautious, that I should protect myself better. I should hate him.

But I can't help it. My feelings for him run deep, and it seems impossible to eradicate all of them.

For now, my only job is to prove my loyalty to him. I trust that Caroline wouldn't steer me wrong, and this is what she suggested I do.

I can do this.

Deep breath.

I can.

I return to the small room after cleaning up in the tiny bathroom. The boat suddenly sways, and I lose my footing. We're so close, I practically tumble into his lap. He catches me with ease, his eyes doing that crinkle around the edge thing that kills me. How can he be so casual about all of this?

"You alright?" he asks in my ear, that sexy-deep grumble of his skating straight between my legs. I bet he knows how he affects me, the jerk.

"Of course," I say. I try to push myself off of him, but of course he doesn't let me go until he's ready.

"Good," he says. "You'll have to learn to get your sea legs." He laughs mirthlessly. "I guess you'll have to learn a lot of things."

Jerk.

He sets me on my feet in front of him.

"Wear this," Stefan says, handing me a tiny black sheath dress that looks as if it's little more than a tube top. I blink in surprise but take it and turn to go back to the bathroom.

"No," he says, sitting on the edge of the bed and crossing his arms on his chest. I look at him over my shoulder, confused.

"No what?"

"You may not get dressed in there. If we are to be master and slave aboard this ship, you'll learn to be comfortable being naked in front of me."

"I... oh, God. Seriously?" Is he going to go all controlling on me?

Well. Obviously.

Sigh.

I stare at him, at the man I once loved, the sexiest man I know, and I wonder if I can do this. How will I?

But then I think of Caroline. The stories she told me. What she's endured. And I decide once again, I will not falter. I will not cave. I'm going to prove once and for all to Stefan that he can trust me, that I will do what he tells me. Because hell... if I'm really honest? I want his approval, and if that means sashaying my naked body in front of him, then... Well. It could be worse.

Lord, what my mother would say.

But something has to give between us. Something has to change. I can't keep vacillating between hatred and want, and if I can show him I'm on his side... if we can both be on the same side... maybe I can turn this around.

So, I give it to him. My trust. My obedience.

My submission.

I don't want to. But it's the choice that's best right now. And sometimes, you need to choose between two shitty options.

"Yes, sir," I say, my voice humble and meek, while I strip out of the rumpled clothing I wore on the plane. My hands shake, the collar at my neck feeling suddenly heavy with the weight of my new role. I grasp the hem of my red top and yank it over my head. Now I wear nothing but a plain white cotton bra and a pair of leggings. This would be sexy if we—no. There is no *if*.

Let's be honest.

This is fucking sexy.

I watch as he shifts uncomfortably, his gaze molten when my clothing falls to the floor like the wrapping of a gift. It thrills me. It *exhilarates* me. Hell, it turns me *on,* and then I realize with sudden vivid awareness, *I'm controlling this.* He might be the one with overtly more power than I, but right here, right now? I'm the one commanding this energy between us, and I love that I am.

I step closer to him, watching his every move as I roll the top of my leggings between my fingers and begin to push them down. I step one foot out, then another, and without hesitation, remove my panties and bra. My breasts feel fuller than normal, my body tight with the tension that rises between us. This room is so tiny, there's hardly any space between us at all, so when I stand in front of him, no longer clothed, he only has to reach out a hand to draw me to him. My breaths mingling with his, we're sharing the same space, the same air, but more... the intimacy of this moment. And he'd have to be made of granite to be immune to this pull between us, our attraction as inevitable as gravity.

When he touches me, I lose my resolve to outwardly obey but remain detached. Hell, did I ever have that much control? I can't be angry with him when he touches me like this, his rough hands at the small of my back, pulling me between his legs, as if he's meant to touch me there. To hold me like this. As if I'm his, like my body's grooved to fit his touch and when he holds me, we're one. My throat tightens and my breath hitches. I'm dancing between logic, desire, and a need so desperate my heart is being rent in two.

Without a word, he dips his head to my shoulder and kisses his way along the slopes to my neck. My head falls to the side, granting him access to the tender skin. I moan when his tongue trails along my collarbone, followed by a sensual suckle I feel straight to my clit. The tenuous hold I had on my resolve crumbles.

Pulling his mouth away, he groans. "Fucking gorgeous," he says in a husky voice. "Jesus *Christ*." I thrill at the sound of his voice. I love that I affect him like this. I wish this were another place and time. It's my every single fantasy come true when he runs his hands up and down my back and over my aching ass, palming each cheek in his firm grip, dragging me even closer until the roughness of his clothes scrapes my naked skin. His blue eyes blaze with hunger, his large, muscled body vibrates with energy. I'm no fool. This is no act.

"Taara," he says hoarsely. *"Ty boginya."*

"Tell me what that means again?" I whisper. I have a vague recollection but want to hear him say it.

He drags his hands up my back, pulling me closer, fluttering kisses anointing my bare skin before he groans, "It means you're a fairy, a mystical, whimsical feature from another world come to steal my heart."

"I'm not," I say, my cheeks flushing in embarrassment just seconds before he squeezes my ass in disapproval.

"Stop that," he chides, but the corrective tone of his voice wavers. "Your only response here is *yes, sir,* or *yes, master.*"

"Yes, sir." I like that better than master, which sounds weird and stilted, but it still doesn't feel quite right. Something is a little… off with the title. But I push the thought away. This whole situation is *off*.

In silence, he holds me to him, kissing the valley between my breasts before he worships the fullness and curves of each one, palming and stroking and weighing them in his hands. I stop breathing when he leans forward and grasps my nipple between his lips.

I buck and moan when he laps and suckles. I've never felt anything like this. He's working my body like a master *should*. He's never even kissed me before this moment and it's not the kind of kisses I've imagined, but I'm not complaining. Of all that's happened in the past day, this is almost worth it.

Almost.

He's still a fucking *jerk,* and a little sexy times isn't changing *that*.

"Good girl," he murmurs in my ear, and the words unexpectedly thrill me. Oh, God, I love when he approves of me like that, his words appealing to a need hidden deep, deep within me. I once again try to remain detached and aloof. I tell myself this is necessary for me to prove my loyalty to him, and this is no more than a job. I'm like a prostitute of sorts or… something. We can't pretend to be a couple aboard this ship without touching each other. Hell, I may even have to whore myself in obedience to him, so that he knows he can trust me. So that I can convince him *we're on the same team*.

Caroline told me to convince him, and I trust that woman.

But right now, this is no act. I don't fabricate the little moans that escape my lips, the way my knees buckle, and I fall sitting onto his lap. The way I lean against him when he cradles me in the crook of his arm and tips me back, granting him access to the most sensitive parts of my body. The way my heart hammers in my chest when he holds me close and dips his mouth closer to mine.

Our breaths mingle in anticipation. Gentle fingers stroke my chin, then cup my jaw. Blue eyes light with unquenchable fire, holding my gaze for long moments before lowering his mouth to mine and brushing my lips with his. I wish this were real, that he wanted me like I want him.

But I shouldn't want that. I know who he is now... who he *really* is... and it's too damn dangerous for me to allow myself to even begin to entertain *any* romantic thoughts.

I mean, God, I'm a *slave on a ship* for him. Does it get any worse than that?

He must feel me tense or perhaps his own inner censor warns him to stop, as quickly as he kissed me, he stops.

"Let's go," he says harshly. He stands, and I tumble to the floor, nearly falling but he grabs my elbow and rights me before I do.

The spell is broken.

The clock struck midnight.

My carriage is turning back into a pumpkin, my riches to rags.

My ragged breathing stills, and I right myself with a heavy sigh.

"You listen well to me, little girl," he warns. The angry, stern taskmaster is back. I clench my fists as I listen.

Jerk. You're such a jerk.

"Yes, sir?" I snap back, not even bothering to mask my anger at this game of cat and mouse. "What is it, sir?"

"I want nothing but utter obedience from you both inside and outside the walls of this cabin. Am I clear?"

"Crystal," I say with derision, barely refraining from curling my damn lip up at him. "Do what you say," I parrot. "Obey your every command. Speak to you with respect, let's see… anything I'm forgetting?"

He weaves his fingers in my hair so hard and fast I gasp when he tugs my head back. "Respect," he snaps. "You forgot *respect*. In your tone, your posture, your actions, and your words."

"Only one problem, sir," I say through clenched teeth. "Respect is earned, not demanded." I know in my head I shouldn't mouth off to him, that this isn't going to end well for me. I can still feel the cut of the cane he wielded on me, and I try to stop my mouth, but I hate how he's playing with me.

He isn't amused. "Perhaps I should school that mouth of yours before we leave this room? Hmm?" And hell, that gives me a little reluctant tingle.

"Whatever you wish, master," I drawl so sarcastically, I literally bite my lip after I say it. But I'm too angry with him to obey without question. I'm not sure what type of reaction I'm trying to get out of him, or if I'm just behaving on instinct. You know, it's a lot easier saying "show him your loyalty" than actually fucking doing it.

And hell, if it doesn't turn me on watching the way his brows snap together and his eyes flash at me, the stern clench of his jaw and the way his grip firms on my arm.

With a rapid, harsh tug, he drags me to my knees and sits on the edge of the bed, pulling me between his legs before he unfastens his zipper.

My mind flashes, *warning.*

What exactly might "school that mouth" mean? I think I'm about to find out, and hell, I'm already wet.

His hand fists around his cock when he freezes, as if he's acting on instinct and just realized what he's doing. My heart stutters in my chest, because I suddenly *know* what he's doing. I suspect "schooling that mouth of mine" would mean his cock between my lips in forced submission.

I really, *really* need to curb my temper and watch my mouth. Though my anger is justified, it's not helping this situation.

I swallow hard, not sure what to do next. Apologize? Push him away?

Or knock his socks off by giving him the best fucking blow job of his life?

He must feel what I do, he has to. This exchange of power is electric between us. Dynamite. The air between us fairly sparks with anger and passion, the pungent scent of arousal so strong I nearly moan out loud.

He works his jaw and reaches for my mouth, grasping my cheeks between his fingers so hard it hurts. "I'm not taking you out there and risking fucking everything up because you don't know how to obey," he spits out. "You're unpredictable and that makes you a goddamn liability. If I can't trust you to watch your mouth, I can't trust you out there with me at all." He looks to the door then back to me. "Is that what you want, Taara? To be cuffed to this bed for hours while I work that floor alone? Take another woman?"

No. Oh God, no. He knows I don't want that, and it makes me want to slap his beautiful face for even suggesting such a thing. I hate that he's playing the jealousy card. It gives him that much more control over me.

"No," I tell him, shaking my head, even with his hand still gripping my cheeks. "No, sir." My words are slurred like this, my voice tight and choked. I close my eyes for one brief moment before I open them again. "I'll be a good girl." I let my eyes drop dramatically to his pants and he releases his grip on my face. "I'll even suck that cock of yours for you if you really want to school my mouth."

God, I will. I swallow hard and lick my lips. I want this. My voice drops to a low whisper, but I'm not manipulating him. I mean this. "Perhaps I can prove my loyalty on my knees rather than in a crowded room of men."

"Perhaps," he says, his voice hoarse and ragged.

I watch as he strokes himself, his eyes boring into me. "Would you, babygirl?" he whispers. "Show me your loyalty on your knees?"

Babygirl.

Oh, God. Oh, I like that. I like that a *lot*.

I nod eagerly, "Yes, sir," I say, but once again it doesn't feel right. Something about this moment is off. I nearly shake my head, because the truth is, *everything* about this moment is off, everything except the palpable need and want and longing that's growing between us.

We are both using our circumstances as an excuse. I'm on my knees before him as his supposed "slave." He's got me in his grip as my supposed "master."

But neither of us are immune to the erotic pull between us.

There's more than role play here.

But before we can take any steps to further this, before either of us does something we regret, he pushes his cock back in his pants and tugs his zipper up. I breathe out a sigh of relief even as my heart sinks.

"I'll tell you only once, Taara. Watch that smart mouth of yours or the next lesson you'll get *will* be on your knees in front of *all* of them."

And I know he means it. This is no idle threat.

But worse? *I want that.*

Then we're walking to the door, his face angry and impassive, my steps quick and hurried to keep up with him.

What the hell just happened in there?

We exit to the hallway, and I'm pleased to see we're alone for a few moments. I need to get myself together before we reach the crowd. We don't speak, though he doesn't take his hands off of me, not for a moment. His large, rough hand holds mine to him protectively, tucking our folded hands by his side, as we walk toward the main meeting area. I don't know what to expect when we reach the crowd, but I know that I have to stop fighting him. At least for now.

Not only do I get a chance to prove my loyalty and thereby my innocence, but he mentioned something else as well. Something about Afghani refugees and my ability to help them. What wicked things do the owners of this ship do? And how can I really help? But it stands to reason that it's in my best interest to observe and not cause any disturbance. I'm hoping all this will become clear soon.

He doesn't lead me to the main welcome area, though, but to another room. My steps instinctively slow when I see the darkened doorway ahead of us, and the crowd of people walking toward the doorway en masse. Couples with an obvious, decided power difference: the men fully clothed and in charge, the women submissive. The slaves.

But something tells me this is no consensual arrangement. There's an air of desperation that warns me this is not a little jaunt to a BDSM club, no consensual rendezvous among friends. These men are possessive but lethal, the women under their absolute control.

A large portion of them have my dark skin and hair, and I could imagine them on the streets of my mother's homeland, dressed in tunbaan and chadoors, the dresses and head scarves that serve as traditional Afghani wear, and it fuels my decision. I may find it near impossible to do

as he says on principle. But I have a choice. I'm not

merely a victim in this. If I play this right… I'm under-cover, and my job with him has the potential of helping my people.

This I can do.

I think.

Chapter 9

Stefan

I HATE HAVING HER HERE, exposed in her too-short dress, but worse, in the presence of people I don't trust. The majority of these men are part of the underground slave trade. The few that aren't only function as paid staff. She knows very little of what is really going on. We've discussed some, but she doesn't know how badly the infiltration permeates all of America.

Sworn to secrecy, with iron-clad non-disclosure agreements, the staff here welcomes politicians, military, and every form of leadership in our country. They revel in lewd acts and debauchery, and if I'm honest, my brotherhood is no exception. Until my son Nicolai interfered, Tomas demanded payment to his Bratva in the form of a virgin bride from auction. He no longer does so and is happy they've cut off ties to the auction now that he knows the Thieves are behind the human trafficking in

America, and the ties to the slavery ring among my brotherhood run deep.

"Stefan." I look up to see a tall, bearded man with his arm around a woman with vibrant violet hair. Her skin is black as night, her eyes exotic and beautiful.

I nod. "Mikahl." I know him to be a former brother in San Diego, and further know that Tomas' dealings with the San Diego contingents eradicated corrupt leadership there. I've kept Atlanta neutral, loyal to neither San Diego nor Boston, and in the past year that decision has paid off.

His eyes go to Taara before traveling back to me. He looks at me questioningly, but I don't answer the implied question. Have I bought her at auction? The less I say, the easier it is to stay consistent with my story.

"What brings you here?"

I shrug. "Same reasons as anyone else. You?"

"Same."

Taara grips my arm tighter when a couple engages in a scene to our right. I hold her close to me, watching myself, as the man ties the woman to a bench and lifts a stout leather strap from a peg on the wall. She flinches when the leather makes contact with the woman, then turns back to me. Her eyes look questioningly into mine.

Would you?

I nod. Yes. I have no qualms about such a scene if she gave me reason. Or hell, even if I just felt like I wanted to or *needed* to. Did she forget her caning?

"Good to see you, brother," Mikahl says, shaking my hand,

before turning away and taking his woman further into the crowd. I'm not sure if I like that I know people here. I'd prefer anonymity. But Mikahl has already moved on, and I hope he forgets me. Though I'm not hiding the fact that I'm here, it's best if I keep my own counsel. For now.

"Oh, God." Taara mutters beside me. I look to where she does, and see a woman tied to an exam table, spread-eagled and stark naked. Her eyes are wide, her mouth parted, and she makes a little squeaking noise.

"Not your kink?" I ask her, my lips twitching. I can't keep the humor out of my tone, because her reaction amuses me. She's either horrified or turned on, and I can't tell which until her nose crinkles in disgust. The brothers I know revel in the power exchange. Men like us enjoy the release it gives us to have a strong woman under our control. I like to dominate and master.

"Um, *no*," she says. "I honestly didn't know that was *anyone's* kink."

"Taara, this ship is a sex club on water. You know that, don't you?"

"Well I... yes, but I... oh, God." She pinches the bridge of her nose as if she doesn't know how to respond. "I didn't know it would be like *this*."

Oh, she has no fucking idea. We've only scratched the very surface of what this world we've delved into holds. Our purpose here isn't play, though.

We watch couple after couple, electric play and impact play, chained slaves on hands and knees beside whip-wielding masters, a foursome bringing a woman to orgasm over and over again until her voice grows hoarse. Some is consensual and some clearly is not.

And I'm curious. Every time we witness a new scene, I whisper in Taara's ear. "That?"

"No," she says, shaking her head, her eyes wide and lips slightly parted in astonishment.

Then a pretty blonde woman wearing a light pink dress walks in front of us. I know without asking them that this is not one purchased from the auction, but the partner of one of the members.

"Oooh," the woman says, and they're close enough we both watch as he takes her hand in his and leads her to a nearby bench. "Daddy, this is something I've always wanted to try. Will you, daddy?"

My chest tightens. How will Taara react?

Taara's eyes widen, and she looks up at me curiously.

"Daddy?" she mouths. I give her a slight shake of my head with a finger to her lips to tell her to be quiet, when the man sits on the bench and draws his woman on his lap.

"If you're a good little girl for daddy," he says, tucking her up against his chest.

"That," Taara whispers, but right after she does, she clamps her hand on her mouth as if she didn't mean to say it out loud.

I look at her in surprise, not sure at first what she's talking about.

"That what?"

She jerks her chin toward the daddy and girl and her cheeks flame, but she doesn't lose her resolve. "*That.*"

And then it dawns on me.

I'm decades Taara's senior, the oldest member of the Atlanta brotherhood. And she's known me for years. I don't think I imagined her feelings for me, however distant they may be right now.

"You like that," I state, drawing her near to me. I finally understand why she's so eager to please me, why her calling me *sir* sounds forced. Why she's served me without question as my paid staff.

Does Taara have a little bit of a babygirl in her?

I aim to find out. I find a vacant bench and tug her over to it. I sit, and without preamble, tug her onto my lap. "Sit on Daddy's lap, little girl."

Her cheeks flush a deeper shade of pink, and she bites her lip between her teeth. "Yes, sir."

I shake my head. "No, Taara. The correct response is *yes, daddy*."

"Stefan," she whispers, burying her head on my chest to avoid looking in my eyes. But I won't have that.

I take her chin and draw her gaze to mine.

"You'll do what I say, little girl, unless you want to find yourself over daddy's lap?"

Christ, I'm fucking hard, my cock a steel rod against her ass just *saying* this. Everything about our relationship is wrong, so it's an easy matter exploring this with her as well.

Fuck taboo.

"Yes, daddy."

And then she drops her head to my chest again and buries her face, unable to look at me. She's trembling.

Through everything we've done, this is the most vulnerable I've seen her yet, and I instinctively know I've stumbled on something she didn't anticipate.

"Good girl," I whisper to her, and hell if this doesn't feel *right*. "Such a very good girl for daddy."

"Stop saying that," she says, but it's a weak plea, as if she has to say it but doesn't really mean it.

"Who makes the decisions here, Taara?"

"You, sir."

I clear my throat. "Try that again."

"Oh, God. You, daddy."

If Taara is a babygirl, I'll have to treat her very differently than I have, but it excites me to know this about her. Seeing her naked made me hard. Having her between my legs, when I was on the cusp of punishing her with my cock between her lips, that was hot as hell. But this?

Fucking hell.

"Daddy" is an American word, and maybe that's why it is easier for me to accept this as *ours,* a taboo power play that turns both of us on. To reach that level of trust with another, for her to be able to give this to me and for me to honor it, could strengthen our relationship.

But hell, is that what I want? Where will that lead us? Taara and I aren't a couple. We've been forced together and now need to make the most of our situation. But if during our time together we find something that makes it easier, we could explore that avenue.

Nothing about this is right or normal, so why shouldn't we do what we want?

We don't speak for a few minutes. I hold her on my lap, her head on my shoulder. I use this time to observe the room, to listen in on the conversations around us, but it's difficult from where we are.

"Stefan?" Taara lifts her head up and whispers. "D-daddy?" she flushes madly.

I nod.

She pushes herself up on my lap and weaves her hands around the back of my head, pulling my ear to her mouth. "Did you hear that?"

I shake my head. "Hear what?" I whisper back.

"The man at the bar." Her voice is so low I can only make out her words with concentration. "He just said *Moscow*."

I sit up straighter. Though it isn't a dead giveaway that he could lead us to something we need, I can't dismiss this clue without further examination. I keep my look casual, as if I'm just glancing about the room. He has no woman with him that I can see but stands with three other men that look as if they could be his brothers. And one of them is staring straight at Taara.

"Put your head on my chest," I whisper, and like a good girl, she immediately obeys. Who is this motherfucker that's looking at my woman? I know it's my own damn fault for even coming in here, but it's the quickest and most expedient way to find the information I need. Tomas said to look for Adam Numeros, the man who runs the auction. A friend to Tomas, his allegiance is to Boston above any other brotherhood, and he knows the inner workings of the slave trade better than any of them. In recent years, he's stepped back from direct involvement, but Tomas promised me he would be aboard this ship.

I look about the room, but I'm aware of every set of eyes that looks toward us. I hate that Taara is dressed so scantily. Though anything more than what she wears would make her stand out, I underestimated the amount of attention this beautiful woman would draw. Christ, I want to cover her so only my eyes can see her. I want to take her back to the room and hide her. Why the fuck did I decide to do this? For one brief moment, I imagine her dressed in the burka of the most traditional Afghani people, and it's the first time I've understood the purpose of such conservative garments. Hiding everything but her eyes sounds pretty damn good right about now.

I'm looking for Numeros, the contact Tomas told me to look for. I try to see the man who's standing at the bar with his back toward us, as it looks like he fits Numeros' profile. "Let's get a drink," I say, gently drawing Taara off my lap. She keeps her head bowed and leaves as little space between us as possible. I need to get her alone. Something happened in here tonight that's affecting her. I'm going to find Numeros, listen to what I can about Moscow, then get the hell out of here.

When we approach the bar, I see a man who's small and lithe, with swarthy skin, when he looks to me, his piercing blue eyes confirm this is indeed the man I'm looking for. I don't go to him at first, the men standing next to him are speaking in low, rapid Russian.

"Vodka," I order for me, "And a glass of Pinot Grigio for my girl."

She grips my hand tighter.

We drink in silence, and I keep our backs to the men, but I'm catching bits and pieces of their conversation. One mentions the *prichal*—a wharf, and another the *otgruzka,* or shipment. We need a place and time, or at the very least names we can pursue, if we're to find the men behind the potential overtake of the American Bratva. I gather little bits and drabs of conversation, but nothing really concrete.

"Come," I say to Taara, tugging her toward Numeros. When I reach him, he lifts his glass in greeting and clicks mine.

"Stefan."

"Numeros." We shake hands. Though we can't speak as freely here as I'd like, he may have information we need.

"And you are…" his voice trails off as he looks at Taara. She looks to me for permission to speak.

Good girl.

She'll be rewarded for that.

"This is Taara," I tell him, but offer no further information.

Numeros sips his drink. "Nice to meet you," he says, then to me, "She looks Afghani, but I have no recollection of her being in any of the auctions." He smiles. "I'd remember."

"You've spoken to Tomas?" I say tightly. I'm not answering the question.

He nods, takes another sip of his drink, and fixes his gaze somewhere over my shoulder when he speaks in a low whisper. "The men behind you. Brigadiers to the

Thieves." He clears his throat. "That's all I can tell you. Watch them."

I nod. "Thank you."

He shrugs a shoulder. "Be careful. And if you follow them?" His eyes go to Taara. "Leave her behind."

Then he waves a hand to someone who greets him from across the room, and leaves that quickly, likely so as not to draw any more attention from those around us.

Leave her behind? Like fuck I will.

"Greetings," says a voice behind us. *"Pervyy raz na bortu?"*

Your first time aboard?

I grip my glass tighter and hold Taara by my side, while I turn to greet the three men Numeros gestured to, the ones he says work for the Thieves. These are the very men who plan to overtake our American Bratva. They know who I am. We've spread word that their comrade, the very man whose body lies in a grave Nicolai and Rafael dug this morning, is still alive, so they don't suspect my motives.

"Hello," I greet. "And yes, it is."

Two of the three men are blond, one with a shaved head, and I'd bet under their suit jackets all three bear the ink of the Thieves.

"Your son's no cruise virgin, though, eh?" The man with the shaved head holds a shot to his lips and downs it, holding my gaze in bold challenge. It's widely known my son obtained his wife from one of the auctions, but that she was sold into slavery by her father. There are varying opinions on how and why Nicolai did what he did, and I will not allow it to come into this conversation.

"And your name?" I ask the man with the shaved head.

He places his drink on the bar before turning back to us and gives me a calculating smile. "Master." He won't tell me his name. It isn't until then that I realize he has a woman on a chain behind him. He snaps his finger and two more women, all dressed in skimpy clothing with bowed heads, approach them.

"Join us?" he asks. "We're going to a private room for the remainder of the evening, and your woman is beautiful." He scoffs at the room around us. "And there are far too few pure-bred Russians in attendance."

I take a second shot, hold up the vodka to toast his drink, and play my part. *"Ya soglasen, brat."*

I agree, brother.

If I'm to get in with these men and find out what I need to know, I can at least acquiesce to solidarity with fellow Russians. In recent years, various brotherhoods have inducted men into their groups without demanding pure Russian ancestry. Throughout history, from Hitler to Genghis Khan, men sought to overthrow political regimes under the auspice of purifying the population. I wonder if the reasoning behind the plotted overthrowing of the American Bratva is related.

Taara looks to me with wide, fearful eyes, but she gives me a slight nod. Being alone with these men is dangerous, but it could also grant us access to information we need.

"Thank you," I say, keeping my temper in check with forced control. "I'm happy to join you, but I don't share her with anyone." There's a limit to how far I'll go to find what I need.

One of the blond men laughs out loud. "We'll keep that in mind. I think we likely have plenty of women to go around, so you can keep your little Afghani whore." He winks as if to soften the blow of what he just said, then turns from me. He walks away which is a damn good thing. I was seconds away from breaking his fucking nose and slicing his throat, and *that* could get a little messy.

Taara turns to me and tugs on my arm, pulling me to her so she could whisper in my ear. "Sharing me with them might grant you more access to information we need."

My body goes rigid, my pulse racing. "No fucking way," I whisper back, and I fully intend on playing the cards I have to ensure her obedience. She responds unpredictably to *sir*, but perhaps she'll respond better to her *daddy*.

My mouth at her ear, I whisper, "And if you suggest such a thing again, you'll find yourself over daddy's lap for a good, hard spanking. Understand?"

She pales and nods, then swallows hard, without a trace of disobedience. "Yes, sir. I mean, y- yes, daddy." It's unlike Taara to stammer. I can't fucking wait to get her alone and delve deeper into what fuels her.

The men are leading us past the bar, and several women follow their lead. "Do exactly what I say, young lady," I instruct her. I hate that we're doing this, that I've brought her here, but I know that if we can make it past this situation, I will find what I need. We go past the bar filled with people and noise to a smaller, secluded area, down a short flight of stairs, deep into the belly of the ship. The room is luxuriously outfitted in black leather furniture, with dim purple lighting, and thick, plush carpet. Fortunately, if my sense of direction is right, we aren't far from our private room here. When I've obtained the information I need, I will bring her back to privacy. But first, we have a job to do.

The men have more women waiting for them, but within a minute, three more follows, until the small room is filled to capacity. At first, those that invited us only speak amongst themselves, until one produces a large bottle of vodka. It seems order is a mere formality, as this group shares freely from the large bottle. They slosh some in my cup, and I down it. I watch as the men strip out of their jackets down to their t-shirts, some revealing the star-tattoo that's widely known as the mark of a Thief.

But they don't speak to us. Rather, the men pair off with groups of women. Taara and I watch in fascination as one man sits beside us and places a woman between his legs. I catch a few phrases that make me stiffen.

"*Minet,*" and "*Naveshat' pizdyley*." He's threatening to beat her if she doesn't suck him off. Taara doesn't hear what he says but watches the way the man yanks her head and forces the woman's mouth on his cock. The woman kneels, her hands in her lap, and dutifully does what he says.

And Christ, it makes me hard. Why an act of lewd violence like this, devoid of any romance or tenderness at all, gets me off makes me furious. When one man comes our way, his eyes on Taara, I almost lose the last threads of hold I have on my temper.

"Look away," I order Taara, yanking her toward me. "And get on your fucking knees."

She falls to the floor, her eyes wide and curious, but she isn't afraid. She swallows hard and licks her lips, her hands folded in her lap like a good little girl. Then in the most submissive, demure voice I've ever heard her use, her gaze holding mine, she whispers, "May I, daddy?"

And right then, right there, I'd give that woman fucking anything. She's in this with me. She knows what's at stake and how dangerous our position is. And instead of fighting me, or running away, she's falling into her role as my slave. When I draw out my cock and line it up at her lips, she actually looks eager and excited.

And hell, if that doesn't unravel my resolve.

"That's it, babygirl," I say when she leans forward and captures my cock between her lips. "Just like that, baby."

And when my cock glides between her lips, her eyelids flutter shut and she moans, the vibration making me hard as fuck.

"*Milaya devushka,*" I groan. *Sweet girl.*

It's been so long since I've been with a woman, and fucking decades since I've been with one that I've had true feelings for. I've shoved the memory of Amaliya and *any* woman I ever cared about out of my mind. It's too painful, and it's easier to be who I am if I get off with women that I have no attachment to. But this woman... Fuck, this girl...

"Just like that," I groan, when she rolls and sucks with ease. Her head bobs between my legs, she's eager to please me. I reach down and grasp her nipples over her little dress, rolling them between my fingers as she works my cock.

"Touch yourself," I whisper. "Work yourself to climax while sucking daddy's cock."

Her hand trembles while she glides it between her legs, and she moans again, the vibration on my shaft hot as fucking hell. My cock throbs in her mouth but she doesn't relent, sucking me hard as she works her clit. The room fades while I draw closer to climax, and she's working herself harder, faster. I tweak her nipples one last time before I chase my release. Hot come lashes in her mouth and she groans, her body shuddering as she brings herself to orgasm on her fingers while sucking down every drop, and it's gloriously fucking beautiful. She groans and sucks, swallowing and writhing until she releases me. We're panting and sweating when we look in each other's eyes.

"Christ, Taara," I groan when I finally settle.

I should feel regret. This isn't right. I've just fucked her mouth in a roomful of predators, and we're not here for pleasure. Not to mention, she's way too young for me. Her mother practically left her to my care for fucks sake.

But I don't. I fucking don't. I draw her to me and hug her. With a sigh, she places her head on my knee. I run my hand over the top of her head.

"You please daddy very much, little one," I whisper in her ear, and for the first time since I was forced to take her... this feels *right*.

Christ, I'm in so much trouble.

Chapter 10

Taara

I LOOK up at his eyes, those beautiful eyes of his, and wonder if what I discern in those depths is real or my imagination because right then? I swear this isn't just sex. This isn't just my captor, the man who's embraced cruelty in the name of justice and his brotherhood. There's so much more I see right then, so much I can't quite accept it, because if I let myself believe that what I hope is true, it will hurt too much if I find out it isn't.

That he actually cares about me. That I mean something to him. That somehow, his feelings toward me have changed, like Caroline promised. I haven't really done anything to merit that change. Not yet. But what if he felt that way before…

No. I have to stay focused.

My heart's still drumming a rapid beat, a staccato rhythm

that thunders through my entire being, after what we just did. And there's more than that, other couples mingling all around us in this close, intimate setting thick with sex and domination.

He slips his cock back in his pants and zips them up, and the sound of the zipper makes me bite my lip and my cheeks heat. Oh lawdy, I just blew Stefan Morozov where anyone could see.

He doesn't take his eyes off of me, and is it my imagination or is the sex-sated blissful look shifting?

"You've done that before," he says, almost accusatory, his brows drawing together.

I'm still on my knees, still weak from coming, the salty taste of him lingering on my lips.

"Done what?" I ask. He reaches for my hand and brings me to my feet, then forcibly pushes me onto his lap. His only answer is a growl.

"Ohhhh." It dawns on me, and I'm a little annoyed. "If you're wondering if I'm a virgin, the answer is no. But yes, you're the first man I've sucked off."

God.

"Don't say that. It's vulgar."

But his accusation annoys me. "Are you kidding me? We're in a room full of people having outright orgies, and you want me to be all discreet?"

He reaches down and slaps my thigh, hard. "Ow! Hey!"

"I should lock you up."

I'm feeling somehow more buoyant after what we just

did, invincible even, so I kinda shrug a little. "Sounds hot."

He isn't amused, his grip on me tightening. *"Taara."*

"Yes?" I ask sweetly.

"You were too good at that for me to believe that you've never done that before."

Hot damn, I like this possessive side of him. I like that the thought of me with another man makes him angry. I like that he said I was good at that. But I told him the truth. I'm not a virgin, but I've never given a blow job. I've never *wanted* to until right now, right here, with *this man*.

"I haven't, I promise," I tell him.

How can I tell him that I have *in my head*? How I've fantasized about just this? How I've sucked down romance novels like they were candy while taking copious mental notes?

I mean, it's a viable way to learn.

"You're lying," he says, but a corner of his lips quirks up a bit, as if he's teasing me now, and he really hopes that I'm telling the truth. But I want him to know that while I might tease him, I might push my boundaries, and I'm no angel, that he can believe me when I tell him the truth. So I look up at him, take his face between my hands, and hold his eyes with mine.

"I would never lie to you," I say, with every bit of sincerity I can muster, because this isn't just about a blow job I just gave the man, but the very premise for my captivity. "Never. I value honesty with you far too much to ever tell a lie."

He holds my gaze for long moments, his hands resting on my wrists, before he leans in closer and kisses me. Just a brief touch of lips to lips. Just one moment of the two of us together in a crowded room. But it's all I need.

I close my eyes and drown in this kiss. This stolen moment. In the truth that will, please *God,* eradicate any doubt he has about me and tether me to him in the way that I long for. The way that I need. The way that we both do. And then he pulls away, and I become aware of the voices and sounds around us.

I want to run. I want to leave this place, burrow myself in his chest and let him cover me so that no one else knows I'm here. I want to be alone with Stefan.

But I have a job to do.

"Thank you, daddy," I say, not shyly this time but with all the hope and confidence I can muster. I can't understand it and don't even bother trying. I'm not the first woman to call her lover daddy and I won't be the last.

Wait.

Wait.

Lover?

What *are* we?

"Thank you for what, little one?"

My heart melts a little every time he calls me that. "For looking at me like I mean something to you. For kissing me."

I close my eyes as soon as the words leave my mouth. I've gone too far, and I can't bring myself to look at him.

I've said too much. Stefan and I have a job to do, and we can't let my ridiculous infatuation with him in any way affect our focus. And what if my honesty has pushed him away?

"You're right," he says with a smile. "Christ, Taara. I know it now."

"What?" I whisper. What's he talking about?

He tugs a lock of my hair and shoots me a brief, crooked grin that melts me into a puddle. "You can't tell a lie."

Then believe me, I want to say.

But maybe… maybe he already does? But it's someone else he needs to prove this to? He takes my hand in his and laces our fingers together, and I smile at him.

"I really can't. My nose practically grows."

"Good to know. Any Pinocchio-like symptoms, and my babygirl's earned a spanking for lying to daddy."

Oh hell, I could get into this, *big time.*

On instinct, I pout, which earns me a good tug to a lock of my hair.

"Behave, Taara."

I drop my head to his chest and breathe him in. We have so much ahead of us, I need to steel myself for what I need to do. For the trials I know we face. If we're going find out what we need to, we'll have to become just like them. And how much can one role play without having a transformation of sorts?

Still cuddled up to him, I'm enjoying every damn minute of this. He's strong and warm and this is utter perfection. He holds me so tight, so close, I wonder if he likes this as much as I do.

I let my gaze roam a few feet away. I catch the eye of a woman who looks so similar to me, we could be cousins, and that gets my attention.

She's one of them. One of the stolen ones. To my surprise, when she catches my eye, she crooks a finger at me. I point wordlessly to my chest.

Me?

She nods, her expression darkening, and beckons me with more urgency. Then she turns on her heel and steps quickly to a door marked *restroom*.

She knows something.

I make a split-second decision.

"I have to use the bathroom," I tell him.

"You'll have to wait," he says firmly. "There's no fucking way you're getting out of my sight and I'm not allowed in the restroom with you."

"But I—"

He holds up a finger to stop me mid-sentence. "When daddy speaks, you listen," he says, and hell I wish he didn't put it that way, because it makes me feel little and submissive, and I need to get shit done. I promised I would work with him to get to the bottom of this trafficking fiasco, and my gut says this girl beckoning me has something to say. But he won't let me go.

"Fine," I say with a sigh, while internally plotting how to get away from him, and thank God right at that moment the men from earlier approach us. Stefan puts me on my feet so he can stand to greet them, and I look about me for my chance. My heart's beating so fast I'm light-headed. He's going to punish me for this. I know he will. There's zero doubt in my mind that he would lose his mind if I got away from him right now, but I have to do my part in this job we have.

So I take my hand from his, pretending I dropped something, and to my relief, he's deep in a conversation with one of the men. I fuss with my shoes and keep my head down and take one step backward. He doesn't notice. This could be my chance. He looks at me for a moment, then someone else speaks to him, and when he turns to look at them, I bolt. I keep my steps at a fast-paced trot. He could see me now, but he couldn't stop me without drawing attention to us.

In six paces, I'm in the bathroom. I open the door and shut it behind me. I'm panting, like I've just run from the police and made my escape. I'm shaking, because not only do I know that what she's going to tell me is important, but I know when Stefan gets his hands on me, he's going to punish me.

The woman I saw on the main floor opens the door and comes in when I do. "Thank you," she whispers. She's about my age but her hair is short, and she's wearing even fewer clothes than I am. I start when I see finger-shaped bruise marks all along her upper arms. What cruelty has she endured?

But before she can speak to me, the door opens again, and the woman with the violet hair I saw earlier steps into the room. Tall and gracious, her exotic, almond-shaped eyes smile at me. She doesn't speak but locks herself in one of the stalls. The woman who beckoned me here catches my eye in the mirror and holds a finger to her lips. I pretend I see nothing, and step into the second stall, pretending to use it while we wait for the other woman to vacate.

A moment later, I hear the flush of a toilet, and watch the silver, pointed-toed shoes of the woman beside me exit, then the sound of a faucet being turned on.

"Ferhana," she says. Her voice is clear and melodic, like church bells. "Are you well?"

"I am. Just needed to freshen up a bit," she responds.

"Your master will be looking for you," the other woman says. My stomach tightens at the warning. He will indeed be looking for her. This woman needs to get the hell out of here.

Her fancy shoes click-clack on the tiled floor. I flush the toilet, so this all looks normal, and hear the door open and close. I come out of the stall and go to wash my hands when the woman who beckoned me in here goes to the door, shuts it, and flips a deadbolt, locking it.

"She's right," she says in a voice just above a whisper. "My master will be looking for me. I have to be quick. But I know, you are not one of the women from the auction, and you are with the man with the beard."

I nod.

"We have to be quick," she whispers. I don't know how she knows she can trust me or how I know I can trust her—okay, I *don't* know that I can trust her, I'm still very much taking a risk here. "They'll kill us as soon as look at us," she whispers, and the reality of the danger we face settles on me thick and smothering. "I've seen him do it. He says we are easily replaceable."

Right outside this door are men that do unspeakable things. And just the fact that we're both standing here, each bearing resemblance we can't deny, it's obvious.

Easily replaceable.

We're expendable, and we know it. They could snuff us out like birthday candles.

But she *isn't* expendable. *I'm* not. Hell, no human being is. Every single human who walks this earth, from the tiniest, most dependent child, to the frailest elderly person is worthy of a life well-lived, respected, and honored. A vision of my mother, so thin and weak, holding my hand, immediately assaults my memory. I think of Caroline, the woman who bears the scar of the cruelty she endured.

And I decide once again that whatever it takes, I'm going to help Stefan end this trade. Even if it kills me.

I can do this.

"I know every single woman who's come to auction since the beginning of the year," she says. "I forget nothing, and you are not one of them. And the man you are with has kindness in his eyes unlike any of the others. Tell me who you are."

Shit.

Stefan is going to *kill me*. Like literally, have my *head*. He's probably looking for me now.

Shit shit shit.

"My name is Taara," I say, not wanting to give too much away. "The man I'm with is one of the Bratva *pakhans*."

Yeah, so that was probably already too much. *Damnit.*

She nods. "He did not buy you, did he?"

I shake my head. "No, but I—" I pause, then say with conviction, "but I belong to him. I am his slave and he my master." But I don't give her any more information than that. I don't know who she is, and I don't fully trust her. "And who are you? Why did you want to speak to me?" I can't let this become a one-sided interrogation.

She shakes her head. "It doesn't matter who I am. I'm nobody." She isn't nobody. The pretty woman with the violet hair and skin as black as night knew her name. She continues in the same hushed, timid whisper. I wonder how she even got the nerve to come here. "The two of us need to make the acquaintance of one another. The man who calls himself my master is a cruel man, and when he finds out I've come here without his permission, he will punish me. And if he knew I told you what I'm about to tell you..." she pales.

She draws closer and take my hand. "Promise me you will help them."

I don't know this woman, and I will likely never see her again, but when she squeezes my hand in hers, we're immediate and instant friends, bound together in this travesty that affects us all.

I nod. "I will do everything I can." She doesn't need to tell me who she's referring to.

We start when someone tries to turn the doorknob. A second later, a large fist bangs on the door, a deafening *boom* making us both jump.

"Open this door!" I don't recognize the voice, but one glance at her and I know she does.

She closes her eyes briefly, as if to steel herself for what she'll face, then her eyes flutter open and she whispers in my ear. "I eavesdropped today. I know where the next shipment will go. Tomorrow night, ten o'clock, at Long Wharf in the city."

I nod. I will remember this. I have to finds Stefan.

She stifles a scream when the fist pounds on the door again. "He'll share me tonight," she says in a shaky whisper, as if she has to tell someone. "He'll make me sleep with all of his men for this." Then her eyes look at mine in desperation and her grip becomes frantic, her eyes bulging out of their sockets so widely it unnerves me. "Take me with you. Will your master take two slaves?"

Jesus, *God*, as if I'd let another woman touch him.

I blink and shrug, not knowing how to respond. "I—I don't—"

No, I want to say, but a part of me wants to rescue this woman so badly, I can almost deny the rampant jealousy that takes hold of me at the slightest suggestion. Another *bang* crashes on the door.

"Get into the stall," she whispers. "It might save you."

Before I can process what she's saying, she shoves me in and shuts the door, then I hear her step away and fumble with the lock. She's so brave. I'm sick to my stomach, but I turn the lock to the stall with trembling fingers. If I let myself be taken or injured, I can't bring what I know to Stefan. I can't stop what's going to happen.

The door yanks open, and from the bottom of stall, I see thick black boots stomp into the room.

"*Ty, blyad', shlyukha.*" She screams, and I can't see what he's doing, but I can tell from the scuffle that he's dragging her out of the room. I hear him slap her, and I flinch, then another scream as she's dragged out. But at the doorway, he pauses.

"Who else is in here? You aren't alone?"

"No, sir. Please!" she screams again, and then footsteps approach my stall. I go as far back as I can, but there's no room in here. Nausea whirls in my belly and my head feels too light. I look around for something to protect myself, but of course there's nothing at all in the bathroom stall.

"Open this door!" he orders. Oh, God. Where am I going to go? What will he do to me?

A second later, I gasp when the door to the stall flies open with a large *crashing* noise. He literally smashed the door right off its hinges. It's one of the blond bastards, glaring at me. Holding her by the hair in one fist, he reaches for me with the second. I smack at his hands but it's useless. He's bigger and stronger, and she's doing nothing to defend herself, likely out of fear of what he'll do. He grabs my arm and hauls me out of the stall. I stumble, banging my head on the door, but before he can do anything to me, a loud, furious voice fills the stall.

"Get your hands off her. I've got this."

Relief floods me so rapidly I'm dizzy with it. *Stefan.* Oh, thank God. But my relief is short-lived when Stefan's livid eyes meet mine. My stomach drops straight to my toes. Right now, I'm not really sure he's a safer bet than the other man.

The other man drops me so quickly, I stumble, grabbing onto the porcelain sink to steady my fall. Stefan is glaring at the man and a muscle ticks in his jaw. His hands are clenched into fists so tight he's white-knuckled, but his voice remains steady and calm. "What's going on in here?"

The men speak in rapid-fire Russian, so quickly and furiously I have no idea what they're saying. The girl hangs her head and won't look at me. I bet she's resigned to her fate, now that this asshole's got her. But when Stefan speaks, she looks up at him. He crosses the room to me and pulls me to him, shielding me from the monster that's still holding the other woman by the hair.

"Is this true?" Stefan asks.

"Is what true? I have no idea what you're talking about." Christ, I'm a terrible liar. My voice shakes and I can't look at either of them.

"He says you two were in here with the door locked. That you are plotting something. Is that true?"

"No, sir!" I lie. "Never! I came in here to use the bathroom. I don't even know who she is. And I think the door must've been stuck. Neither of us locked it."

"She lies," the man says to Stefan, spittle forming in the corner of his mouth like a rabid animal. I shudder and bury my head on Stefan's chest. "They locked the door. They were conspiring."

"Conspiring against whom?" Stefan says, smiling at the man, and I know this is an act. He's feigning nonchalance, but he wants to shake the living daylights out of me and maybe hurt the man.

"Us, of course," the man says, but Stefan's question seems to set him off.

"How, brother? We already own them. And this little one here knows that anything less than honesty and submission will get her punished." He gives me a look that's no longer playful. *"Severely."*

Yeah, I'm toast.

They speak again in Russian, until another man comes to the doorway. The blond man turns to him, says something under his breath, then drags the girl out with him. Stefan's voice stops him before he leaves, though.

"Just one more thing?" he says, almost casually but for the ticking of his jaw. Blond guy turns and quirks a brow in his direction.

"Don't ever touch her again. Not one solitary finger." He shoots him a chilling smile that promises pain and retribution. "In fact, it would be best if you never even *look* at her again. Do we understand each other?"

Blond man swallows hard. "We do. My apologies, brother."

Stefan shoots him a chin lift, and the other guy leaves. I'm alone with Stefan in the bathroom, shaking so badly I can hardly stand. He turns me around to face him, wraps his arms around me, and hugs me to his chest. I bury my face on the fabric of his shirt and breathe him in, then out, tucking my arms around his back and holding onto dear life. He brings his mouth to my ear and whispers, "You scared the shit out of me."

"I'm sorry. I had reasons."

"Reasons," he scoffs. "You are in *so much goddamn trouble*."

I swallow. "I know. But I have to speak to you alone. Can we leave?"

"Oh, you bet your ass we're leaving," he says, taking me by the hand and dragging me out of the bathroom.

I repeat what I know so I don't forget.

Tomorrow night, ten o'clock, at Long Wharf in the city.

Chapter 11

Stefan

I'M SO ANGRY, I can hardly see straight. I grind my teeth together so I don't say something I regret. I'll have her alone shortly, and she will tell me exactly what the fuck she was doing. It's bad enough she left my side without permission, in blatant disobedience to my commands. But when I saw that man's hands on her —*fuck*, I need to hit something. *Break* something.

My muscles contract and sweat forms on my brow, my body vibrating with anger as I escort her out of the room. What the fuck was she thinking? She better have a good goddamn answer for what she did. I'm about to redden her ass so badly she won't sit for a damn week.

I never should have brought her here. *Never.*

Thankfully, no one follows us as we make our way to our room. And what a fucking waste. I found out literally nothing in that little private party than I knew before I came. Has this entire visit to the ship been in vain? We should've flown straight to Moscow.

But if I hadn't brought her here... my mind goes back to that scene we shared before she left, and hell, my dick's hard again just thinking about it. Would she have done what she did?

Daddy.

I shake my head and open the door to our room. I don't care how sweet that moment was or how sexy, I have rules for her, and for good reason, and this little girls in big fucking trouble.

I drag her in the room and slam the door.

"Stefan," she begins, but a swift slap to her ass has her quickly amending herself. "Daddy!" We are not on equal footing here and we might as well get that cleared up.

I spin her around and pin her against the door before I grasp her shoulders. I want to pound this door with my fist, until it splinters and shatters, find that motherfucker who came near her and knock his fucking teeth down his throat. "What were you thinking?" I say, my voice taut with anger. "You disobeyed me. You risked your safety. Christ, Taara, if I hadn't come in there right then—" I want to shake the truth out of her before I take her across my lap for the spanking of her life.

"I had to," she says. "Please. Listen to me. I'll tell you everything. Please, daddy."

My cock hardens and instead of punishing her, I frame her face in my hands and bring her mouth to mine. I give thanks for this moment, that she's safe with me, that I found her in time, and that no one hurt her. Her soft, sensual mouth melds with mine, her hands wrapping around my waist as if to steady herself. She moans, and one lone tear falls down her cheek. With great reluctance, I pull my mouth away from hers and whisper in her ear, "Why, Taara?"

"She had answers for me," she whispers back. "I have the location and time we need."

I close my eyes. "It wasn't worth the risk to your safety," I tell her. "If I wasn't so angry with you, I'd take my belt to your ass for this. Hell, I still will. You'll learn that daddy says what he means." I kiss the softest part of her cheek. "*Always.*" I can't believe she has the power to make my anger evaporate so easily. A moment ago, I wanted to throttle the girl for what she did, but now, I want to wrap her up and tuck her away. Take her to a place where no one will ever find us. Strip her clothes off and make sweet, lazy love to her until she comes beneath me, then falls asleep beside me, her body one with mine.

There's no use denying what's between us anymore. I've never allowed myself to have feelings for her. She was too young, too innocent. But now that we're alone in this… the two of us thrown together in a situation where neither can back out now… I have to accept the truth. I'm falling in love with this woman.

"I—I believe that you meant what you said," she says in a soft voice, the sound skittering along my skin like fairy dust, almost, *almost* weaving me into its magic. "And I knew you'd be angry. But please listen to me, daddy. I had to do it."

"Like hell you had to."

"I did," she says, and a fire lights her eyes when she looks at me. "And I'd do it again."

That does it.

"Oh, really?" I ask, pulling away from her and standing her in front of me. "Would you?"

This is not okay. Not at all.

And that little firecracker puts her hands on her hips and flashes those beautiful eyes at me. "I would. Because it's important. And because I need to prove to you that you can trust me!"

"By disobeying me?" I ask, reaching for the buckle of my belt.

"Yes!" she says. "Well... I mean..." and then her gaze travels to my hands, and she watches in wide-eyed fascination as I unbuckle my belt and tug it through the loops.

"By helping you," she says.

"Go on," I say, folding my belt into a loop and giving it a good, hard *snap,* which make her jump.

She backs toward the bed, and now I've changed my mind. I *like* the tiny size of this room. There's nowhere for her to go.

In one step, I've caught her.

"Stefan!" she protests, when I flip her over and push her belly down on the bed. "Don't!"

"Don't what?" I ask. "Whip your pretty little ass for disobeying me? I'm sorry, little girl. I think you've woefully underestimated me."

In one quick tug, I rip the little dress and it practically disintegrates in my hands. A firm hand on her lower back pins her in place and with the other, I snap the folded leather across the fullest part of her ass.

"Ow!" she howls. My dick's a steel rod at the sight of the red stripe on her creamy, gorgeous skin. I lash her again, and again, ignoring her mewls and howls of protest. The way she wriggles beneath me makes me even harder, but I don't let up. This little girl is going to learn that I mean what I say, if I have to take my belt to her every damn day.

"You'll obey your daddy," I tell her. "Am I clear?" Our mission is urgent and deadly, and I won't let her strong sense of justice and fearlessness endanger her life.

"Yessss," she wails, as I whip her again, the *thwap* of leather and her protests making me almost lose my resolve. "Yes, daddy."

I bring the belt down three more times in quick succession, red stripes lining her pretty skin.

"Will you ever go against my instruction again?"

Thwap.

"No, daddy," she wails. "I'm sorry, daddy!"

"This matters, Taara," I lecture. "This fucking matters."

She howls when the leather falls across the crease at the top of her thighs. "I know," she moans.

"Then *please*, Taara. Never again. You'll do what I tell you."

Thwap.

"You'll trust me to take care of you."

Thwap.

136

"Do *not* disobey me."

She's mewling little protests into the bed and nodding her head. She's had enough. I lay the belt down beside her and run my hand along her heated, reddened skin. She still bears the marks of the caning I gave her, and now my belt. At first, she flinches and moans, until she relaxes into my touch. Allowing me to make it better.

I massage her tender skin, my palm cupping each of her ass cheeks as I rub out the burn and sting. My cock's aching for release, straining against the zipper of my pants, but I need to tend to her. A daddy's job is more than enforcing rules. I have to be sure she's okay.

"Come here," I murmur, turning her around and lifting her up into my arms. I cradle her to me and walk to the head of the bed, sitting down and holding her to my chest. I rock her, whispering soothing, calming words.

"I don't care how urgent you think it is," I tell her. "You don't know the evil some of these men are capable of. How easily they would end your life."

And as I hold her to me, rocking her back and forth in consolation, I know. She's more than my charge. I've cared for Taara for as long as I remember, but not in this way.

I love this woman. *Love* her.

"How could I have found out what I needed to?" she asks, her voice shaking.

"You could've trusted me to find out. Or told me who I needed to speak with. I could have at the very least orchestrated you talking to the girl without the danger of someone accosting you."

She doesn't speak at first. "I suppose that would've worked," she finally admits with a sigh, and I actually laugh.

"I suppose," I concede. I sigh. "Taara. When I saw you were gone, I thought the worst." I close my eyes, remembering when I realized. I looked to my left, then my right, and over every inch of the small, private room before I heard a commotion near the bathroom. And when I saw that asshole breaking down that door, I knew. I fucking *knew* she'd be in there.

I kiss one cheek, then the next. She took that spanking without shedding a tear. Taara is my brave girl.

She watches me, wide-eyed, her eyes bright and damp.

"You thought the worst?" she whispers. "What do you mean?"

"That you were gone," I say, my voice choked. "That someone hurt you. These men are capable of terrible evil, Taara. They don't even think twice."

Her eyes drop to my chest, and she runs one finger along my shoulder, as if testing to see if I'm real. That she didn't make this up. Like she's fantasized about this very moment.

"They are," she whispers. "Which is why I want to defeat them."

"I'm not an innocent," I tell her. "I'm not a good man. But I will do whatever I need to protect you."

"You killed that man because you had to," she says, her voice stronger now. "If you didn't—"

I put my finger to her lips. "I never, ever take a life without good reason. But we will not sugarcoat who I am or what I do. We do not justify what I've done. *Ever.* Do you understand me?"

I know then the spanking I gave her got through, because she nods submissively and swallows hard.

"We don't ever justify my actions. I'm the leader of one of the most dangerous organized crime rings not only in this country, but this *world.* You know that, don't you?"

She nods again. "Yes," she says, then she pushes herself up on my lap so she's facing me. "But I want you to know something. I'm not as naïve as you might think, and anyway, I…" I watch as she swallows hard before she says with conviction, "I… I lo--I still care about you anyway."

She was going to say *I love you.*

Christ. But she held herself back.

She has to. I have to. Fucking hell, we both do.

"I…care about you, too," I tell her, feeling like an idiot. But I do. I fucking do. "It's why I punished you just now." My voice breaks when I admit the truth to her. "Because if anything ever happened to you—if anyone had taken you—" I can't finish the sentence.

I take her in my arms and lean her back, silencing her with a gentle, tender kiss. She tastes like fine wine in summer, decadent and sumptuous, and with her tucked against me like this, all feminine curves and exotic temptation, molded to my body, she feels as if she belongs here. Just like this, just this way, and the very thought of anyone taking her from me fires me with conviction.

I will keep her safe, no matter the cost.

With that knowledge, I deepen the kiss. When her lips

part I slide my tongue between them in exploration. She sighs into me, her hands grasping for purchase around my neck. Standing, I take her with me and lay her on the bed, still locked together in a kiss. In silence, we declare our vows to one another, held in this unbreakable bond.

My hands ride up her body, bunching what remains of her tattered dress in hand. I release her mouth so I can tear her clothes off over her head, but as soon as she's divested of the dress, I go back to kissing her. When my lips are locked with hers, I can breathe more easily, my breath and hers one. Unwilling to take my mouth off hers, I cup her jaw and mentally tell her everything I want to say. What I wish I could.

I love you.

I will protect you.

I will keep you safe from whatever threatens us.

This is no mere girl I've just met, but someone I've watched grow to be the woman she is now. Fearless and brave, brilliant and loyal.

But I can't let myself fall for her. I won't.

She's supposed to be my fucking prisoner.

The need between us builds, and I don't bother to stop her hands gripping my shirt, yanking it up my body. I tear my mouth off hers with great reluctance but find solace in the fiery eyes that meet mine.

"Take your clothes off," she whispers.

"Your ass is still striped with my belt and you've got the nerve to tell me what to do?" But my lips twitch. She wants this as much as I do, and it's goddamn electrifying.

"You bet your ass I do," she whispers, gripping my ass cheeks in her hands. "You bet this glorious, tight ass I do."

"Naughty girl," I say with a cluck of my tongue. "Such a naughty little girl."

I take the hem of my shirt and yank it over my head, loving the way her eyes drink me.

"Oh Lord, have mercy and salvation," she whispers, running one long, tapered finger over my shoulder, tracing the faded ink there. "I was probably in grade school when you got these."

"That matters?"

She shakes her head. "No," she says. "It makes me want you all the more. Something tells me you're like whiskey. You get better with age."

I chuckle, tossing my t-shirt to the floor, where it falls into a tumbled heap while I allow her to continue to explore my body. Her hands roam up and down my sides, over my abs, and as she explores my muscles and ink, my cock aches to be in her.

"Wow, you are so damn hot," she says. I chuckle, lift her hand to my mouth, and kiss each of the tips of her fingers.

"I like your hands all over me like this," I say. "But if I have to wait one more minute to feel your pussy wrapped around my cock, I might have to punish you again."

She giggles, and it's the cutest damn thing I've ever heard. "That isn't fair."

"Fair? No. Necessary? Yes."

"Then let's take care of that, hmm?"

Our hands meet at my waist, mine fumbling with the clasp of my jeans and hers helping push them down. They join the t-shirt and I take one quick second to give her a reassuring squeeze. When my cock springs free, she grasps it in her hand, stroking it with her eyes on mine.

"Daddy likes what he sees, hmm?" she teases. I love this side of her, all saucy and sweet and bold.

She strokes harder and faster. I can only groan in response, rocking my hips into her perfect touch. I cup her breasts and skim my thumbs over her peaked nipples. Her hips roll beneath me, and she strokes me faster.

"Stop," I groan. "Stop, Taara." She obeys, and I give her a smile of approval. "That's daddy's good little girl."

"Oh, God, that's so hot," she moans. "Are we really going to do this?" she whispers. "Or am I dreaming?"

We're locked aboard a ship with men ensnared in evil, her body still bearing the marks of my punishment on her. I dragged her from her home and brought her into the middle of danger, and she wonders if *she's* the one dreaming?

"Shh, Taara," I whisper, my finger to her lips. I fetch a condom from my wallet, her little mewl of displeasure from losing my touch making me that much harder.

"Patience, babygirl." I come back to her and slide the condom on, kneeling beside her. "Trust me, Taara."

A pretty little smile plays on her lips. "Yes, daddy."

My cock twitches in response, and she bites her lip, her

eyes on mine. Leaning down, I capture her wrists in one hand and secure them above her head. My voice at her ear, I whisper, "We do this in silence, little one. Understood? No more talking."

Her eyes gleaming, she nods slowly, but mouths the words, *yes, daddy*. She looks at me with such adoration, such hope, I want to make every wish she holds in her heart come true. The utter trust and adoration she gives me fuels me. I can do anything when she looks at me like that. I anchor myself above her, holding onto her wrists, and line my cock up at her entrance. She bites her lip and I bend down, kissing the tension away. "Trust me," I whisper in her ear. She parts her legs, welcoming me closer. I've forbidden her from speaking. This is her showing me trust.

The first stroke shakes me to the core, it's so fucking perfect. Her tight pussy milks my cock with ease, and she moves her hips while I rock against hers. I thrust, and she moans, I press her wrists harder and her hips rise to meet me. With every stroke of my cock her lips part wider, every thrust and her mewls get more frantic. Silently, like a lover's waltz, her hands clasped in mine with her pinned beneath me, we chase heaven.

I could come just like this, just from her hot cunt wrapped around my cock and her sweet, supple body bending to mine, but I wait, I hold on until her head falls back and her eyelids flutter closed, her lips part in a moan, and I warn her. "You ask permission before you come, little girl."

"Please, daddy?" she whispers, and those words make my cock twitch inside her.

Fuck.

Flushed cheeks. Parted lips. Sweet, seductive moans of pleasure.

Jesus *fuck*.

I groan out loud, "Come, babygirl," and when she throws her head back in climax, I lose my mind. I come so hard my vision's blurred, I've lost my voice, she's moaning and wriggling in my grasp. I groan out my own climax, rocking my hips with hers. On the tail-end of her climax she writhes again, a second spasm overtaking the first, and her voice rises in pitch. So fucking passionate. So fucking beautiful. So graceful and impassioned, I'm losing myself to this woman like I never have before.

I never let myself imagine that Taara could be mine. She is too innocent, too sweet, and way too damn young. But when I kiss her lips and touch my forehead to hers, I know.

Tarra was created for this moment. Taara was created to be mine.

I roll over and bring her to my chest. "Come here."

She tucks her head under my chin, hikes one knee up on my legs, and drapes her arms around me as if to put every cell of our naked bodies next to one another. It isn't until I feel dampness on my chest that I realize she's crying. She took a whipping with my belt and didn't shed a tear, so I wonder where this comes from.

"Baby," I whisper. "Are you okay? What is it?"

When she looks at me, her lashes are dotted with tears like tiny diamonds. "I don't know," she says. "I didn't mean to cry. It's just... I mean, there's no point in holding it back anymore."

I tighten my arms around her. "Back what, baby?"

"I've admired you for so long," she says, shaking her head. "I only wanted attention from you. I never dreamed that my feelings…" She falters. "That you would want me, too." She squeezes her eyes together and another tear rolls down her cheek, and when she speaks, her voice is barely above a whisper. "I'm sorry for what happened, Stefan. Do you believe me?"

I know then that I do believe her. How could I have ever doubted her?

"I do," I tell her. "Forgive me, Taara."

We needed this. I had to ask her forgiveness. I know now that I want Taara for my own, and we can't move to that place until I've asked pardon.

For everything. Christ, for punishing her in front of my men, for humiliating her. For dragging her here and putting her in this position. I've been a class-A douchebag. What she said to me back in Atlanta was right. I'm the fucking *pakhan*. I didn't have to do this.

"Of course, I forgive you," she says. "I mean, I fucked up, too."

"Shh, baby." I won't hear of it. She was in the wrong place at the wrong time, and she's innocent in this. My voice firms as I make up my mind. "We won't speak of this again. What happened is in the past, and we'll put that behind us now. We start right here. Right now. Understood?"

She smiles at me through her tears, so beautiful and sweet and nods. "Yes, daddy." I'll never get tired of hearing those words, of holding her like this, of kissing her tear-stained cheeks. That she grants me this privilege is a damn miracle I won't forget.

And as I hold her to me, my arms wrapped around her as she sighs into my chest, I make a decision.

I will end whatever threat is posed against us here. I will take Taara back to Atlanta where she's safe.

I know I love this woman. And because I do...she's not coming to Russia with me.

Chapter 12

Taara

STEFAN HAS something on his mind. I don't want to ruin this moment, with the two of us still lying together like this it feels sacred, stolen even. But it matters to me what he thinks. I need to know what concerns him.

My feelings for him are resurfacing. I know that now, and while a part of me yells *warning* in my head, I can't help but want to *let* myself love him again. Can I go there?

"What is it, Stefan?" I ask, then I gentle my voice. "Daddy? Is something bothering you?"

I know it is by the way his gaze is distant and clouded, but when he looks back to me, he smiles, his eyes crinkling around the edges, and he kisses my temple.

Predictably, he doesn't answer the question but turns it back on me.

"Tell me what's on *your* mind," he says.

"No fair," I respond. "That's what I asked *you*."

In response, he tugs a lock of my hair. "Who's the daddy?"

Aw, hell, that *really* isn't fair. "You," I say. It's like he pushes a button when he says that and I get all melty and submissive, which isn't really me at all, but apparently *is* me when I'm with Stefan and he pulls the daddy card.

"It's crazy how hot that is," I tell him.

"Crazy?" he repeats, his lips quirking upward.

"*Crazy*," I repeat.

But he only shrugs a shoulder. "Not sure why."

"No?" I ask.

"And anyway, I like crazy," he says. "So yeah, this is hot to me. Having you on me like this, all starry-eyed and disheveled…" He strokes his fingers through my hair, his voice rumbling and unhurried. "The way you came with my name on your lips. Your ass still hot to the touch and striped with my belt." My heart thumps. "And yeah, baby. The way you call me daddy."

He holds me to him wordlessly for a moment before he continues. "And I don't need to ask why or how or what the hell this means. I just know that I like it."

I rest my head on his chest. I guess his quiet reassurance is good enough for me, too.

"Now," he says. "Where were we? You were telling me what's on your mind. Where do you go when you get that distant look in your eyes?"

"I get a distant look in my eyes? Me? I was just thinking that about *you.*" Seems we're both distracted.

He chuckles, ignoring my mention of him. "By my calculation, you're somewhere in the Far East right about now."

That makes me smile. "I don't know," I say truthfully. "I go lots of places, I guess."

"Tell me one," he suggests. "It'll be a good start."

"You want to know what's on my mind?" I clarify.

"Yes," he says earnestly. "But more than that." He smoothes his large hand over my elbow. "I want to know what's on your heart. What you fear. What you hope for."

"Really?" I ask.

"Why do you question me?" he asks, his brows furrowed. "Why wouldn't that matter to me?" I suppose it shouldn't surprise me if what Caroline told me is true.

"Well," I say carefully. "It isn't like we have a long history of trust between us. I mean, I think we're sort of on the expedited path..." my voice trails off when he chuckles. "What?"

"The expedited path," he repeats. "That's one way to put it. You're a treasure, you know that?"

No, I don't know that, but hearing him say it makes me feel tingly and warm all at once.

"Thank you," I say softly.

"You didn't answer the question."

"What was that again?"

"I wanted to know why you question that I care about what matters to you."

"Well," I begin, thinking before I say something silly or foolish. "Truthfully, it's hard to imagine that a man of your stature cares about such trivial things."

His brows draw together, and his stern features harden. "Taara, those are hardly trivial things. They matter, more than you know."

Just when I think I couldn't love him more, he starts tearing away the wrappings of my heart until I'm helpless to stop him. I'm only human after all.

My heart does a little dance in my chest. He wants me to talk to him.

"So, tell me, Taara."

"Okay, then. But you might not like what I tell you."

"Try me."

I draw in a shaky breath. "I am sad about losing my pictures."

His brows furrow together and his lips thin. He doesn't remember. "Pictures? What pictures?"

I sigh. "You told Rafael to destroy my phone, remember? I had…" I pause, my voice shaking. I swallow hard. "I had hundreds of pictures I've been taking for months on there. And they… they were important to me."

My throat feels tight and my nose a little tingly when I remember the way Rafael ground his heel into my phone on Stefan's command, like some overgrown playground bully.

"I'm sorry," he says. "At the time…" his voice trails off.

"I know why you did it," I whisper. "But that doesn't mean I'm not still sad about it."

It might seem to him that with all we face, I'm fixated on something trivial, but I'm not. This matters to me.

Nodding, he runs his hand over my head and down to my shoulders, then back again, as if trying to console me. And oddly, it does.

"Would you take more pictures if I got you what you needed?" he asks.

I swallow. "Of course."

Hugging me to him, he gives me a quick kiss. "Good girl. Now tell me what else is on your mind."

I think for a moment before I reply. "My mother," I say without hesitation. "I was supposed to see her this weekend. But now that we'll be in Russia, I won't be able to."

He nods. "That can be arranged, and soon."

I push up and look at him curiously. It makes no sense to me how that's possible if we're going to Russia. "What? How?"

"We'll talk of that later."

"No, Stefan," I begin, insistent on hearing what he has to say. "I want to know what you're talking about."

But he shakes his head, and his voice hardens. I know by now that when he looks like that, there's no point in trying to convince him otherwise. "No."

I sigh. He's as immovable as a mountain.

I wonder if his reluctance to tell me what he's planning

has anything to do with the faraway look he had just a few minutes ago.

We speak easily for a little while. He asks about things that interest me and shows that he's been paying attention when he mentions the foods I've cooked him, the books I've left lying around in the living room, and the classes I've taken. It's so comfortable like this, in the warmth of the room, on his chest with the blanket pulled up over us, I yawn widely. We've been through so much, and I'm utterly exhausted.

"You need sleep, little one," he says finally. "Let's get you to bed."

I've been a strong, independent woman for years now, but when he calls me *little one,* I actually *feel* little. I have to admit, I like it.

He helps me clean up and I climb between the sheets, still sore but blissfully content. Heaviness descends on me, and my eyelids suddenly feel too heavy to fight. I'm familiar with this feeling, but usually have a hard time falling asleep and if I do, staying asleep. But tonight, for the first time in years, I fall into a blissful, dreamless slumber.

I wake the next morning to dazzling light streaming in through the window, and a knock at the door. I blink in surprise. I never sleep until it's light out. I look up to see Stefan standing by the door fully dressed. How long have I slept?

He opens the door and takes a silver tray from someone on the other side, says a few murmured words, then shuts the door with one hand while balancing the tray in the other. Turning to me, he smiles.

"Good morning, sleeping beauty," he says.

"Morning. What time is it?" I ask on a yawn. "How long have I slept?"

"It's nearly noon," he says.

I sit up quickly. "I've slept half the day away!"

He chuckles. "You did, but something tells me you needed that."

Sitting on the edge of the bed, he slides the tray on the table beside me. The smell of bacon makes my stomach rumble with hunger.

"Sit up, little one," he says. I do, eager for some food, but when I reach for it, he shakes his head. "Let daddy do it."

So that part wasn't a dream, then. I bite my lip and nod, not sure how to respond. How do I feel about this? But when he puts a large forkful of eggs in front of my mouth and says, "open," it's easy enough. I take the bite between my lips and eat the eggs, then after I swallow, he follows it with a strip of bacon.

"Mmm," I whisper. "This is delicious."

"Good," he says approvingly. "It should tide you over for a little while, anyway."

He got up and showered and dressed, ordered food and everything. Wow. And I slept through it all.

After feeding me another bite of eggs, he continues. "We'll dock in about an hour, and I want you well fed before the next leg of your journey."

Your journey?

Wait. Why mine, and not "ours?"

It seems an odd choice of words, but I don't question him as he feeds me a bite of toast, another strip of bacon, and a wedge of orange. I finally hold up my hand to indicate I've had enough, and he lays the fork down on the tray.

"Aren't you going to eat?" I ask him.

He smiles, but for some reason the look in his eyes is distant. "I ate hours ago. And anyway, I want you to get ready before we dock, so let's get moving."

I throw the blanket off me and push to my feet, my body aching in reminder of what we did last night. All of it. Somehow in the bright light of day, I feel a little bashful about it, but he doesn't seem troubled at all.

"Get ready," he says, pointing to the bathroom. I do, and just as I finish, I hear Stefan call to me from the other room. "We're here. Let's go."

I come into the room where he is, and he already has our bags packed and ready to go. He takes me silently by the hand, then to my surprise, pulls me to him and kisses me so fiercely, I gasp, falling back a little, but he catches me. His touch feels nearly desperate, his kiss hurried.

"What was that?" I whisper, giving him a curious look. "Stefan? Is everything alright?"

There's a fire in his eyes and a firmness to his jaw that unsettles me. "Everything's fine," he assures me.

But I'm not so sure. I want to know that nothing has changed between us. That everything is still in place. "Tonight, we need to go to the wharf." I tell him what I found out, and watch as his jaw tightens.

When he shakes his head and doesn't meet my eyes, my stomach tightens. *"I'll* be going to the wharf," he says, busying himself with folding the blanket at the foot of the bed. "Tonight, you're getting a plane back to Atlanta."

I'm having trouble making my mouth work. "I—Stefan," I whisper, then on a whim, "Daddy. What are you talking about?"

"Don't do that, Taara," he says, his back to me. "Don't question me in this. It was hard enough to make this decision."

But no. I'm not going to cave that easily. I didn't work this hard and give up so much just to turn tail and run, leaving the rest of this battle for him to fight.

"What decision?" I say, unable to mask my anger. "To send me away from you?" I can't keep the hurt out of my voice.

"I'm not sending you *away* from me," he spits out. "And watch your tone of voice, Taara." He shoots me a warning look over his shoulder that makes my pulse spike, but I don't care. He has one hell of a nerve going all master on me after dropping a bomb like that. I don't care if he takes his belt to me again or canes me or does whatever the hell he thinks he has to, to get me to obey him. I'm not agreeing to this. No *way.*

"Watch my tone of voice?" I repeat, my voice rising in pitch. "Are you kidding me?"

"You really want to push this envelope?" He turns to me and crosses his arms on his chest, and I swear for one minute, I almost lose my resolve. He can be scary. His deep voice rumbles, warning me. "Keep it up, little girl, and you know exactly where this will land you."

"*Stefan*," I plead. "You just told me that everything I've done was for no reason."

"Don't *do* that," he says, and it might be my imagination, but I swear a tiny bit of his resolve begins to crumble. I push on.

"Do what? Speak the truth?"

"Taara," he warns, taking a step toward me, but I hold up my hand and take a step backward. Not that there's anywhere to go.

"No, Stefan. I've earned the right to speak the truth, haven't I?"

With a sigh, he concedes, but when he stands in front of me with his arms crossed on his chest, looking so intimidating, I almost cave. It's funny how quickly I forget how big and strong and muscular he is until he's standing in front of me. I've seen full grown men quake in front of him, so I know it isn't just in my head how scary he is. I take a deep breath, let it out slowly, then plead my case as best I can.

"You told me I had a chance to help the Afghani women," I tell him. "And if you didn't have me here with you, you wouldn't have found out what I did about tonight, would you?"

He lets out a breath and opens his mouth, but before he can speak, I plow on. "After what we've been through, what we've done, what we've confessed to one another, I'm not backing down. And I don't want to be separated from you," I tell him. "It matters to me. It matters *so much* to me. I can't even tell you."

His stone-like features soften at that, and he takes another step toward me. He's within arm's reach now, and I want to let him hold me, tell him everything he means to me. I've confessed my deepest dreams and wishes to him, my biggest fears. I've come to him at my most vulnerable and survived to tell about it, so I can't give up now. I *won't*.

My throat feels scratchy, and my nose tingles.

"Please, daddy," I whisper, and when I blink, a tear rolls down my cheek. "Don't make me leave you."

He gathers me to him and it's messy, my hair is all tangled in his beard and I'm crying, my tears dampening his shirt. I've cried before with him, but that was different then. That was before he broke me open and folded me all back together again. That was before I believed he loved me.

"Taara," he says brokenly. "I can't put you in danger again. If anyone hurts you, I'll have to kill them." And when I hear those words, I know, the weight of the lives he's taken anchors his heart and mind, and he's loathe to go there again.

"Then protect me, Stefan," I whisper. "I trust that you will. I know that you can." It's a lot that I ask, but I can't turn away now, and appealing to his inner need to look after me is my only chance.

He holds me in silence for long minutes, our hearts beating in time and my tears streaming down my face, before he speaks.

"Promise me you'll do what I tell you," he says, and I know then that he's softening, that he's considering my plea.

"I promise," I tell him.

He holds me tighter. "I mean it, Taara. This is no game we play."

I swallow hard. I'm willful and stubborn, but I can give this to him. I have to. So, I look up into his eyes and blink away my tears and give him nothing but the bald truth. "If you give me this chance, I promise you, Stefan. I will not let you down. I will trust you." I go up on my tiptoes and brush my lips across his before I speak again. "I promise. You have my word." I weave my fingers through his. "We're a team now, you and I." I use the last card I have, and I go out on a limb. "And do you really want to trust my protection to someone else?" I shoot him my most winsome smile, but this is the most important thing I've ever asked him. "This, from the man who insisted on feeding me breakfast by hand?"

"*Chert poberi*," he curses.

"I promise, if I even *think* about disobeying you, you can flay me alive."

"I fucking will."

"You won't have to, but I still promise."

He laughs, and I breathe freely for a moment. "Please."

Before he answers, he tangles his fingers in my hair, and closes his eyes as if steeling himself to do this. Then he captures my mouth and kisses me so hard it's bruising and punishing, as if he's warning me what I'm up against. My lips burn and tingle when he pulls away, his mouth just inches from mine.

"Alright," he concedes. My heart sings with hope. "We'll

do this together. You and me. And I'll hold you to everything you said, Taara."

"I know you will."

A knock comes on the door.

"Sir? Do you have luggage for us to take?"

"I've got it, thank you," he says. He waits until the footsteps retreat before he slides his phone out of his pocket. Still holding me to him, our hearts still hammering together, he brings his phone to his ear.

"Nicolai," he says with a sigh. "Cancel the flight. She's coming with me."

Chapter 13

Stefan

THERE'S no tenderness in my touch, no gentleness in my voice as we leave the ship. I take Taara by the hand and half drag her with me in grim determination. I can't believe I've let her talk me into this, but at the same time, I'm relieved. I *hate* the idea of being apart from her. And if she's with me, I can be the one to protect her, instead of trusting her to someone else.

There are no easy choices in this.

I observe everything I can as we load our bags into the car I've called for us to take us to the hotel, but there's nothing out of place. I recognize a few faces, but nothing stands out. Tonight, we'll stay at the hotel that's adjacent to the airport so we can easily catch our early morning flight to Russia. But before then, we have work to do.

We.

Jesus.

"Don't look so happy," she mutters, when I hold open the door for her. "Your face might freeze that way."

"Taara." My warning is a grumble, and I swear to God I remind myself of my father. My ruthless, asshole of a father, who spoke in grunts or fists, however the mood struck.

She only sighs and slides into the seat, and when I join her, gives me a little smile. "Yes, daddy?" And if that doesn't just melt my goddamn heart. She knows it does, too. I reach over and tug a lock of her gorgeous, midnight hair, but don't let go. I wrap it around my finger and rub my thumb along the strands. She watches me, her eyes bright and beautiful, but she can't move too far from me.

"Behave yourself."

She opens her mouth to speak, but something out the window catches her eye. I let her hair go and slide my hand to her upper thigh before I give her a little squeeze.

"That fucking asshole," she says under her breath. I look where she does and see the woman she talked to and her master from the night before. Her head hung low, and she's walking as if she's in pain. He drags her around beside him, careful not to make too much of a scene because we're in public now, and no longer aboard that godforsaken ship. But he hurt her, and it's obvious. He says something in her ear which makes her cower and cringe, and I make up my mind right then. It isn't just about the threat against the brotherhood. I'm no saint. Hell, I've earned damnation ten times over the for the shit I've done. But I will do whatever the hell I need to, to end this bullshit once and for all.

"Taara," I say, this time my warning more meaningful.

"Careful, baby. If you're going to work with me, you have to keep your temper in check."

"Says the man who nearly killed that guy last night," she mutters. "Ow!"

I tap the leg I just squeezed. "That smart mouth will get you in trouble."

She sighs and shakes her head. "It already has. Like *many* times."

We fall into silence as the car begins to drive toward the hotel. The streets of Boston are always teeming with people: pedestrians and bikers, business people, and construction workers. Our ride will be slow through the city streets. For now, though, I'm grateful for the tinted windows on this car, it allows me to get a good, long look as people leave the cruise ship. Many of the men from the private party come out first.

"That's funny," Taara murmurs to herself. "That's really weird."

"What is?"

"That woman over there," she says, jerking her chin toward the woman with the violet hair who accompanied Mikahl the night before. "She's holding someone else's arm today. It isn't the man from before."

I look, but shrug. "That's not unusual, sweetheart," I tell her. "Few in this game are monogamous."

"No, I know," she says, shaking her head from side to side. "But there's something else off about this. I can't quite put my finger on it."

But soon we pull too far away to see them as we head toward the hotel. I take a few minutes to make some calls, checking in on my men in Atlanta. All is well, and it pleases me to hear Rafael relay that Nicolai is leading well. Though in my heart of hearts, I'd prefer my son not entangled in the danger of Bratva life, I know how this works, and I know Nicolai. He's as dedicated to the brotherhood as I am.

I can't speak freely to Nicolai in the car, but I give him enough information that he knows things are going as planned. I'll fill him in on a secure line on a burner phone after tonight, on our way to Russia in our private jet.

Taara looks at me curiously, her head tipped a bit to the side while she worries her lip.

"She isn't a submissive," she finally says.

I look at her in confusion. "What are you talking about?"

"The woman. The tall one with the violet hair and dark skin. The beautiful one."

"Yes?"

"She isn't a submissive."

"How do you know?"

"She seemed out of place, because she was the one giving commands," she says. "It took me a minute to figure it out, and when she was with a second man, I knew. She's the one in charge in that relationship."

I shrug. "So? That doesn't mean anything. It's not uncommon for women to be dominant, sweetheart."

"I know," she says, shaking her head. "But it isn't that. I don't know. I can't really explain it, I just—" she sighs. "Last night, when I spoke with the other slave, that woman came into the bathroom behind us. And I don't think it was an accident. I think she was either spying on us or wanted us to know that she didn't miss a thing."

"Did she?" That is a little curious, given what happened last night, but still nothing I'm overly concerned with.

She shakes her head. "I have good instincts, Stefan," she tells me, as if defending herself.

I smile at her. "No doubt."

"And my instincts say we should watch her."

"Noted."

She huffs out an irritated breath. "You don't believe me!"

I shake my head. "I do. But I need more than 'she was in the room with us,' and 'she's not a submissive,' to go on."

We pull up in front of the wide, circular entryway to the Boston Harbor hotel. I pay our driver and take our bags to check in. Our check-in is quick and painless, and within a short time, we're in our room. I toss our bags in the closet and make a few more phone calls.

"Wow," Taara breathes, looking through the pamphlets on the bedside table.

"What is it?"

"There's like a spa here, a pool, a cocktail bar, and restaurants." She flips through the pages. "They have a valet service, and there's even this option to book a private appointment to get a haircut." She laughs. "Oh, the lives of the rich and famous."

But I'm not paying close attention, because I'm mapping out where we'll be tonight at the Wharf. There's an outside bar that overlooks everything, and I'm confident that if we get there at the right time, we can blend in with the crowd before we observe what happens. I have no doubt the finer details of the trade will be well hidden, but we can at least have a good reason to be there.

What if nothing happens? What if we show up and no one else does? What if the information she got from the girl is incorrect? I suppose we get our flight to Moscow in the morning and take it from there.

"They will even come to your bedroom just to paint your nails!" Taara is still leafing through the pamphlets.

"I'll paint your nails," I say, suddenly realizing that I have her alone in this room and there are several hours before we need to leave. After tonight we need to get some rest before our ten-hour plane ride to Russia, and we won't have the luxury of being alone together for probably another twenty-four hours.

And I want this woman. I want her so badly my mouth's dry at the prospect, at the knowledge that she's just mine for this short time, that we're sharing this luxurious room, and that what we have together is special.

She smiles at me. "Actually, I could totally picture that," she says, sticking out a foot and kicking off her black flat. She peers at her toenails. "I could use a little attention in that area, too."

I sit beside her and take her foot in my hand. "Could you?" I ask massaging my thumbs along her graceful foot. "A little attention, you say?" It feels nice to hold her slender foot in hand. I rub my thumb along her insole, and she groans. I smile at her. Damn, she's cute.

"Oh, *wow,* that feels super good," she says, putting her head back on the pillow. "Continue, please."

I pause the massaging. "Ask the right way."

"Please, sir," she says, but the teasing glint in her eyes tells me she knows exactly what I'm aiming for, and she wants to string me along a little.

I tug her little toe. "Taara."

Her face lights up and she grins at me, so lovely and winsome my heart squeezes. Holding my gaze, a few seconds pass between us before she lowers her voice and whispers, "Please, daddy?"

"Of course, baby," I tell her. I won't admit it to her, but when she asks me like that, her eyes all lit up and sparkling, in that sweet voice of hers, I'd give her damn near anything.

After a few moments, she sighs and closes her eyes. I lay her foot gently down on the bed and take her other foot in hand, remove the shoe, and begin massaging that one as well. Between her soft skin beneath my fingers and the little sighs she lets out, I'm getting hard just watching her.

Her head falls to the side and I wonder at first if she's sleeping, she's so at rest and comfortable, until she speaks.

"Isn't this a contradiction?"

"Contradiction?" I ask, rubbing my thumb in a circular motion, covering every inch of her skin.

"You're the master," she whispers, her voice pitching off into a yawn. "And I'm the slave. Yet you're the one massaging my feet. Serving me."

"Ahh. No, it's not a contradiction. Not at all. Masters can serve their slaves. In fact, the sign of a good leader is the ability to be meek. To serve."

Her eyes flutter open and she smiles softly at me. "Then you're a good leader," she whispers.

"Why do you say that?"

"Because you're here," she explains. "Serving your brotherhood by finding out who's behind all this."

I shrug. I haven't done anything for them until I've actually accomplished what I've set out to do. But she isn't finished.

"Because you treat them all with this... paternal care or something. You watch out for them, instruct them, set a good example. They respect you, and that's because you've earned that respect." I don't deserve her praise, and I shrug it off, but then she smiles at me. "You're a good daddy, too."

My already-hard dick tightens. Holding her gaze, I let my hands travel from her foot to her ankle. Pushing aside the fabric, I caress her bare skin. I love how her mouth parts and her breathing grows heavier. I'm impatient to have her again, to be inside her, to feel her hot, wet cunt and hear her moan in climax.

"Take 'em off," I say in a low, rumbling whisper.

"What? Take what off?"

"Everything."

Her cheeks flush pink and she bites her lip, but she doesn't hesitate to comply.

"Yes, daddy."

As if she's as eager as I am for this, her movements are frenzied, but my cock aches and I long to be balls-deep in her so badly I can't wait for her. My hands dwarf hers as I yank off her clothes. We toss them in a tumbled heap onto the floor.

"Stay right here," I instruct. Kneeling one knee beside her, I yank the bottom of my t-shirt and pull it off my hand, roll the fabric into a rope, lean down and twist it over her wrists. I pull it taut, then take a moment to admire her stunning, naked body on display before me. Her perfect dark skin, full breasts studded with hardened nipples, her rounded belly, and trim waist that give way to voluptuously curved hips. Her pretty tapered fingers fold above her head as if in prayer, her eyes meeting mine in challenge.

"You know, daddy," she says thoughtfully, shooting me a teasing look. "I'd love to lick my way up and down that body of yours." She swallows hard, her voice shaky and affected. "Those *tats*. Those *muscles*. I want to touch every inch of you and worship you with my mouth."

She's grown bold, and I have to admit. I love it. Taara owns what she wants. So brazen.

"Do you?" I ask, tracing my finger along the very edge of first one nipple, then the other. She moans and squirms, but the t-shirt holds fast. "I'm the one that's supposed to do that."

"Oh?" she says in a breathy whisper. "And why's that, daddy?"

This girl knows how to play me like no one ever has.

I lean down and kiss her cheek, then take her earlobe between my teeth and bite, reveling in the way she bucks beneath me. "Because, baby," I whisper in her ear, and though my words are a seductive whisper, I mean every one of them. "Daddy's the one in charge."

"Clearly," she moans. "Doesn't mean I don't want to."

I chuckle, while working her nipples between my fingers. "Of course. Someday, I'll let you. Deal?"

"Deal," she manages to croak out. I work my way from her ear to her cheek, kissing down her jaw to her neckline. When I reach the very top of her breasts, I drag my tongue lazily along her naked skin. She's sweet and salty, and I can't get enough of her.

"Do I taste good, daddy?" she whispers.

"I don't know," I respond, holding her eyes as I bring my lips further down her belly to her naval, where I lazily lap and suckle. "I haven't tasted you yet."

"Stefan." My name is a garbled, ardent plea I feel straight to my cock, but a quick pinch to her ass makes her amend herself. "*Daddy*."

I move lower, until my mouth hovers over her pussy. I breathe hot air over her, and she shivers and moans. I brace myself on my elbows on either side of her, cupping her ass in my hands to raise her pussy to me.

"Oh, fuck," she whispers. I draw the very tip of my tongue to the top of her pussy.

"Not yet," I counter.

"*Stefannnn*," she moans.

"Quiet now," I instruct. I push the tip of my tongue to where she pulses and groan. She tastes sweet and sultry and I need more.

I meet her eyes. "Don't move," I whisper. "Don't talk, until you're ready to come. And the only word I want to hear then is *please.*"

Biting her lip, her vibrant eyes wide and eager, she nods. With a sigh of deep contentment, I lower my mouth and drag my tongue along her slit. Her legs part further and her eyes flutter shut, as I lose myself to this, licking and sucking until her hips buck and she breathes the word I'm longing to hear.

"Please."

Chapter 14

Taara

OH, hell, this is good. His hot, wet, expert mouth on my pussy works me so perfectly to the edge of climax, I'm losing my mind.

"Wait, baby," he says when I beg for him to let him come, his hands traveling the length of my body until he reaches my nipples. I thought I was going to lose my mind before, but God this is even better. I lift my hips to meet his mouth when he tweaks my nipples and laps my pussy.

"*Please,*" I repeat.

He lifts his mouth just enough to whisper, "Come, baby," before his tongue returns to its wicked assault. He flicks my nipple, sucks my clit, and I sail headlong into euphoria. I moan as my body pulses and he works my orgasm to utter perfection. My breath hitches, and I curl my fingers above my head as spasms of ecstasy rock my body. I'm moaning and whimpering while he suckles and laps, and I've never felt anything like this before, so intense, so wickedly delicious, stars dance behind my eyes.

And then he's on me, his large, muscular body dwarfing mine. He gathers my secured wrists in his hands and kisses my temple.

"I want in you," he whispers in my ear.

"Go for it," I manage to croak out, and that makes him grin, actually *grin,* something I hardly ever see him do. And then he's pushing off his pants and rolling on a condom and joining me on the bed, his hot, swollen cock between my legs.

"Open," he commands in my ear. My legs fall open. I'm pinned beneath him, still hot and tingly from coming so hard on his mouth, when he lines his cock up and thrusts deep inside me. Oh, God, this is better, even more satisfying than his tongue on me. Because this is Stefan, and I love him. And there's nothing I need or want more than to be joined with him like this.

He works a blissful rhythm while holding my pinned wrists down.

"Fuck, that cunt's so tight," he groans in my ear. "*Fuck,* baby."

And then he trails off in Russian, probably saying something ridiculously filthy and hot, but I have no clue what he says and I don't care because the only thing I care about right now is his cock between my legs, the way his powerful hips thrust, the way my pussy clenches around him, and the fact that I know I'm going to come a second time, and soon. I'm getting closer and closer to the precipice of orgasm a second time while he moves in perfect rhythm inside me.

"Baby," he groans, pulling himself nearly out of me then thrusting in again to the hilt. *"Christ*, Taara."

And then I shatter. I fragment. I push my wrists against his impenetrable grip as bliss devours me. He pumps in me and groans, and I relish his every sound as his own pleasure overtakes him while I'm still rocking from my own orgasm. He milks every drop out of me, thrusting and gliding while I lift my hips to meet him.

It's perfect and lovely and painfully sweet and lasts longer than I could've imagined but not long enough.

And then he's whispering things in Russian and weaving his fingers through my hair, kissing along my forehead and cheek and chin then mouth, his soft lips in such contrast to the roughness of his beard it gives me a happy shiver.

I love this man.

Will he ever love me back?

It's easy to love someone when you're wrapped in the throes of ecstasy like this, but I know this is more, so much more, than sex-driven. Our lovemaking is only a culmination of what had to happen, a declaration of truth that needed to be said. He's claimed me as his own, and I've claimed him, and it's like we both think this at the same time, because he holds me tighter to him, and I return the embrace. His cock still hot between my legs, my body molded to him, we're one in this.

We lay like that, wrapped in each other's arms, the sheets knotted and twisted around us like spun cotton, and still we don't let each other go. I can't, and he won't.

Our stolen moment together needs to last as long as it can, because if we didn't capture this, the uncertainty of what lies ahead could tear us apart. His phone rings, and he doesn't move, lying his head on my chest.

"You should probably get that," I say, running my fingers through his damp hair, but his eyes are closed and he's breathing heavily. "Stefan? Are you sleeping?"

A corner of his lips twitches, and I know he isn't.

"No, but whoever that is can wait a goddamn minute while I enjoy this time with my woman."

I smile and bite my lip. *His woman.*

"It sucks we had to go through what we did to get here, though," I muse. "I mean, all you had to do was knock on my door."

I know he's laughing when his shoulders shake.

"I wouldn't have said no," I continue. "Hell, I'd have given you anything you wanted."

"You shouldn't say that," he says softly, but the pleasure in his voice mitigates any correction.

"Why not? It's the truth," I say, still weaving my fingers through his hair. His whiskers are rough on my bare chest, but his body is warm and cuddly, and this feels so right.

"Because it isn't right for a girl like you to be with a man like me."

"Since when do you worry about what's right?" I tease, but he shakes his head to stop me.

"Don't, Taara," he says. "Since it affects *you.*"

"But if I hadn't—"

"Shh, baby," he says. "Let's not question this. Let's not wonder what's happening or what will happen next. Let's enjoy this little bit of peace, hmm?"

"Yeah," I breathe, closing my eyes and drawing in a deep, ragged breath. This little bit of peace. But his phone rings a second time, and he curses under his breath. Pushing himself off me, he reaches for his phone and answers it.

"What?" he snaps. I give momentary thanks *I'm* not the one calling him. But as he listens, he sits up straighter on the bed, taking his warmth and whatever consolation that gave me with him. His brows are drawn together and his lips thin. "Do whatever the hell you need to," he says. "And tell me as soon as you know anything."

He hangs up the phone and drags his hand across his brow, exhaling. "San Diego's gone dark," he says. "All our contacts gone, the neutral men we had in position say it's like they vanished overnight."

"Vanished?" I shake my head. "How can that be? Don't they have a large compound like yours?" I don't know much about it except from what I once overheard Marissa say after a visit there.

He nods. "Vacated. No one knows where they went." He pushes himself out of bed. "I've got some calls to make." But before he does, he reaches out and strokes the back of his hand along my cheek. "You make this easier, you know," he says so softly I barely hear him at first.

"What?" I whisper. "I make what easier?"

He bends down and brushes his lips to mine before he answers.

"Everything."

I watch him in silence, drawing the blanket up over my shoulder and laying on my side. I like that I make everything easier for him, and the knowledge fills me with satisfaction. I don't really know what will happen to us next. But he asked me for forgiveness, and hell I granted that. The road he walks is narrowed and treacherous, and the position we found ourselves in compromised us both. But we won't let it change who we are, or the fact that two are better than one.

He gets dressed, and after a while I get up to take a shower. I catch bits of conversation as he makes call after call, and I can roughly gather that he's confirming with his associates that San Diego has indeed gone dark.

"This is like one of those military things," I tell him, as I slide on a pair of shoes. It's getting close to time for dinner, and I know Stefan wants to go to a little restaurant near the wharf.

"Military things?" he asks. He's tidying up our room and preparing our bags, since we leave first thing in the morning.

"Like a covert operation," I mutter. "Like a stealth bomber or something."

"Yeah," he says.

"Those planes you can't see, they fly overhead so they can't be sighted before they attack, right?"

My backs to him, so I don't know he's come closer to me until he hugs me from behind.

"Exactly, baby."

I swallow. I love the feel of him behind me, but I can tell

he's distracted and worried. "So how do you fight an invisible target?"

He sighs. "You draw them out."

"And that's what we're doing tonight?"

"Not yet," he says. "But we will. Tonight, we find out who's flying that plane."

I turn to him and lay my head on his chest for a moment, then go up on my tiptoes to kiss his cheek. "You'll do it," I tell him. "You'll find out where they are, and you'll activate the men around you. I know it."

He smiles sadly at me. "Do you, Taara? Tell me how you know it."

"Because you're the king," I whisper.

He shakes his head. "I'm no king."

But two can play at this game. "You sure as hell are," I say. "I've watched how the *pakhans* of literally every other Bratva group in America pay you homage."

"Have you?" He runs his hand up and down my back.

"I have. Tomas calls you for advice about everything he does. I mean, you even officiated at his wedding. I don't know every detail, of course, but I've seen how they treat you with respect. And when we get to Moscow, I bet it will be the same."

He smiles. "We will see about that." But I can tell by the way his eyes dance at me that he's pleased.

As we close in on the time when we need to leave the safety of this room, my heartbeat begins to quicken. I'm not sure what will happen next, but something tells me it's going to change the course of everything.

"Listen to me, Taara," Stefan says after we're ready to go. He's got the location we're going to mapped out on his phone and plans in place.

"Yes?"

But he doesn't speak at first. He draws me to his chest and crushes my face against the black t-shirt he wears, then kisses the top of my head so fiercely, I draw in a sharp breath.

"What is it, Stefan?"

"This is fucking dangerous," he says. "That's what. Fucking dangerous, and I wish you weren't here with me."

I push myself away from him and plant my hands on his chest. "It's going to be okay," I tell him. "Trust me to help you with this."

He sighs. "Promise you'll do every goddamn thing I say," he demands in a tight voice.

"I promise to do every goddamn thing you say," I repeat.

He narrows his eyes. "Promise if I tell you to be quiet, you'll be quiet. If I tell you to hide, you hide. And if I tell you to run, you run."

"I promise," I tell him, reaching for his hand and giving him what I hope is a reassuring squeeze. "*I promise.*"

His eyes probe mine for long minutes before he finally gives me a curt, reluctant nod.

"Let's go."

It's slightly cool and breezy outside in downtown Boston, but the dogwoods are in full bloom, and everywhere I look, feisty green sprouts are poking out, unhindered by the chill in the air. Spring in Atlanta is much warmer than this, and I shiver when a chilly wind nips at my neck. Stefan wordlessly draws me closer to him, shielding me from the cold.

"There," I say, pointing to the restaurant that's right near the wharf and open late. We'll eat here and observe what we can before we make our way to the Wharf. If we can see anything from here, we may not rouse suspicion. Stefan chooses a table underneath the faded awning and gestures for me to sit. He'd probably prefer we sat inside tonight, but we'll get better visibility here.

I order fish and chips and a lemonade, and he orders a fish plate. We eat in silence, both of us observing every-thing we can. And at first, I don't see anything at all. Where we sit, the waterfront spans out below us, dotted with couples and teens and parents with their babies. Someone plays a guitar and someone else sells large bouquets of flowers. Many ships are docked, quiet, lazy water lapping at their sides as the tide goes in and out. Few move at all.

But as I take a pull from my glass, something catches my eye. I sit up straighter, pausing with my mouth still to my glass. Stefan notes my sudden stillness and his eyes follow mine. Three large black SUV's have pulled up to one of the largest boats in the harbor, and several tall, tattooed men step out.

I move on, pretending I don't see anything at all. Ice hits my lips, and I swallow hard, when I recognize the man Stefan greeted the night before. The man he calls Mikahl. He's with another man, and he's gesturing angrily toward a boat, clearly upset.

"All done, baby?" Stefan asks. I nod, and he places

several bills on the table to cover our bill. "Let's go." To anyone else, it would look like a casual date night coming to an end, but I know it's my signal that it's time to move on the real purpose of our evening.

We move swiftly, down to the wharf.

"There were several pallets of deliveries and shipments on the main deck," Stefan says. "You go there, and I'll go aboard the ship when the other men of the brotherhood come."

"What if they know you're not with them?" I ask.

"I'll mention the contact we have through Tomas." I remember the man at the bar we met the night before. "And say he orchestrated this."

I go where he tells me, grateful for nightfall that covers my tracks, and he's reluctant to let go of my hand. "I don't like this," he mutters. "You shouldn't be here."

"Well I am," I say stubbornly. "And you promised."

"Speak to no one," he commands. "You have my cell phone number if you need it." We both carry burner phones that he acquired before coming here, and his number is the only one programmed in. He holds my face in his hand and draws me to him, giving me a fierce, almost angry kiss before he lets me go.

And then he's gone. I take my place and crouch behind the cargo, listening to everything. And for long minutes, nothing happens at all. Men come and go, and some speak in Russian, so I know we're in the right place, but nothing's happening that would give us a clue at all. Nothing to go on. My legs are falling asleep, when someone stops just on the other side of where I'm hidden.

"I have news that impacts our plans." The voice is clear and lyrical, and I immediately recognize it as belonging to the violet-haired woman. I hazard a peek through a tiny space between the pallets, blinking when I see that her hair is no longer violet but black. Her back is to me, and she's pointing toward a ship. "The shipment's delayed."

Ugh. My stomach drops. If the shipment's delayed, we may not find any information at all.

"Why?" I can't see the man beside her, but his shadow shows him to be large and formidable.

"Complications in Moscow."

"Doesn't mean we can't make our plans happen," the man beside her says.

She nods. "Indeed."

"You're the boss. You give the orders, and all this ends."

She turns to him, and her voice takes on a chilling edge. "Why would all this end? Do you think I've come this far to give up now?"

"No, of course not," the man says.

"Then shut up before I silence you myself," the woman says. "And find Stefan Morozov. My sources say he's in a hotel room in the city. I don't trust him. I want him dead."

My pulse spikes and I stifle a cry. I'm vaguely aware of the man agreeing to do just that. I stand stock-still, my hands trembling as I reach for my phone and I send a text to Stefan.

Get out of there. Now.

I hear her heels clicking as she walks away. I'm shaking so badly I can't think straight, but when my phone buzzes back I look at the screen.

Are you okay?

Of course, his concern is *me*. I want to shake him.

I'm fine. MOVE.

Heavy footsteps fall on the dock, and I hold my breath. Someone's getting closer to me. I take another peak, but it isn't the familiar face I hope to see, but the man Stefan calls Mikahl. He's glaring in front of him, pacing back and forth. He pauses once just beside me, and I hold my breath. What will he do if he sees me here?

I can't leave my place and Stefan can't come to me if he's here. What do we do now? I bite my lip and look for some way of escape but see none. I text Stefan again.

You'll have to create a diversion. There's a guy here and he's not leaving.

Got it.

I wait impatiently, tapping my foot and biting my lip, because I'm that afraid that someone's going to get to Stefan before he can leave.

A loud, obnoxious blaring sound pierces the night air. Shouts come from a few paces away, and there's the scuffling sound of someone running.

"Fire!" someone shouts. I'm holding my breath, waiting for Stefan, when a hand comes over my mouth from behind, and I stifle a scream. But a second later, I smell his familiar scent and know that it's only Stefan.

"Easy, baby," he says in my ear. "You're alright."

He releases me and pulls me to him. "We need to move."

I nod, and we both creep away from our hiding place, immediately toward the restaurant where we dined earlier. I feel as if everyone's watching me, as if someone's going to pull a gun on us at any second, but it seems all are distracted by the fire alarm. When we reach the restaurant, I take a near-empty glass off the table and pretend to drink it. Stefan follows suit, and the two of us pretend we belong here. We're not going to run. We're sitting right here until we know we can leave safely.

I lean over the table, bracing myself on my arm, and whisper to him, "They're after you."

He doesn't react, but feigns a yawn, leans in closer and whispers back, "Who, baby?"

"I'll tell you after," I promise. "But the person in charge ordered you dead, so they've got to be after you."

"Let's get back to the hotel room."

"It isn't safe."

He frowns. "We need to get to Moscow."

"We do. Can you have your jet ready to go *now?*"

"Now?"

"Yes, now. Aren't you listening to me at all?" I'm feeling desperate. Sirens get louder around us, and emergency vehicles pull up outside the restaurant. I don't need him to tell me he pulled this on purpose to cause the distraction.

"Let's go," he says. "We'll grab our things and go."

"I'm telling you, it isn't safe," I insist, but he shakes his head, as if he's some kind of mind reader and knows we'll be okay. A guy stands beside me and gives me a once over, the *jerk*, and Stefan gives him such a withering look, the man literally cowers and backs off.

"Whoa. Easy, there, killer," I mutter. He only growls in response while he makes a call.

"Have the jet ready to go. We aren't waiting for the morning."

Chapter 15

Stefan

I CALL for a car to take us to the airport, and everything passes in a blur. We have a long flight ahead of us.

"Our bags, though…" Taara's voice trails off.

"There's nothing of importance in any of them," I tell her. She looks out the window and doesn't respond. Everything of importance to her is back at the compound.

We need to talk, but not until we're in a place where we have total privacy. "Wow," she whispers. "That quickly you summoned someone to fly us over the ocean… I didn't really think you'd be able to do it."

But we don't have time to talk. I take her by the hand and drag her to the runway, and in minutes we're secured. Soon, we're high above it all, heading to Russia. It isn't until we're settled back in our seats that I breathe more easily, though I know that even in Russia we may not be safe. I don't like operating without my brother-hood physically near, prepared to defend. When we get to Moscow, we'll be that much closer to bringing down the operation, and I'll have Demyan at my back.

I'll do whatever it takes to make sure Taara isn't in danger, but this is the first step.

"Tell me what you heard," I ask her. We're both disheveled. Her hair's wild and crazy, her eyes wide. I reach over and smooth her crazy hair out in the pause before we continue speaking. I don't want this for her. I want her to be safe and secure.

"It was the woman we saw," she says. "But she must've been wearing a wig at one point. Her hair wasn't violet anymore."

"No?"

"And she was the one giving instructions. She said the shipment had been delayed, and she was the one that ordered you killed."

I blink in surprise. In our line of work, our brotherhoods are run by men, and traditionally those in charge within our circles are men. It's rare for a woman to have any place of authority in our ranks.

"How odd," I say. "What else did you find out?"

"Not much," she says, worrying her lower lip. "But we know she was with Mikhal, we can surmise that she's somehow joined with San Diego."

"Yes," I agree. "And what little I heard tonight also confirms this. So, our next course of action is to find the source in Russia and join with Demyan's men to bring them down."

She nods and yawns widely. "Yes."

"Get some sleep. We have a long flight ahead of us."

"I will, daddy," she whispers, before she closes her eyes. I take a blanket and drape it over her shoulder, tucking it in around her, and think about what happened tonight.

She could have been seen. What would have happened if *I'd* been seen? It's too dangerous to have her so close to what happens in the brotherhood. I close my eyes and think of Amaliya.

Nicolai has a half-sister. Rafael's wife, Laina. They shared a mother, and their mother was the only woman I've ever loved. Amaliya and I were lovers long before any of the issues between the brotherhoods arose. I was barely out of high school. We split up after she had Nicolai—her choice, not mine—and she fell for Yuri, the former head of the Thieves who died at Rafael's hands years ago.

It wasn't until many years later we reunited. After she had Laina and found out what a despicable piece of shit Yuri was. *Years* later. And we enjoyed the hell out of one another before she was taken from me.

I thought her death accidental until Laina told me otherwise. And now... now I go back to mother Russia, and brush shoulders with the Thieves, the very group responsible for my Amaliya's death.

Am I destined to repeat history? It's too dangerous for me to be going back here with Taara, but hell if I didn't try to stop her. I did, damn it.

But did you try hard enough?

I let her talk me into taking her tonight, and that could've ended in disaster. *Christ.*

She's too young. Too innocent. This isn't right at all.

Finally, after stewing for hours, I fall into a fitful, restless sleep. When we wake, we're getting ready to land. I pull out my phone and call Demyan.

"Brother, we've landed."

"I've got a car waiting."

I fill him in on what happened tonight. "I have no idea who she was, but she's got to have connections here."

"No one will know you're here."

I hang up with him and call Nicolai. After I tell him what's happened, I tell him we're heading incognito to Moscow's compound.

"All good here, except there's something I need to tell you," he says.

I rub the back of my hand across my brow and nod into the phone. "Yeah?"

"It's Taara's mother."

Shit.

"What about her?"

"She's not doing so well. A few hours ago, they found her in her room, and it appears she's had a heart attack and a fall."

Jesus.

"It's not looking good, if we're being honest."

And we just fucking landed here. Part of me wants to turn right back around and take her home, but that makes no sense. Taara meets my eyes and smiles. She has no idea how the information I'm hearing will impact her. I force a smile and squeeze her hand.

I sigh. "Alright. Thanks for letting me now." I'll tell her, but not now. Not when we're twenty minutes out from the compound, on the run, having undergone so much in a short time and only *just* arriving in Moscow. *Jesus.*

"Thank you. And how's Marissa?"

"Doing alright," he says. "Little bit of a scare earlier. It looked like she might've been in pre-term labor, but thankfully fine."

I should be there, not here. Ready to help my son usher another child into this world. Back where Taara can visit her mother. But hell, if we don't find out why they want me dead, what possible good am I there?

Taara hears my phone conversations, but doesn't interject or say a word, until we're just outside the Moscow compound.

"Anything I should know?" she asks.

"No one knows we're here."

She nods slowly. "Alllrighty then…" her voice trails off. "Got it."

I don't tell her about her mother. There's nothing she can do right now, not when we're this far away from home. I will tell her when the time is right.

We exit the plane and head to our waiting car. I recognize the men who wait for us and greet them each in turn. Part of Demyan's Moscow strike force, they visited us a year or so ago when they had dealings in Atlanta. They're strong and brawny, each bearing the signature Bratva ink.

Taara's head bobs to the side as we head to Demyan's. She's so tired. Soon, we arrive, and the sun is high on the horizon. Thanks to the length of our flight and the time zone change, it's early evening here in Russia, and the cities are alive with merchants and their wares. But my only concern is to get Taara back to safety.

"How do you know you can trust him?" she asks.

"Trust who?"

"This man in charge in Moscow."

"You'll know when you meet him."

One of the men in the front of the car looks at us in the rearview mirror but doesn't interject in the conversation.

"Your flight was good, then?" one asks.

"Yes, thank you."

"Larissa's prepared dinner for you," a second says. These men, unlike the men in my Bratva group, have heavier Russian accents and bear different ink, though all have the same stern and formidable air.

And we don't have to wait long for me to prove to Taara she can trust Demyan. The ride from the airport to the compound is swift, the roads clear.

"Does Larissa cook, too, like Caroline?"

The man driving us smirks and shakes his head. "Not quite. But the staff does whatever she asks, and she's arranged this for you.

Taara nods and yawns. "So weird how we're here, and we basically flew the whole day away."

"Have you flown this far before?"

"Well, not that I remember," she says. "I was a child when we flew to America."

Yes. She was a child. It's a stark reminder of how much younger she is than I am. But in the back of that car, with her head on my shoulder, I don't care. I don't fucking care. I've long since discarded any proper notion of love and relationships. Taara is honest and kind, and she's put up with my shit better than any other woman I've known. That matters.

"Here we are." The driver pulls into a long driveway, our tires crunching on gravel.

"Is that him?" Taara whispers, pointing to the muscular blond man standing by the entry.

"It is."

"Okay so he looks terrifying." Her voice shakes. "There's something ruthless about him."

"Baby, there's something ruthless about all of us." Did she forget she witnessed an execution?

"Yes, but—"

"You're not used to the way Russian men carry them-selves. Russian Bratva are feared, and for good reason."

"I'd say so," she mutters.

"Demyan is a stern *pakhan*," one of the men says. "But he is loyal and fearless, and the most well-respected leader our men have had in decades." He gives Taara a reas-suring smile. "As you're here as Stefan's woman, you have nothing to fear."

Her eyes widen and she bites her lip, but nods.

"Stefan's woman," she whispers in my ear. "I like the sound of that."

Jesus, so do I. *So, do I.*

I get out first and open the door for her. It's cooler here than in Boston but temperate. A light breeze brushes her hair off her shoulder, and when she steps out of the car, the golden beams of the setting sun kiss her shoulders and the top of her head, giving her an almost angelic appearance.

"You look like an angel," I say to her, taking her hand.

"Ha," she laughs. "I think you'd know better by now."

"Brother, welcome." Demyan reaches us and extends his hand. A pretty, petite woman with jet black hair stands by his side. She wears a wedding ring on her left hand. His wife, then.

I take his hand and shake it hard. "Demyan. Thank you, brother."

"Meet my wife Larissa," Demyan says with pride, ushering Larissa forward with his palm on her lower back. She smiles at me, gracious and beautiful, but she has a steel about her that reminds me of both Marissa and Caroline. I'm convinced now that Bratva woman are tenacious. They have to be to withstand life married to one of the brotherhood.

"Pleased to meet you," I say, shaking her hand warmly. "And this is…" I hesitate. What do I call her? "This is Taara," I say firmly.

"She's yours?" Demyan asks, shaking her hand.

I place my hand on her lower back and draw her to me. "She is mine."

Larissa gives Taara a smile. "Forgive me if this is too forward. You two are the most unlikely couple, but you look as if you belong together."

Taara laughs out loud, and I swear I fall in love with her all over again at the sound.

"Thank you."

Larissa meets my eye. "The King's ransom," she says softly.

I don't respond but give her a curious look. Taara doesn't hesitate, though.

"What do you mean?" she says.

Larissa smiles at her. "It's an expression," she says. "It means of exceptional worth. Years ago, the king's ransom was the money demanded for the return of a captured king, but the expression's evolved. It simply means of great value. And I can tell," she says softly, eying my hand on Taara's back. "That you are his treasure."

"I see," Taara says softly, her cheeks flushing. "Well, that's cool."

Larissa grins.

Taara is so damn cute.

Demyan gestures them inside impatiently and takes Larissa by the hand. "*This* king is about to forfeit over half his kingdom for a meal. Let's go."

"He's always like this when he's hungry," Larissa says. "And when he isn't. And when he wakes up in the morning and when he's—ow!"

Demyan tugs her hair and gives her a mock look of reproach. Taara smiles then yawns widely.

"Anyway, let's feed these two so they can get some rest."

Over dinner, I fill Demyan in on everything, but it seems Nicolai has already told him most of what I need to. Nicolai, once a member of this Bratva group, is well respected among Demyan and his peers. I'm grateful. It makes my job here that much easier.

"So you want to end the slave trade?" Larissa asks, signaling for waitstaff to bring us a tray of desserts.

"I do," I say, taking a tea cake. The buttery cookies dotted with nuts and drenched in powdered sugar are my favorite, and I haven't had any in years. "God, it's good to be back in Russia."

Taara gratefully takes a large chocolate brownie studded with chocolate chips. "I can make those for you, you know," she says. "They're easy enough." She takes a bite. "Oh, I love chocolate," she says. I didn't know that. There are many things I don't know about her, but I will note each one.

"I'd like that," I tell her, though right now the idea of getting back to my brothers in America seems like a distant one.

"What was your role in Atlanta, Taara?" Larissa asks.

Taara swallows her bite of brownie, and casts her gaze to the table.

"I was his housekeeper," she says. "And caretaker."

"I see," Larissa says. "Then how did you get roped into this?"

Demyan doesn't bother to stop Larissa from asking questions. Though some of the men prefer their women not be party to the inner workings of the brotherhood, he allows her free reign. Taara looks to me, and I nod my permission to tell Larissa what happened.

"I saw something I shouldn't have," she says, her cheeks flushing faint pink. "And I..."

"She came as my prisoner," I supply. "Taara witnessed an execution."

"Oh," Larissa says, her eyes wide. But a second later, her voice hardens. "And the brotherhood thought it best to get rid of her, I'm presuming? Though she's served you for..."

"Decades," I tell her, my own voice tight. I understand why she's upset, but she doesn't walk in my shoes. "And that's why she's with me."

Larissa holds my gaze for a moment before finally nodding, accepting this. She sighs and looks to Taara. "I fear for you, but you're not ignorant of the workings of Bratva life, are you?"

Taara nods and reaches under the table for my hand.

"And she's no longer my prisoner," I explain. When did she stop being captive to me? When did she become so much more?

"Brother, how do you propose ending the slave trade, when the Thieves have such a stronghold in America?" Demyan asks. He sips coffee from a teacup.

"That's why I'm here. I need to find who commands this and end any insidious plans from the top down."

Demyan nods. "But someone ordered you dead, so they already presume you know too much."

"Correct."

He strokes his chin and looks over my shoulder. Contemplating.

"Then tonight, we will form a plan. We have confidantes and spies we can utilize that work with the Thieves."

I exhale in relief. "Thank you."

"But it might not be as simple as you think," Larissa says.

"I never said it was simple."

Larissa nods. "Yes. It's just that those that run the operation are many and varied. You'll have to find all that want this to happen and eliminate all of them."

Tarra squeezes my hand tighter.

"I'll do whatever I have to," I tell them, looking from Larissa to Demyan. "I have no choice. If I don't, the Bratva in America is all but done."

Demyan's eyes cloud and his jaw firms. "We cannot have that," he says. *"Bratstvo ne padet."*

I swallow hard and repeat, *"Bratstvo ne padet."*

We get up from the table, and Larissa takes us to a room.

"Leave a message for me or Demyan, and tell us what you need."

"Thank you."

She smiles and leaves, and we enter the room. The bed's turned down, and the bathroom filled with toiletries. It's nicer than a luxury suite, but I breathe easier knowing I'm once again surrounded by brothers at my back. Tonight, we rest. Tomorrow we'll begin our next job.

But I can't stop thinking of Taara's mother. I take my phone and text Nicolai.

How is her mother?

But he doesn't respond. I have to tell her. I cannot delay it much longer.

I turn to Taara, who's looking about the luxurious room with wide eyes. She yawns widely.

"Sleep for you, little one," I say. "Let's get you ready." I have a burning need to help her to bed. To tuck her beneath the sheets and see that she's safe. Taking care of her feeds a need in me I didn't know I had until she came along. And when she looks at me with those wide, luminous eyes and whispers, "Yes, daddy," I know. She is a gift to me. The King's ransom, as Larissa said. So precious. I don't deserve this—any of this. Her trust or loyalty. Her kindness and steadfast obedience.

"I'd like to shower first, though," she says. "After traveling and all."

"Of course." I take her by the hand and lead her to the bathroom.

"I can do this myself," she says sheepishly, biting her lip, but I can tell she doesn't want to. She gets all submissive and shy when I take care of her like this.

"Of course, you can," I respond. "But I enjoy being the one that does. And no more protests from you."

Her eyes grow concerned for just the briefest of moments, before she nods her head and smiles at me. "Alright, then."

I help her out of her clothes, slipping each garment off her beautiful body and tossing them into the laundry hamper. Who knows how long we'll be here. We might as well make the most of it.

I kiss her naked shoulder and run my hand down the length of her back to her ass. I put the shower on, placing my own hand under the steaming hot water to check the temperature.

"Are you joining me, daddy?"

Fuck, I love when she calls me that.

"Of course." She doesn't have to ask me twice. I quickly strip and join her, then take a washcloth and soap it up.

"Come here," I murmur, pulling her to me. I clean her hair and lather her body, enjoying the sweet scent of honey and vanilla. And Christ, predictably I'm getting hard again. But not tonight. Not now.

"Tonight, we're just getting clean," I say.

"If you say so," she says with a grin.

"I do," I groan.

She drapes her arms over my neck and kisses me. "Okay, only more question."

"Yes?"

"What did Demyan say to you?"

I frown. "I'm not sure what you're talking about. When? He said a lot of things."

"No, in Russian,

Ah. *"Bratstvo ne padet?"* I ask.

She nods eagerly. I sigh, squeezing out the washcloth and

turning the water off. "It means the brotherhood must never die."

"Ooooh." She captures my face between her hands and draws my gaze to hers. "He's right. *Never.*"

I kiss her, silently thanking her.

Chapter 16

Taara

I SLEEP SO SOUNDLY that when I wake, I actually feel a little groggy. I open one eye, then the other. It takes me a minute to realize where I am and I must make a sudden move, because Stefan's arms wrap around me.

"You alright?" he asks. "You jumped." His voice is all gravelly with sleep, and the sound makes me feel warm and comforted. I roll over toward him, and he pulls me to his chest.

"Just didn't remember where I was," I say.

"Does this help you remember?" Cupping my face in his hands, he brushes his lips to mine.

"Mmm," I say when he lets me go. "I'm with Stefan."

"Sure as hell are," he says with a grin that makes his eyes crinkle around the edges. My heart thumps madly in my chest, and he brings his hand under the blanket, one massive palm covering my breast. I sigh and move closer to him. Without a word, he rolls over on top of me and pins my wrists down while kissing me, gently at first then more persistent, his erection pressing between my legs.

It seems Stefan likes morning sex, and he doesn't have to ask me twice. I part my legs for him, moaning when he moves one hand to grasp my nipple between his thumb and forefinger and pulls at the hardened peak. The thin nightie I wear does nothing to protect me, but I'm not complaining. It feels fucking awesome. He yanks up my leg and spanks my bare thigh, making me yelp then groan.

"Over my lap," he says.

"What?" I ask.

He's already spinning me out and yanking me over his knees. "You'll come for daddy with your ass aching," he says.

My pulse spikes, and I moan as he yanks off my clothes and bares my ass over his knee.

"You're a naughty little thing," he scolds, clucking his tongue just before he crashes his hand on my ass. I buck and moan, but this isn't like being punished. It's hot and sensual and my clit throbs. I scissor my legs when he crashes his hand down a second time, then a third, before he weaves his fingers through my hair and yanks my head back.

"Tell me. Tell me you're daddy's naughty little slut."

I mewl a little in protest, but when he spanks me again, I breathe, "I'm daddy's naughty little slut."

In reward, he glides his fingers to my pussy and pumps hard and fast. "Whose pussy is this?"

"Daddy's," I moan, and he spanks me again, and again, his huge palm covering every inch of my bare ass. Then he drapes me over his lap and squeezes my ass cheeks.

"And whose ass is this?" he asks.

"Daddy's," I whisper, flushing red hot at the insinuation. Oh, God. I gasp when his thumb glides across my asshole.

"Who's gonna give that ass to daddy to fuck?"

"Okay, now, wait a minute--*ow!*"

Another hard spank.

"Yours, daddy," I finally say, not because I'm afraid of him but because I want him to do just that, to fuck me every which way he wants and can. Stefan is the master of my heart and master of my body, and nothing thrills me more than being fucked by him.

In minutes, he's got me divested of my clothes, his own quickly discarded. He lays me onto the bed and I part my legs, my spanked ass aching on the silky sheets but making me impossibly wetter when he rolls on a condom. He glides his cock between my thighs, and in silence, with perfect, vicious, exquisite strokes of his cock between my legs, he fucks me.

He bends his mouth to mine and kisses me, pumping his cock in me in flawless rhythm, working me to ecstasy. This is unlike our lovemaking before. This is hot and hurried, but sweet and sensual, and I come with his lips still on my mouth, his own release on the heels of mine.

When we're panting and satiated, he brings his mouth to my ear.

"Now do you remember?"

I grin. "Yes, daddy."

We dress in amicable silence, though the shower together nearly delays us even further. I remind him Demyan and Larissa are likely waiting for us, and I get away with no more than a quick, teasing slap to my ass. When we make our way down to the dining room, we hear heated voices in a doorway to our right. I look at Stefan curiously, and he meets my gaze. It sounds like Demyan and Larissa.

"You *know* it's the only way," Larissa says. "None of our sources are on the inside of the trade. But if she could get in... and with her profile and coloring, she easily could... she could get us information no one else could."

Stefan steps to the door, not one to eavesdrop. He clears his throat.

Demyan looks up and nods to him. "Hey. You two hungry?"

"Very," I say, grateful for something to say, because I'm shaking with the knowledge of what she wants me to do, but more importantly, I'm shaking with the knowledge of what I *must* do. And I further know that I'll have to fight Stefan tooth and nail.

We walk in silence to the dining room, and when we arrive, Stefan pulls out a chair for me. I sit and gratefully take a cup of coffee. After a simple breakfast of eggs and toast are served, Stefan clears his throat.

"We overheard part of your conversation," he says. Demyan sighs, and Larissa nods.

"Did you?" she asks. "Which part?"

"You suggested 'she' go on the inside. I'm assuming you mean Taara?"

Larissa nods and Demyan growls low and angrily, but she ignores him. "As I was saying to Demyan, there are no other options here. We have men on the inside, but they're not privy to the type of information she would be." She shrugs.

"Yes, but the only problem is, no way will I allow that."

"And what if I want to?" I interject. Stefan shoots me a murderous look, but I look away from him and speak to Demyan and Larissa.

"You have men on the inside, yes?" I ask. "Well, why couldn't you have them prepared to defend me if anything went wrong?"

"Because it's too dangerous," Stefan says, but Larissa interrupts him.

"Not necessarily. You told us yourself last night that you were in danger of losing the entire American Bratva. And you have Taara here to prove that she's loyal to you, no?"

"Yes, but—"

"And do you not trust that our men would protect her?"

"Larissa, *enough*."

"Please," I say. "I'm the one who's safety is on the line. Don't I have a say in this?"

None of them know that it isn't just important to me

that I find the information Stefan needs. I want to prove to Larissa, and, if I'm honest, to Caroline as well, that I am made of Bratva girl mettle.

Demyan and Stefan meet each other's eyes, and Stefan finally nods.

"Go on."

"I can defend myself if need be," I tell him. "But I also want this chance to prove myself innocent once and for all. *You* might know that I am," I tell Stefan. "But does your brotherhood?"

"No," Stefan says staunchly. "I won't allow it." He squeezes my leg in warning, but I push his hand away. It doesn't work, though, because he's right back at my leg again and squeezing me even tighter and higher, and this time it works, because I know he means what he says.

"If you let me in on this, a few things can happen," I explain. "I can get insider information no one else will know. I can prove that I'm not a threat to anyone. We can find who's responsible for taking over America and end this."

"Taara," he growls.

"She has a point," Demyan says, stroking his chin.

"The fuck she does," Stefan growls. "You'd let Larissa go?"

Demyan grits his teeth and meets Larissa's eyes. "Against my better judgment, but yes. I have let her work with us."

"A true king's ransom," I say to Stefan on impulse, but it was maybe not the smartest thing to say because his eyes narrow dangerously.

"You are *not* my ransom," he says. "Not at all."

I place my hand on his leg. "But am I the king's ransom?" My voice wavers as I hold his gaze. I need him to know he can trust me. I want to do this.

"*Ty moye sokrovishche,*" he murmurs, his voice husky. "You are my treasure."

I forget that we're right there with Demyan and Larissa and that his men could likely see us. I forget everything, as I lean over and place my hand on his chest.

"Then let me help you. You will protect me." I lift his hand off my leg and kiss his fingers to my mouth. "I trust you. *Please.*"

He curses under his breath, but finally, shaking his head, concedes. "We're meeting with the rest of the brotherhood, no?" he asks Demyan.

"We are."

"Let's see what we can find out."

But he's already made the decision. He's already decided.

We meet with the men, and it's much like the meeting with Stefan's own brotherhood, only this is a much smaller group. The inner circle, I surmise. They sit and stand, arms crossed, with grim expressions, as Demyan and Stefan relay the purpose of their meeting.

"Fucking Thieves," one man growls. "Who was this woman in America who ordered you killed?"

"She commands some of them, but we aren't sure who."

They continue discussing options and a strategy, until Larissa brings up her proposition.

"She looks the part," one of the men says. "Are you Afghani?"

I swallow hard. "I am. And I'm willing to do what it takes."

"Can you play the part of frightened slave?" another asks. I tremble when I answer, because I know the part of frightened slave all too fucking well.

"I can."

"They've captured half a dozen more women as of tonight," one man says. "Bringing their current total to two dozen."

"Do they count them?" Stefan asks, his expression grim.

"Yeah. We'll have to take one and hide her."

I stifle a groan. This is starting to make me a little nervous.

"Okay, okay, so... let me get this straight," I say. "The new shipment comes in and I go in as one of them. We somehow sneakily hide one, so they don't mess up on the count. I find out what I can, and report back to you."

"Christ," Stefan says.

"You'll have a comm device," Larissa says. "Something in your ear if you need to talk to one of us."

"And a weapon," Stefan says grimly.

"That's too dangerous," one of the men says, but Stefan turns on him so furiously that the man slams his mouth shut and stops talking.

"Brother, he's right," Demyan says gently. "She can't carry. Far too fucking dangerous."

"Fine, then," Stefan grits out. "*I'm* her weapon." He stands to his full height, and all the men in the room look up to him. He's taller than most, and with the silver in his beard and massive stature, he looks like a Viking God. Are they all looking at him adoringly, or is that just me?

"You be my weapon," I say, tapping his arm. "I love that idea."

Larissa catches my gaze with twinkling eyes.

"Son of a bitch," Stefan grits out, but we manage to continue our plans despite his blustering and anger. It's the only plan, and it has to work.

We finally get out of the meeting, and I'm taken with Larissa to get outfitted for my undercover job. Stefan follows, scowling at his phone. "Motherfucker," he whispers.

"What?" I ask. "Everything okay?"

But he won't meet my eyes. "It's fine," he says. Then to Larissa, "How much further?"

"Oh, just up ahead, Stefan," she says, but he's impatient and irritable. "We should get her there within the hour, so she can quickly amass with the others before any of the guards begin to recognize faces.

"Fine," he snaps. Thankfully, she's used to grumpy, bossy men, because she barely reacts at all.

"Here, Taara," Larissa says. We made it to a storage room of sorts. She pulls out a white sheath from a pile in the closet. "You'll have to wear this." She can't hide the way her lip turns down in disgust.

Stefan grabs it. "This? Are you fucking kidding me?"

"Stefan, you agreed to this," Larissa warns. "Can you *please* just try to get used to the idea?"

"No, I will not fucking get used to—"

I place my hand on his shoulder and whisper in his ear. "Daddy. Please." That softens the worry line at his brows, but he doesn't speak. I know he's concerned, but is there something else going on that I don't know about?

I actually wonder for a moment if I mean to him what I hope I do. Or has this all been just a game he's been playing? Gone is the tenderness I've come to expect, gone the gentle touch and soft words. I can still feel the residual effects of our lovemaking this morning, but it seems so long ago.

Stefan's phone rings, and he scowls at it before he answers. His eyes come to me before he turns away, cursing.

What the hell?

"What is it?" I whisper. "Stefan?"

But he turns away from me and doesn't answer. Larissa won't meet my eyes when I look to her for answers, but instead helps me into the sheath.

"Come, Taara," she says. "Let Stefan take the call."

But my gut instinct says something is off. Is he hiding something from me?

I'd convinced myself that I mattered to him. That he cared. But now…

In minutes, I'm ready. Wearing the simple sheath with no makeup, no jewelry, it's a stark reminder of my past and the women who've been in this position before me. I swallow hard, determined to give it my best. For me. For my mother. For every woman who's been mistreated or abused. For Stefan and his brotherhood.

"How does she look?" Larissa asks him.

He only grunts in reply, then turns away, as if disgusted with me. My heart sinks. I hate this. God, I hate it so much.

"Stefan..." my voice trails off as I look to him for something, anything to give me reassurance that I still mean something to him. How could I have fallen in love with a man like him? Someone so brutally possessive and fierce, who can turn like this? He's unpredictable, and that scares the hell out of me.

"She looks fine," he says to Larissa, not meeting my eyes. His phone rings again, and he curses, taking the call and stalking out of the room.

Larissa must note my hurt, because she puts an arm around my shoulder and whispers in my ear, "He's just concerned. Don't think too much of it. He hates the idea of you being put into danger."

But no. There's more to it than that, and I know it. When we get into the hall, some of Demyan's men, the ones who brought us to the compound the night before, wait for me.

"Abram is in place," one of the men says to Stefan.

"He your mole?"

"Yes. He'll help swap out your woman with the other."

Your woman. As *if.* I want to roll my eyes and stomp my foot. I hate that I don't know where I stand with him.

Demyan enters the room and walks to Larissa. Without a word, he draws her to him and kisses her.

"All well, my love?"

"Yes," she says, taking his hand. "She's ready."

Their brief gestures make me feel bereft without Stefan's support. I want to know that he cares. His aloof attitude makes my heart ache. But I have a job to do.

I get into the car that waits, Demyan's men joining me.

"I'm going, too," Stefan says.

"Bad idea, brother," Demyan warns. "If anyone sees you, you'll draw suspicion."

"I'll make sure no one sees me."

"And I don't need his help anyway," I interject. "I'm *totally fine* not having his help." I don't miss the way his eyes widen in surprise then narrow. He's not happy with me at all.

"Like hell you are," he says. "Are you out of your mind? I'm going."

Demyan holds up his hands in resignation, and I huff out an angry breath. He slides in beside me and slams the door.

"Go," he orders the driver, then he turns to me once we take off. "What the *fuck* was that about?"

"What?" I say, turning away from him. I don't look at him, because a lump has risen in my throat and I don't want to cry.

"What?" he repeats. Trees whiz by our windows as we speed toward the Thieves location. "*What?* The sudden ice show," he says. "You're freezing me out. Why? What the hell is your problem?"

"I don't have a problem," I say through gritted teeth. "Seems like *you're* the one with the problem."

Asshole.

"My problem is there isn't enough space in the back of this car to haul you over my lap and spank the truth out of you," he growls.

I roll my eyes. "Naturally."

He grips my leg and squeezes it. "Taara, you talk to me." But I don't know what to tell him. I want his attention? I want some affection from him? I'm sick of wondering if I matter to him at all? I'm questioning why I ever let myself fall for him in the first place?

And even if everything was just *peachy*, where does this leave us? If we take down our rivals like we're planning. How will his group ever welcome me as one of their own? I shake my head. There's so much to say, that I don't say anything at all. It pisses him off, but I'm almost beyond caring.

Almost. My heart aches. I long to lie my head on his chest and let him comfort me. To feel his arms about me and know that I matter to him. But the time has been too short, his actions toward me inconsistent. And I can't take the whiplash.

"We're here," one of the men says. Thank *God*.

"Stay here," the guy in front says over his shoulder.

"You wait until Abram gets you," Demyan insists. "Do not get out of this car."

I sigh and wait, until the door opens. "Come with me," a man says.

"Are you Abram?"

He nods politely. "I am."

He's the one supposedly on the inside with the Thieves. "It's lunchtime," he explains in a hushed whisper. "Though it isn't the safest place, lunchtime makes it easier to avoid notice. The surveillance is a bit more lax. And the girls are hidden in the back, so it will be easy enough to swap you." He sighs. "It's dark in there."

I nod. I can feel the other men surround us, though they quickly make themselves scarce in the woods surrounding the compound. They're here for one reason only, to be sure to protect me.

Though it's still daytime, it's dark where he takes me. Devoid of both artificial and natural light, he has to shine a flashlight beam from his phone just to see where we're going. The air is heavy with anticipation, the stench of body odor permeating the air. My stomach clenches with nausea. This is the place where they take the women they sell for auction. It should come as no surprise to me how disgusting it is.

"Stay there," Abram says. He opens a gate that swings from a chain link fence.

Yeah, I'm not going anywhere. I keep my head down as I suppose a good slave should. I don't want to draw any attention to myself. But I catch the glimpse of silver, and when I look up, Stefan is standing only a few yards off. I wish it gave me the reassurance it once did.

There's a scuffle and the sound of footsteps, then Abram's standing before me. I blink in surprise when I recognize the girl from the slave ship in America, slave to her blond master. I open my mouth to say something, but Abram cuts me off. "Stay right here and do not make a sound," he whispers. I watch in stunned silence as he takes the woman and brings her to Stefan. He reaches for her, and my heart squeezes when I see him pull her close to him.

Of course he does. He doesn't love me. I don't matter to him. He's only taken care of me, like he will her, because it's who he is, not because I'm anything to him.

No.

"Come," Abram says, grabbing my hand and dragging me inside. I go blindly, my eyes are blurry with unshed tears.

Chapter 17

Stefan

ABRAM SHOVES the stolen woman into my arms before I can say a word. I look at him in surprise, and Taara stares at us just before Abram whisks her into the compound. She takes a piece of my heart with her. I can't believe I agreed to this. I can't fucking believe I did.

"Sir?" the woman in my arms looks at me questioningly, her voice soft but plaintive. I look down in surprise when I realize she's the woman from the ship. The one that Taara snuck off with. I don't know what to say, but she does.

"He said to come with you," she whispers. "That you will protect me. If my master realizes I've gone…" her voice trails off and she bites her lip, then looks up at me curiously. "Did you come to rescue me?"

"Partly," I tell her. "But we're here to bring this operation down. "Now be quiet while I get you to safety."

"Yes, sir," she says meekly, and I hate it. I fucking hate it. She isn't my girl and I am not her master. But I have no time to dwell on this. I take her to the car that waits. With quick, hurried movements, I shove her into the car and buckle her in. I dismiss the wide-eyed look she gives me.

"Stefan," one of the men asks. "You're supposed to be coming back with us."

Like hell I am.

"Go," I tell him. "Now." I turn and leave.

In the comm device that I wear, I can hear Demyan cursing.

"For fuck's sake, Stefan."

"Shut up," I growl. "Like you'd leave Larissa."

"Fair," he mutters. But then we both lapse into silence because we need to hear what Abram and Taara are up to. I want her the fuck out of there *yesterday*.

Earlier today, I got a call from Nicolai updating me on her mother's condition. The prognosis isn't good at all. I need to get her back to America. I never should've brought her here. She isn't safe. This is so damn wrong. She should be at home, with her mother, not pretending to be a slave in this underground movement that threatens the safety of all.

Then Taara's voice comes through the comm.

"Yes, sir. Certainly, sir."

I slide my phone out of my pocket and pull up the feed, and when I do, I freeze.

Fuck.

She's standing in front of Mikahl, and beside him stands the woman from America. The one who ordered my execution. They haven't seen her, but if they do this could be lethal for Taara. What if they recognize her?

Never should've brought her here.

Once I get her alone again, I'm gonna lock her up and never let her out of my goddamn sight again.

I can hear two people speaking to one another, and when one says 'Boston,' I listen harder. "You are the only two that want to do this," one man says. I don't recognize him but wonder if Demyan will.

Want to do what?

"The rest of us believe having ties in America strengthens us. It's a terrible idea to eradicate America."

My heart momentarily soars. Does he speak for all, or just himself?

"I agree," someone else says.

"Do you know what America stands for, though?" the woman asks. "They are the ones that diluted our brotherhood by allowing those with American blood to infiltrate their ranks."

"But they maintain the demand for Russian blood," one says. Several other concur.

"I've had it with this trade," one says. "We've made our money and forged our power for decades without stooping to this level."

Demyan's voice comes into my ear. "That's Makar. Head of the Zelenegrad Bratva. His interference at this juncture bodes well, brother. Very well."

This might go more smoothly than we feared. I peer at the device in my hand. Mikhal and his woman stand at the head of the room, the rest standing around them in a circular group. Instead of being the ones in charge, they're now on the spot, as it seems those in front of them are not as keen on following their plan as they thought.

But Taara is still in there. Abram isn't allowed in the inner circle, though a few of the trusted slaves are there to serve their masters. As the tension in the room becomes more highly charged, my need to get her out of there builds.

"It's enough. We have enough to go on. We know who wants to take down America, and it seems the majority don't favor this move. It isn't as insidious as we thought."

"Maybe not," Demyan says. "But be patient. It's too dangerous to move her out just yet." I disagree. I fucking disagree. Every second she's near their greedy hands is too long. She's served her purpose.

I start to move, but pause when Demyan speaks up again.

"Wait, Stefan," Demyan insists. "We need to know more before you take her out." But on the feed in front of me, I see Mikhal take a step toward her.

"Why is she here?" he asks.

My need to protect her takes a grip on me so vicious I can't breathe.

Stay safe, Taara.

Mikhal's woman reaches for Taara's hair and yanks it so her head falls back.

I will kill her.

"Good question," she says icily. "This one actually looks familiar, though I can't quite place where I know her from." She shoves her away, instantly dismissing her. I breathe again.

"In any event, I'm disappointed in your lack of support, Makar."

While we watch, she draws a pistol from her hip, turns it on Makar, and with no warning, pulls the trigger. Taara screams, but no one moves. I watch in horror as the man's body slumps to the floor. She shot him in the chest. He isn't dead yet.

"Someone has to stop her," Demyan grates into the phone. "She's out of control and unpredictable."

I make up my mind in an instant. "I'm going in."

I'm running through the woods without a care now who sees me or what they'll do if they catch me. "Call a medic!" I shout to Demyan. Makar may still make it. I'm banking on the fact that Mikhal and his cohorts are in the minority. Killing a fellow Bratva *pakhan* brings certain war and turmoil. We need to save his life. I need to get to Taara.

I rush through the doors of the compound, only to be instantly flanked by two large guards. I drop to the floor and roll, as they point their guns at me. I shoot one right between the eyeballs and the other in the chest. One falls dead instantly, the other falls to the floor, howling. I apparently missed anything too vital so I shoot the second man in the leg, certain to keep him from coming after me. He screams and swears at me in Russian, but I plow on. I'm not leaving until I have my Taara safely secured.

I burst into the room, rage nearly obscuring my vision. Men are on their feet, their guns trained on me. Taara's eyes meet mine, wide and surprised.

"Stefan," Mikhal says, unperturbed.

"I told you to kill him." I look into his woman's eyes. She looks straight at me, her gun pointed to me. No one moves. No one says anything while she shakes her head. "Who the hell do you think you are, storming in here?" She cocks her pistol, but I'm not giving her a chance. Taara lunges at her, pulling her down. Her shot ricochets somewhere off the ceiling, and I shoot her. I don't hesitate when Mikhal points his gun at Taara. I pull the trigger. He, too, falls to the floor.

They obviously made more enemies than friends in this compound. No one, literally not a single one even tries to stop us. Within seconds, Demyan's reinforcements who were stationed outside this warehouse arrive while I go to Makar. He's breathing, still conscious.

"Moscow," one of the men says. "It's Moscow. Thank you."

She didn't kill Makar. It's confusing and bloody, the bodies dragged away, but when Demyan comes into the room, they all fall to silence. He's earned the respect of the Russian Bratva in all corners of the country.

"See to Makar's immediate wellbeing," he orders.

I pull Taara to me, but she stiffens, and she won't allow me to embrace her. What the hell?

Demyan addresses the room while a medic rushes in to tend to Makar. "But the bigger question here is where this leaves us." His voice rings out, loud and certain and deep. The others pay attention. "We've been told the insidious plan to overtake Stefan and the American Bratva ran deep."

"No more, brother. It was Mikhal and Farrah who were plotting to overthrow America." I look to see one man standing in the front of the room. I don't know who he is. "Since Tomas backed away from the slave trade in America, the rest of us decided we wanted to follow suit." Murmurs of agreement surround us.

Demyan nods. "Good. We have better ways of ensuring our income and influence than in slave trade." He nods to Makar. "Brother, we'll meet again when you've recovered. Do you have room for his recovery here on your compound?"

"We do," the man says. On his arm he bears the signature star tattoo of the Thieves.

"I will be in to see you," Demyan promises. Makar is taken out of the room, then momentary silence descends.

My hatred for his group runs deep, but when the brigadier comes to me, he holds his hand out to me. "Stefan," he says. "On behalf of my brotherhood, we'd like to extend the olive branch." I blink in surprise when he reaches for my hand and shakes it. This isn't just about what happened now, but runs much deeper, back to when my Amaliya was victim to the Thieves. I swallow hard and take his hand. I could go the rest of my life and not make peace with the Thieves, but I can't blame modern day leadership for the sins of their ancestors.

"Thank you," I tell him. "We will talk at Demyan's?"

He nods, smiling in agreement.

Taara stands awkwardly by my side.

"Let's go," I tell her. Demyan nods, giving me permission to leave, and I take Taara to where our ride waits outside. But she doesn't hold my hand. She walks apart from me and barely acknowledges I'm there. I want to yank her to me, to kiss those pouty lips of hers and remind her that she's mine, but I can't.

And it's better off this way. We've come this far for something that's already over and will be dealt with by high ranking brothers within our brotherhoods. I've fucked up bringing her here. She needs to get back to America.

So when we get to the waiting car, I reach for her, and when she pulls away, I let her. I fucking let her. Because it's too dangerous for her to be with me. She's so much better off not being attached to a man like me who dwells in the dark and dangerous places. So much better. But she's trembling. She's been through fucking hell, and it's all because of me.

"You did well," I say to her, keeping my voice distant and aloof. "Thank you for helping us achieve our mission."

"Sure," she says.

Sure?

I clear my throat. "Tonight, you're getting back on a plane for America."

"Wait... what?" She asks.

I ignore the way she looks at me, the betrayal in her eyes

slicing through my heart. I have to steel myself against it, because I want to gather her to me and hold her close. I want to tell her that I love her, and that I will go to whatever lengths it takes to protect her... even if it kills me. Even if sending her away from me is the most painful thing I've ever done.

But I have to. Being in that room with the Thieves... It was impossible to forget what they did to my Amaliya. And though we've made our public peace, I will not, I will *not* put Taara through that kind of danger.

She needs to be home. Home in Atlanta, with her mother. Sitting on the porch of the facility where her mother lives, drinking sweet tea. Waking up in the morning and taking pictures of the flowers that bloomed in her absence.

I can't fully love another woman. I can't fully give myself to a woman again, knowing that she's in mortal danger by being connected to me in any way.

But Christ. My head says one thing and my heart another.

I love her. And it's going to kill me to send her away.

"Why are you sending me back to America?" she asks. Her voice wavers, and she doesn't even bother checking the tears that fall. It's a knife to my heart seeing her like this, so distraught and knowing I put her in this position. "I came here to help you."

"You know where to take her," I say to the driver.

"Aren't you going?" she asks.

But my going with her puts her in more danger. I won't

go with her. I can't, even though it kills me that I have to trust her to the care of others.

I don't kiss her. I don't hug her. If I get too close to her, I will not let her go *and I have to let her go*. It's been a mistake allowing myself to draw too close to her. A huge fucking mistake. But when the car pulls away, and I see her face buried in her hands, I am instantly filled with regret and the need to go after her has me following. One step, two, until I'm running, but I can't keep up with the speed of the car. I finally give up, panting, bent over from the exertion. What the fuck is my problem?

A car pulls up beside me, and I suddenly realize where I am and that I'm nowhere near safe. But when the driver's window rolls down, I see Demyan.

"You let her go," he says, and I swear there's judgment in his voice. "Get in."

I don't say anything to him but walk to the passenger side and yank open the door. I slide into the back, and he shakes his head at me from the driver's seat. "Why'd you let her go?" he asks, as he peels out of the parking lot.

So I tell him. I tell him everything. And when I finally finish, I realize he's turning away from the compound and accelerating, not entering like I thought.

"Where the hell are you going?" I ask him. "We need to get back."

"Bullshit," he grits out. "You're a fucking idiot for letting her go."

"Hey!"

But he only shoots me a withering look and shakes his head. "Fucking idiot," he says, driving so quickly I swear the tires are literally burning rubber, leaving streaks of black on the pavement in our wake.

"I can't go with her," I tell him. "If I do, we'll never be able to stay away from each other. It's too dangerous for me to be with her, and I swear to God if—"

"Too dangerous for her?" he asks tightly. "Or too dangerous for *you*?"

"What the fuck are you talking about?" I demand. "I'm not afraid of anyone coming after me. I can handle myself."

He snorts, and I wanna deck him. "It's not an outside danger I think you're afraid of," he says. "You're afraid of falling for her. You don't want to fall in love."

"Fall in love?" I ask incredulously. "I'm not afraid of falling in love. That's bullshit." I huff out an angry breath. "And anyway, it's too late."

"I know it," he says. "Christ, do you think I don't know it?" He shakes his head again. "You know the girl we rescued? She begged to be yours. Said she'd be a third and serve you."

He looks at me curiously.

"What?"

"She wanted to be yours. The man who was her master was killed today by Mikhal. She doesn't even know it yet. She's with Larissa at the compound."

"Good for her," I mutter. While I'm glad the blond douchebag is gone, I don't want any other women for my own.

He smiles. "And that, my friend, is the right answer."

He turns the corner and I suddenly see where we are. In front of us lies the runway, the plane with Taara on it right before me.

"Go," Demyan growls. "Christ, Stefan. *Go to her.*" He shakes his head. "If I had a fucking eject button..."

But I'm already gone.

When I reach the plane, the pilot recognizes me and steps to the side to grant me access.

"Ride for two, sir?" he asks amiably.

"Thank you."

I don't know what I expect from her when I got on the plane. A hug? A kiss? A tearful reunion? It isn't the stone-cold silence I get. She raises a brow to me, crosses her legs, and picks up a magazine from the selection beside her. Opening one of them, she scowls, then shoves it back in.

"I don't know *that* much Russian."

"There are American versions, too."

"Oh? Excellent. I'll have to get those when I'm back in *America.*" She spits the word out as if it's a poison I just fed to her. "But at least you decided it was time to high-tail it back, too, hmm?"

"Enough, Taara," I tell her. I'm in no mood to spend the next twelve hours listening to her getting mouthy.

"I don't even know why I'm going," she says, her voice laced with fury, "Or why you suddenly decided to grace me with your presence, but I want you to know something. You can fuck. *Off.*"

And with that, she takes the one lone English magazine from the stack and practically buries her face in it.

I don't bother talking to her. I refuse to tell her that her mother's ill and may be dying. I don't want her worrying the whole way. I also know that if we don't make it in time, I'm the only one to blame. *Christ.*

We're served food, and I think I eat it. I don't pay attention. I'm blindly reading magazines in front of me, Russian and English alike, until the entire stack lays discarded on the table beside me. I look over, and Taara is asleep. Her head to the side, she looks so young. So innocent. Fuck, she's still wearing the little white sheath for crying out loud.

I try to sleep, but I'm plagued with memories of the stand-off. My dreams are troubling, and I wake up to dark outside the window and Taara gently snoring. I stare into the darkness for hours, mulling over my choices. What I've done. What I have yet to do.

We're going to land soon. "Taara," I say, gently shaking her shoulder. She wakes with a start and a little yelp.

"You're alright," I tell her. "Don't worry. You're safe."

But is it true? She's with me.

She looks at me in silence for a moment but doesn't reply. Then she finally huffs out angrily.

"Gee," she says sarcastically. *"Thanks. I'm safe."* But she can't mask the way her voice cracks. I want to hold her so badly and comfort her it's physically painful, but I can't.

The two paths in front of me mock me, neither the right option. On the one hand, I could choose to go with her, but if I do, she's joined to me, and it's too fucking dangerous for her. The other...my life without her. And that path seems dreary and dismal.

But I have to choose what's best for Taara, not me.

Love isn't a choice of what's best for me, but for her.

If I love her, and I know now that I do, I have to let her go.

Chapter 18

Taara

WHEN HE GOT on the plane, it took every bit of self-control I could muster not to break down. I wanted to run to him, to throw my arms around his shoulders and ask him *why*.

Why he made me leave. Why he sent me on this plane back to America alone.

Why he came back.

What have I done to deserve his dismissal? It hurts so badly I can't even think about it, so I bury myself in magazines and finally welcome sleep when it comes, though it's fitful and restless, and the weighted pain of his rejection settles back on me as soon as I open my eyes.

Why is he here? If he wanted to send me back to America, he could've stayed back and saved me the torture of his presence.

I get off the plane, disheveled and barely dressed, and it surprises me that Marissa waits outside with Nicolai. I don't want to see them right now. If I were to become Stefan's, those two would be like *family*. And I can't mentally go there. I *can't*.

Marissa reaches her hands out to me. "Welcome home, Taara," she says. "How are you feeling?" She looks at me so probingly, I become concerned.

"I'm fine," I say, baffled. Nicolai looks at me sternly, though, his eyes narrowed, and arms crossed on his chest. Does he still not believe me? Does he still think me a spy? Well he can fuck *way* the hell off, because I have no interest in wasting an ounce of my breath convincing him I'm innocent. Nope. Not gonna do it.

"I just feared that you'd be worried, once you—"

"Marissa." Stefan's sharp voice cuts in from behind me. "No."

I turn around to look at him curiously. What the hell?

"No what?" I say, confused.

Nicolai sighs. "She doesn't know."

Stefan shakes his head.

Know *what? God.*

"Sure," I say. "Go ahead. Keep talking like I'm not even standing *right here before you."*

But they don't even bother to acknowledge that I'm there. Instead, they talk right over me.

"I didn't want her worrying uselessly for the entire flight. She needed rest," Stefan says.

Nicolai nods. "Fair."

Wait. What's going on here?

"Do you have something to tell me?" I ask Stefan coldly, crossing my arms over my chest in an effort to self-protect.

But I'm unprepared for his response. I'm not ready for the cold tone of his voice, the aloof and detached manner, but most of all? The news he tells me.

"Taara, it's your mother," he says, and when he looks at me, I swear I read sympathy in his eyes, but it quickly vanishes. "We got news that she's very ill. And I—" his voice trails off before he clears his throat and turns back to me. "I wanted to be sure you were here, actually able to see her, before I told you."

"Thanks?" I ask, huffing out an angry breath. "I could have made that decision myself, you know?"

A muscle ticks in his jaw, but he doesn't respond at first. I turn to Nicolai. "Who knows how she's doing?" I demand. "Where is she? What are her symptoms?"

"Let's go see her," Nicolai suggests. "And we can talk on the way."

"Thank you." I look down at the clothes I'm wearing and up questioningly to Marissa. "But what about…"

"Her clothes, Nicolai," she says. "Let's get her back to the compound so she can at least change."

He sighs. "We have so little time."

And that's when I realize what's happening. My mother's dying. He's flown me back to America to see her.

How long has he known this?

"I'll bring them to her," Stefan supplies. "Drop her off there now so she doesn't have to wait."

Nicolai pulls onto the highway. We ride in stony silence. Marissa clears her throat.

"So, how was your trip to Russia?"

I sigh. "Fine. I met Demyan and Larissa."

"How are they?" Nicolai asks. "I was once a member of that group."

"They seemed well enough," I say with a shrug. "They were very kind to us, and their brotherhood was welcoming as well."

The rest of our ride is silent.

We finally pull up to the nursing facility where my mother lives, but no one greets us on the ample front porch as they usually do. My mother likes to sit on a rocker with a cup of tea or by the checkerboard table so she can play a game with a friend. But she isn't there.

My nerves are fraught by the time I get out of the car. My hands shake, and I'm still wearing the stupid sheath. I sure as hell hope Stefan will bring me clothes to change into. We aren't far from the compound.

I don't want to go in here alone. I *don't*.

"Would you like me to go with you?" Marissa asks. I shake my head. The only person I would have wanted with me yesterday was Stefan, but after he's acted today, I don't even want him there.

"I'll be fine, thank you," I tell her, but I know it isn't the truth. I won't be fine at all. My nerves are frazzled and I'm wearing practically nothing. And my mother, *God*, my mother. She could be dying. I'm steeling myself for what I'll see when I go in. For what I'll face.

"Take this," Marissa says, taking off her own sweater and handing it to me. It's such a small gesture, but when I place it on, my nose tingles and my throat gets tight.

"Thank you," I whisper.

She squeezes my hand. "Stay strong."

And I know she isn't just talking about my mother, but more. She knows things aren't right with Stefan. She doesn't know exactly what I've been through, but she knows it hasn't been all sunshine and daises.

Caroline's words come back to me. *The women of the Bratva stand together.*

They do. They *do*.

When I enter the lobby, my stomach churns with nausea from the strong scent of antiseptics. The overwhelming hopelessness of this place makes me want to run, but I have to stay. I can't leave now. If he flew me here from Russia with the clothes of a slave still on my back, this is important. Something is very, very wrong.

I go through the routine of checking in and giving them my name. The guard at the main desk gives me a curious look at my weird outfit, but the sweater does make me look a little less conspicuous. I make my way to my mother's room, and when I arrive, I see a familiar nurse, Leah.

"Oh, Taara," she says, coming to me. "Thank God. We were told you'd traveled outside of the country and no one could reach you."

A lie, but whatever. This all happened so quickly, I

imagine that I couldn't have really gotten here any faster than I did.

"How is she?" I say. "I got here as soon as I could."

She sighs and shakes her head. "Not good," she says softly. "She suffered a heart attack and has been moved to the intensive care unit on the hospital side of the facility." She gives me a look of sympathy. "She's holding on, though. We aren't sure for who or what, but perhaps you're the answer."

"Oh." *Oh.*

Oh God, this is not good. I let her lead me in a sort of stupor to the other side of this floor, past rows and rows of people in wheelchairs or walking on wobbly walkers. But my mother will be in bed. Who knew how much I'd want to see her in one of the wheelchairs today?

"Be prepared," Leah says softly when we reach a closed door. "She isn't well at all. She has breathing tubes and an IV and may not be conscious."

I nod, unable to speak. The lump in my throat is so tight I can't even swallow.

Leah opens the door. When I go in, the first thing I notice is how dark it is. The second thing is how quiet it is.

"Mom?" I go to her bedside, only to see that she is indeed, asleep. And God, she looks terrible. Breathing tubes and apparatus surround her.

"I'll leave you," Leah says softly. "Ring if you need anything at all."

I take my mother's hand. "I'm here," I tell her. At first, I think she isn't going to even know I'm there. She's so deeply asleep, she doesn't even hear me. But after a moment, her paper-thin eyelids flutter open briefly. "I knew you'd come," she whispers, then she closes her eyes once more.

I sit beside her and I take her hand, placing it on my cheek. Needing to feel my mother's touch.

We sit in amiable silence. I listen to the sound of her oxygen, and the quietest beeping of the machines she's hooked up to.

"Where were you?" she whispers, and it's odd, but I know then that my mom is at her most lucid. I haven't gotten to talk to my "real" mother in so long, it feels a little out of the ordinary.

"I had to go on a small trip," I tell her. Oh God, as if. A long trip, and it involved a plot to take down the men responsible for the kidnapping of women from our homeland.

"Did you enjoy yourself?" my mother asks.

"Yes," I lie. "Very much."

"And who did you go with?"

"Stefan," I say before I can stop myself.

She actually opens one eyes. "Did you really?" A corner of her lips quirks up.

"I did. Really." But I don't offer anything else at this stage. I don't want her thinking that there's anything at all going on between us, because *there isn't*.

"Good," she says softly, and to my surprise, she lifts the hand I'm not holding, and places it atop mine. "He'll take care of you now."

Her words send panic through me. She's saying goodbye. I can't stand it. "What?" I ask. "Mom, no!"

But her eyes fall closed like she's too exhausted to say more, and when she coughs, it's ragged and desperate. She's barely hanging on. Barely alive. And I can't keep her as mine anymore.

A soft knock comes at the door. I don't look up. I don't want to see any more nurses or really anyone right now. I want to hold onto this moment. Hold onto my mother.

But when I see Stefan through my blurred vision, I don't look away. I don't tell him to fuck off. I take his hand with my free one and he takes my mother's. And we stand like that, in silence. And even though I want to hate him, or even feel indifferent toward him, I can't do it. I don't want to deny my mother time with him, but if I'm honest, I don't want to be alone right now.

I forgive him for being an asshole, because right now that doesn't matter. Nothing matters. He came. He didn't leave me to bear this alone but came.

He's murmuring words in Russian, and I don't know exactly what he's saying, but they sound like a sort of prayer. And I love that. I blink, and a tear rolls down my cheek. This man, this man that I love, he's done terrible things, but he holds my mother's hand and prays with her on her last moments on earth, and *I will never forget that*. I don't know where we go from here, but I don't care.

"You came for her," my mother says, her eyes closing again, as if it's too much effort to keep them open. Then they flutter open again, and she looks from me to him. She takes our hands, the two that she holds, and she joins them. She pulls in a deep, ragged breath. "You have each other now."

She closes her eyes and my heartbeat spikes because I think she's gone, but she isn't, yet. Her breathing comes in ragged, shallow gasps for long moments, and we don't let go. Standing over her, holding one another's hands, we look at each other.

I don't need to say anything. I forgive him for what he did. I love him. And if some stupid misguided notion got him to push me away as he did, I can forgive that.

He isn't getting rid of me that easily.

He holds my gaze and I hold his.

"I love you," he mouths, and it hits me in the chest so hard and fast the tears I've held back begin to flow.

He does. Oh, God, he *does*.

"I love you," I mouth back.

We don't move, not an inch. I look from him to my mother, and I grab at ragged bits of prayers I learned in my youth. I wipe away tears and gently stroke the top of my mother's hand while holding Stefan's with my other hand. And finally, when the sun is setting outside her window, fingertips of orange casting a gentle glow in the room, my mother breathes her last.

It isn't as dramatic as one would think, watching life usher out of this world and into the next. No one comes running. No angels play their trumpets. But her body goes completely still, and right then, I know she's more at rest than she ever was in life. I drop my head to her chest, now still, and I know she's gone. A deep sob racks my body. Though my mother wasn't perfect, and the past few months have been difficult to manage, she was still my mother. The woman who brought me into this world, who taught me right from wrong, who sacrificed countless days and months and years for me, to bring me to America and see to my education, my safety, my wellbeing.

But right now, my mind is blank, and I ride the waves of grief.

I cry until I have no more tears. I'm vaguely aware of people coming in the room and Stefan lifting me into his arms. I don't speak but put my arms around his neck, and find that actually, I *do* have a few more tears to shed. I didn't realize how badly it devastated me to have a rift between us. But I need him now, and I don't want him to let me go. He holds me, speaks to the nurses in the room, and places a call on his phone.

"Let's go, babygirl," he whispers in my ear.

"We can't leave her," I whisper.

"We didn't," he whispers back. "But she's gone now."

I'm grateful he's a take-charge kinda guy right now, because it makes it easier to know what to do next. To walk with him out to the car that waits. To place my head on his chest on the ride home and cry some more. To follow him as he leads us back to his house on the compound, and up the stairs. To walk in a sort of trance to the bed, where he strips me out of the clothes that I wear and tosses the bag of forgotten clothes he fetched on an overstuffed chair.

He leads me to the bathroom and takes my hand in silence, making me take a hot shower. The water feels good and washes away my tears as I cry yet again. I don't realize he's joined me until I feel his strong arms around me. I lean on him, and it feels perfect. It feels right.

Though there's nothing sexual in his touch tonight, it's deeply, beautifully intimate. He's concerned and gentle with me, and it's so damn sweet I let it soothe me. When I'm done showering, he helps me out and towels me off, slinging a towel around his own waist and leading me back to the bedroom.

Then he turns down the bedsheets.

"Hungry, baby?" he asks. I honestly don't even remember the last time I ate. I nod dumbly but lay my head on the pillow and close my eyes. A short while later, someone knocks on the door. He says something to the person on the other side, takes a tray, then shuts it before he comes to me.

"You awake, baby?"

"Yes, daddy." My eyes flutter open. I didn't mean to say that. I feel small and a bit shy now that I have. But it feels nice right now, when I'm hurting and sad, to call him that. And he likes it too. I know he does when he sits on the side of the bed, slides the tray beside me, and bends down to kiss my forehead.

"You're a good girl, Taara. You know that?" he whispers. He brushes his rough fingers along my cheekbone. "Daddy's good little girl."

His praise warms me through. I sit up and take the cup of soup he hands me, as well as some crackers.

"Aren't you going to eat anything?" I ask him.

He just shakes his head.

"You should eat," I say, unnaturally focused on how important this is.

"You let me worry about that," he says, his eyes boring into mine with concern. I sigh, when the memory that I lost my mother today resurfaces. I swipe at my eyes but it's no use. I'm full on crying again with no help for it. Quietly, he draws me to his chest and holds me while I weep, until I'm completely spent.

"Sleep, baby."

"I'll sleep better if you're next to me," I confess.

And then he slides into bed behind me, wraps his arms around me from behind, and gathers me into his chest. And I fall asleep like that, tucked into his arms and as safe as can be. I wake several times in the night and remember the sad reality of what happened. I cry again and again. And every time, he holds me until I'm done, then tucks me back in.

I don't make myself think about tomorrow or what happens next. I lost my mother today. But I found Stefan.

Chapter 19

Stefan

THE DAYS after Hesther's death pass in a blur. It takes a week for us to prepare for the funeral, and Taara opted for cremation. We plan to give her the highest honor burial as one of our own and take care of Taara. Demyan and Larissa even fly out from Moscow, though their purpose is two-fold. Demyan came to convene with me and Tomas regarding where we stand with San Diego and the Russian Thieves. But they arranged their visit so they could be here early enough to be with Taara.

Larissa, Caroline, and Marissa help Taara prepare for the funeral. They get her clothing and shoes and help her dress in black, fix her hair and shoo me out of the way when I check in on her.

Things have gotten worse between me and Taara, but I tell myself it's because she's grieving. And because she's grieving, I need to give her space.

"She's fine, Stefan," Caroline says cooly to me. "Now go drink some vodka or something." And she shuts the door. I stand, bereft for a moment. I don't know what to do with myself. I earned that, though, and I know it. I have no idea what Taara has told them about us, but it's clear it wasn't good.

I should be happy about that, but it makes me want to break a fucking wall.

"Let them take care of her," Tomas says behind me. I didn't realize he was here. I turn to face him with a sigh, but don't speak.

"I don't know what's going on with you and Taara, but it doesn't take a genius to see it's not good," he says. "Death has a strange way of either bringing people back together or driving them further apart." He holds my gaze before he finishes. "See to it that it doesn't do that latter, and you two will weather this."

I walk to him, my hands shoved in my pockets. "How the hell do you know that matters to me?" I ask, feeling like a petulant child. "Her mother's death fucking killed her. And if she's with me, she only experiences more tragedy. More violence. More fucking *death*."

We walk together toward the compound, where our men are convening this afternoon.

"Larissa called Laina, who told Marissa, who told Nicolai, who told me," he admits.

"That's bullshit. Like seventh fucking grade."

He shrugs. "Unions within the Bratva matter," he says.

"Of course they do, but this is no fucking union."

I wish it was. God, I wish it was.

Tomas just raises a brow in my direction and doesn't speak at first. Finally, he shakes his head and chuckles. "You mean to tell me you have no feelings for Taara?"

My silence makes him laugh out loud.

"Fuck off," I mutter, not wanting to deal with him right now.

"Christ, we're having a pissing match now, are we? I haven't even had a shot yet." Demyan stands outside the entrance to our meeting room, rolling his eyes heavenward.

"You can fuck off, too," I tell him, though I love these two like the brothers they are, and even if they sometimes make me want to beat the shit out of them, they are family.

"Stefan," Demyan says, sobering. "I saw you two in Russia. You can't hide the way you feel about her any more than she can hide the way she feels about you."

I shake my head. "I don't want to have this conversation," I mutter.

"Right," Tomas mutters. "Who was the one who pulled away first?"

"I said, I don't want to have this conversation," I say through tight lips.

Demyan smirks. "If you don't, I'll call the girls down and we can get Taara's side of the story."

"You wouldn't."

But now he's deadly sober. "Sure as hell would."

I curse him out in Russian, but he doesn't even flinch.

"Fine," I finally admit. "I decided it was too dangerous for her to be with me. She's too young, and she has her whole life ahead of her. I can't let her get close to someone like me." I swallow hard. "Seeing her in that room, knowing they got their hands on her—"

"Tell me about it," comes a voice behind me. Nicolai joins us, his hands in his pockets and his blue eyes that mirror mine meeting mine unblinkingly. "Tell me what it's like seeing her at the mercy of another man."

I know Nicolai knows this pain badly. He witnessed his own woman fall victim to the slave trade himself.

I sigh.

"Or mine," Demyan says. "You do know Larissa was captured by my men as punishment for theft against the brotherhood?"

"And you know Caroline was arranged to be wed to me by her brother, to pay off his debt," Tomas finishes. "So, go on, Stefan. Tell us how you don't want your woman endangered." Tomas reaches for my shoulder and squeezes. "Just because Amaliya died doesn't mean Taara will suffer the same fate. For all you know, she'll outlive you by decades, bury your sorry ass and live in the lap of luxury with your money for the rest of her life. And honestly, with the age difference between you, there's a fucking good chance."

That makes me unwillingly smile.

I look at each one of them, and it finally seems so clear. So damn clear. *They're right.*

Tarra is withdrawn, but she just lost her mother. She's deep within the throes of grief, and I can't fault her for literally anything she does right now.

"Let's have our meeting," Demyan says. "Taara is in good hands. Give this time to pass and take good care of her in the meantime. And when all is said and done? You make your move."

I swallow hard. "I will," I say. Christ, I love these men. "Thank you."

He punches my shoulder. "Good, then let's get this meeting over with. Someone told me Caroline's cooking us dinner?"

Tomas' eyes light up. "Wait until you see what she has planned for us." The two of them enter before us, and Nicolai lags behind to walk in with me.

"You alright?" he asks me.

I nod and scrub a hand over my brow. I've been taking care of Taara and seeing to her own wellbeing, but I haven't slept well in days.

"You need some sleep," he states.

"I do."

"I have an idea," he says. "We're still a few weeks away from Marissa having the baby. Why don't you take Taara away for a little while? Just the two of you. Head to the mountains or beach or something."

I shake my head. "Not now," I tell him. "But thank you, I'll think about it."

He nods. "Anytime."

Today, the entire brotherhood is here, as well as conference calls joining us with the rest of Tomas's crew in Boston and Demyan's in Moscow. We have to deal with the aftermath of what happened in Russia and decide where this leaves us. I take my place at the front of the room and sit at the head of the table. My brothers join me.

"Welcome, to the *pakhan* of both Boston and our sister group, Moscow," I say. The men clap their hands in greeting, then silence descends on the room. "We need to debrief all of you as to what happened in Moscow and where this leaves us."

The meeting is well underway within minutes. Tomas confirms that those in America who were undercover for the slave trade have taken down the operation, the most duplicitous among them now in jail. He assures us that because he and I did not partake in the trade and are on record for denouncing any connection with the group, as well as being responsible for the ending of the trade in America, we will not be subjected to the legal prosecution the others face.

Demyan explains that the Thieves have extended peace, and they've formed a solid alliance with the Moscow brotherhood. "That strengthens the power we hold in Russia," he says. "And now that the corrupt leaders of their organization have been outed, they no longer pose a threat."

"That isn't the only threat against us," one of my men says. "The last time we convened, you were taking Taara Khan as prisoner because she witnessed an execution."

"Yes," I say. "Taara has proven her loyalty to us." I tell them at length what she did in Moscow, how she put herself on the line. And to my surprise, Demyan shows them footage from Taara's undercover job.

"I believe she is an innocent," Nicolai says. "I no longer believe she is a threat to any of us."

I can see in my men's faces that his words carry weight. He's earned creditability as their leader in my absence, and as the leader now. Though I'm still *pakhan,* they know he is the future of our brotherhood.

"As do I," says Demyan.

"And I," says Tomas.

My throat tightens at the show of allegiance, at their defense of Taara.

"Taara Khan is not only innocent, there's something you should know," I say, getting to my feet. "I love her. She belongs to me. And as such, you will all treat her with the respect due to a woman of the Bratva."

They murmur in agreement and nod their heads. My chest expands with pride, and I swallow hard. "As you know, she's lost her mother. We will bury her with the highest honors and take care of Taara."

We conclude the meeting taking care of all orders of business, and I'm confident my men will honor me in this. Taara is not a threat. She is one of our own.

Now I just need to convince her of the very same.

Chapter 20

Taara

THE DAYS PASS IN A BLUR. We bury my mother's ashes, and Stefan sees to it that she's given high honors, her funeral and arrangements made with painstaking care. It's beautiful. It's brutally painful.

I am so thankful for Marissa, Caroline, and Larissa, for all they've done for me and helped me with. But though my heart aches for the loss of my mother, I long for connection with Stefan again.

Nothing's been the same since we returned here from Russia. He touches me with concern and tenderness... but like a brother.

Is that all he is to me?

At first, I wonder if he's giving me some space, knowing that I'm grieving the loss of my mother. But as the days go on, and he doesn't give me anything more than the most platonic affection, I wonder.

Has he moved on? Is he no longer interested in me at all?

It's the weirdest kind of break up in history, because it's a break up that never happened. We share the same bed. He holds me and tucks me in and kisses my cheek or forehead tenderly. But I want more. I want so, so much more.

I haven't called him daddy since the day my mother died.

And I want to. I want to so badly my throat gets all tight when I think about it. But there's a chasm between us that feels miles wide, and I don't know how to bridge it.

I feel helpless to make the first move. If he rejects me, it will kill me. I don't think I'd survive the pain of that. How could I? I've never loved anyone as I love him.

Demyan and Larissa fly back to Moscow tomorrow, and Tomas and Caroline to Boston the following day. And I wonder... what does his brotherhood think of me?

Before Moscow I was his captive. His prisoner. Before that, his housekeeper.

What am I now?

So, I do what I always do. I clean his house and fold his clothes and arrange his bed—our bed?—so it's neat and welcoming. And I wait. I sit on the steps, wearing a ratty old pair of jeans, scuffed flats, and a sweater, because it's air-conditioned and chilly in here. And I wait.

The sun's already set by the time he comes to me. He opens the door, steps in, then gives a start when he sees me sitting on the steps.

"You alright?" he asks.

I only shrug, because I'm not super sure how to answer his question.

He kicks off his shoes and hangs up his keys, then steps over to the stairs.

"Taara," he asks. "What's wrong?"

But I can't speak. If I do, I'm afraid I'll cry again, and I'm so, so tired of crying. I finally take a deep breath and let it out, take another one, and finally get the courage to speak. So I walk downstairs, and head for the couch. I fold myself in the corner and think about what I want to say before I speak. Finally, I take in a deep, shuddering breath, and let it out slowly, while I turn to him.

"So… I have a question for you."

"Yeah?"

He leans against the doorframe and arches a brow at me, and holy hell is he hot. God, he's so fucking hot it hurts, all muscles and tats and badass leaning all casual against the rail.

I swallow. "Am I still your prisoner?"

His eyes gentle, then. He uncrosses his arms and walks toward me, then sits beside me. He takes my hand in his. "No, baby," he says. "Hell, no. You're not my prisoner. When we had the meetings of the brotherhoods, we made that as clear as possible. You are *not* our captive. Demyan even showed footage of the work you did."

My nose tingles as it does when I'm about to cry, but I rub it with the back of my hand. Where does that leave me? Where does that leave *us*?

"Really?"

"Really."

I clear my throat. The next question is harder. But I'm a woman of the Bratva now, and Bratva women are brave.

"Thank you. So now I'm your… housekeeper?"

"My housekeeper," he repeats, his voice taut and his eyes narrowed on me. I watch as his nostrils flare. "*Housekeeper?*"

Okay, so maybe not the right response.

"What… well, what *am* I?" I ask, feeling my own anger at his rejection boiling up. I look down at the floor, because his eyes are beautiful and I'm going to cry. "I mean… where do I stand with you?"

"Baby. Look at me."

So, I do. Even though it kills me, I do. I lift my eyes to his questioningly.

"You're mine, Taara," he says, in a low whisper. "Don't you know that?"

I shake my head. "How can I?" I whisper back. "You've pulled away from me. How am I to know what I am to you? It isn't…it isn't something I can take for granted."

"I didn't want to hurt you," he says. "I couldn't, Taara. Being involved with a man like me puts you in danger."

"But you'll protect me," I say. I swallow hard, take a deep breath, and square my shoulders. "And if I'm yours, I've got the power of the Bratva to protect me as well."

He's so close to me now I could touch more than his hand, and I'm waffling between shoving that barrel of a chest away from me, and wanting to touch him.

"You do," he says, reaching for me. I don't push him away. His voice softens when he draws me close. "You do, babygirl."

Babygirl.

It's the sun breaking through clouds after a storm. The sound of songbirds tweeting after a long winter.

The sweetest, most tender word I didn't know I needed to hear until he said it.

I close my eyes. I take a breath. I gather my courage, and ask him, "Then why don't you treat me like your babygirl anymore?"

With one hand on my back holding me to him, he runs his fingers through my hair. "You were mourning the loss of your mother," he says, and for some reason that makes me *angry*.

"So?" I ask, and this time I do push him away. "What does that have to do with anything? Are you crazy? You make *literally* no sense, you know that?"

"Taara," he growls.

"What?" I ask, trying to get away from him. "Hey, you're no innocent in this," he says. "You pulled away from me, too."

"You pulled first," I say petulantly, and that makes him laugh. The sound of his laughter makes something inside me melt, and a warm tingling suffuses my limbs. He smiles at me, and that easily, I smile back.

I shouldn't. I should fight him, make him earn me back, but hell, when those blue eyes of his crinkle around the edges and his lips tip up, I'm a goner. I'm a fucking goner.

"So, who will make the first move, then?" he asks, in a suggestive voice that makes my toes curl.

Oh, God, I want him.

"The first move?" I ask, and that stirs all *kinds* of things in me. Panty-dampening, nipple-tingling, dry mouth things. "Well I dunno. What do you have in mind?"

"Oh," he says teasingly. "I'm not so sure. Maybe… something like this?"

He cups my jaw between both his hands, bends his mouth to mine, and brushes our lips together. I am so ready for him, my body goes all full-tingle just from the kiss, and I press my thighs together because the throbbing between my legs is instant.

And then he's tugging me to his chest, and my hair is wrapped all around his fingers, and I'm sniffling a little onto his shirt and he's rocking me right there on the couch. "Get upstairs," he finally whispers in my ear, "before daddy has to make you."

Daddy.

I moan and kiss him again, but I must not move fast enough, for the next thing I know he's lifting me up and over his shoulder, his huge palm crashing on my ass as he ascends the steps. I wiggle my butt and kick my legs because *God that feels good*, and he smacks my ass again, harder this time. I squeal but I close my eyes and breathe him in, because this is Stefan. He's back. I'm his girl, and he's carrying me off to his cave, practically dragging me by the hair and pounding his chest *and I love it. I need it.*

He kicks open the door to his room and brings me in, tossing me on the bed as he tears at his clothes.

"Clothes," he grates out, tearing his t-shirt over his head. "*Off.*" I'd rather just lay here watching him strip and drinking him in with my eyes, but I know that look he's giving me, and there's no doubt in my mind that if I don't do exactly what he says right now, he'll spank my ass.

Not that that would be a bad thing.

So I whip off my top and toss it to the floor, followed by my bra and jeans, and just when I'm yanking them off my feet, his hands are on me, pulling them down before he rips my panties off. Soon, the clothing roadblock has been removed, and he presses me down onto the bed, his heavy, muscled body above mine.

"I love you, Taara Khan," he rumbles in my ear. "And I'm sorry for being a dick."

"I forgive you," I say. "And yes, you were *such* a dick."

He punishes me by pulling my hair back, but I love the way my scalp burns and tingles. "You didn't deserve that," he says. I don't respond, because I'm all choked up again. All I do is cry these days, and I don't want to anymore. I want to laugh. I want to scream in ecstasy and let him bring me to pleasure over and over again. I want to lay on his chest and tell him my dreams. I want to listen to him when he comes home after a bad day, when he's had to make a difficult decision. I want to cook his meals and make his bed and do all the little domestic things I *always* have for him, because I love taking care of him. I love it so much it hurts to think of not having it.

But then I can't think anymore, because he's pressing his swollen cock between my legs and teasing the head along my clit. I moan and spread my legs wider. He pins my wrists and kisses my temple, then drags his lips along the side of my face to my jaw, kissing along the way.

"I love you, babygirl," he says. "I love you so much."

He loves me.

He really, truly loves me. And I know then that men like Stefan show their love in more than words. They show it in selfless giving, in vigilance and protection.

"I love you," I whisper back, my voice trembling. "I love you so much it hurts."

He holds himself above me, his eyes piercing mine with intensity and passion.

"Yeah, baby?" he says teasingly. "Then give that pussy to daddy," he says, and my insides melt into a puddle.

The first thrust has me moaning, the second, forgetting who I am or how I got here. By the third, I'm riding the first crest of ecstasy and he's building the sweetest, most perfect rhythm of pleasure. The feel of him in me, gliding in and out, electrifies me. I wrap my legs around his back as he anchors himself above me, his gaze never leaving mine with every vicious, perfect stroke of his cock.

"Come with me," he orders. I nod mutely, focusing on doing just that.

"That's my girl," he says. "So gorgeous." He palms my breasts and tweaks my nipples and I moan on the cusp of orgasm. "So perfect. I love every inch of you and always will."

I can't talk because I'm going to come. He nods, his eyes falling closed as he loses himself to pleasure right along with me. My breath hitches and I shake beneath him, riding the waves of ecstasy as he throws his head back and gives himself over to this perfection. We're fused together, joined in our pain and longing, and I know this is what we needed. *This is what we needed,* just this, me and him joined together like this.

He rocks against me, and the spasms begin to subside. He lowers his forehead to mine and our breaths become one in the stillness.

"That was fucking beautiful," he says in a choked whisper.

"It was," I agree. "Thank you."

He captures my mouth with his and folds our fingers together. There's so much to say… so much to forgive… but now we're putting that behind us. We have to. For in Bratva life—or in any life, really—there's pain and sorrow, tragedy and heartache. But real love forgives. Real love takes the ashes and transforms the tragic into something beautiful.

We don't speak for long minutes in the quiet aftermath of our lovemaking. We clean up in silence and come back together, and I lay, naked and vulnerable, beside him. He pulls me up to him and tucks my head under his chin, holding me. I lay my hand on his chest and breathe him in. I fall asleep like that. I wake in the night when he does, and he slow-kisses me until I'm wet, then rolls me over and makes sweet love to me with tender, languid strokes until we're panting and sated. We fall asleep again, and when we wake with the sun, we lay together in silence. We've already said everything we need to.

I love this man. And I'll weather whatever we have to. I'll fight for him. I'll fight for *us.*

Because our relationship—what we fought for, what we have—is the true king's ransom.

Chapter 21

Taara

I'm in a deep, luxurious sleep when I hear Stefan stirring about the room. It's warm in here, and last night was utter perfection. Simple, utter perfection. Instead of his usual late-night brooding in front of the fireplace, I joined him. I always do, now. I pour him a drink and sit beside him. He lights the fire, and we sit together. Sometimes I put my head in his lap, sometimes I sit in his lap, and he holds me close as we watch the flickering flames and listen to the soothing crackling sound. Sometimes he tells me about his day, and I love to listen. I always have. But sometimes he doesn't want to talk to me about it at all.

After the fire died down, we came up to bed, and he seemed a bit preoccupied. I didn't push, though. He'll tell me when it's time.

"Wake up, sleeping beauty." His deep, rumbling voice,

sleep-filled and sexy, wakes me up. I smile up at him, still groggy.

"Mmm?" It's Saturday morning, and I usually sleep in. I never have sleep issues like I did before but sleep like a rock now. "What time is it?"

"Ten o'clock," he says. "And I was hoping someone would make me some pancakes."

"Oh?" I ask teasingly. "Maybe we should call someone."

"You know I would," he says. He's mentioned a few times now hiring someone to come in and take my job, as if now that we're a couple I somehow weirdly don't want to cook for him anymore.

I give him what I hope is a withering glare, though my crazy bedhead and daisy pjs might lessen the impact.

"I am perfectly capable of making you pancakes," I tell him haughtily. "And I swear to God, if you mention hiring someone one more time—"

He's got me on my back and pinned beneath him in ten seconds flat.

"You'll what, babygirl?" he says, moving his body over mine. "Give daddy an ultimatum? Hmm? You know where that will land you, don't you?"

My breasts tingle and my core clenches. I swallow hard, because my mouth is suddenly dry.

"Over your lap?" I say, giving him what I *mean* to be a pout, but which is probably pathetic bedroom eyes. My ass still stings from a session the other night, and I'm not exactly against the idea of going over his lap again and letting him renew that sting. I love being dominated by him.

259

I love being held by him.

I love being cherished by him.

Hell, there isn't much I don't love about the two of us together.

"Exactly," he says.

"Kinda hard to make pancakes when you're trapped beneath a big badass," I mutter.

"Pancakes can wait," he whispers in my ear, kissing his way from my cheek to my breasts, then lower still. I don't fight him. I love it. He worships my body and masters my heart. I'mfalling with no safety net in sight, and I wouldn't have it any other way. I don't try to control this. Every time I let myself go, he shows me he's got me, and I love him a little bit more. Turns out he wants to eat *me* for breakfast, and I'm not complaining about *that*.

He says he likes watching me go about my day with a blush on my cheeks, and I'm totally happy with that plan myself. Not complaining. Nope.

I finally pad down to the kitchen wearing nothing but one of his t-shirts, my hair slung up in a messy ponytail, and make the man pancakes. He watches me, nursing a cup of coffee, sitting on one of the kitchen stools wearing nothing but a pair of faded jeans.

Some people want riches or fame. I've got what I want right here.

I place the platter of pancakes in front of him and hop on a stool beside him. We slather butter and syrup on stacks of pancakes and eat in amicable silence. Outside the window, some of the men walk by, and I see a car I don't recognize. I swallow my bite of pancake, then turn to him.

"What's up with the car out there?"

"What car?" he asks, looking at his plate. "I don't see a car."

Normally, he'd be on his feet and at the door, never one to miss a single happening at the compound, so his reaction is a little suspicious.

"Stefannn," I say, hopping off my stool and trotting to the window.

"Get your ass over here."

I stop and turn around to look at him.

"Do you know something I don't know?"

His blue eyes are twinkling at me. "I know lots of things you don't know. I'm the *pakhan*, remember?"

I pout a little.

"No pouting, little girl," he says. "I'll clean up the kitchen. Why don't you go get your shower?"

"Alright," I agree. "I shall do that." When I walk past him, he gives me a teasing swat. I smile to myself. I like this domestic arrangement.

I trot up the stairs to the clinking sound of the dishwasher being loaded and get my things out for the shower.

I frown, looking at my drawers. I swear I just did my laundry. But I'm definitely missing things. I look in the shower, too, and realize a few of my basic essentials seem to have disappeared. Weird.

I shower as usual, but a few minutes in, when I'm shaving my legs, I hear the door open and he joins me.

"Gotta speed it up," he says, lathering me up and rinsing my hair.

"Why?" I ask. Now I know something's up. "What are you hiding from me?"

"You'll see in a minute."

And then it dawns on me. Maybe something's wrong. Maybe he's shielding me from another show-down with a rival group, or they have plans to do something dangerous today and he doesn't want me to see.

"Is everything oaky?"

He frames my face between his large, rough hands, and holds my gaze. "Yeah, baby," he says softly. "Everything's okay. Hell, everything's *perfect*."

He leans down and kisses me, all wet and slippery and sensual, before he releases me, spins me around, and finishes rinsing me off.

We towel off and go to the room, and I pull on a pair of jeans and a t-shirt. But when I towel dry my hair, I cast a glance outside the window. The car I saw earlier is parked right out in front of our door. I don't bother asking him what's up again. He knows, and he'll tell me when he's ready. If there's anything I've learned about managing this man, it's that he does things on his terms, but there's nothing wrong with that. He's more than leader to all these men. He's the father-figure, the one they all look up to for guidance and support. And I love him for that.

I've never been able to trust anyone the way I do Stefan.

But he's proven himself worthy of my trust so many times now. *So many times.*

He dresses beside me in silence, but I can feel how tense he is. When I look at him, his eyes are still twinkling though his mind is elsewhere.

Stefan has a surprise for me.

"You ready?" he asks, after I've fixed my hair.

"Depends," I say teasingly. "Ready for what?"

"You're incorrigible, you know that?"

I shrug. "If I were... corrigible... that's a word, right? Then where would the fun be in that?"

He tugs my hair and grins at me.

"Too true."

"Yeah, daddy," I say, smiling at him. "I'm ready." Because I am. Whatever he's going to tell me, I'm ready to go with him. I don't really care where we're going or what we're doing. I just want to be with him. Wherever he is, as long as I'm with him, it's my happy place. It's home.

"Leave the bed," he says, nodding to the tousled sheets and tangled covers. "I've got someone coming here to clean while we're gone."

Gone? A little thrill goes through me.

I don't argue the cleaners point. Though I want to be the one that still cares for him, I've got no objections whatsoever to letting someone else make the bed and mop our floors.

Where are we going?

He reaches for me and draws me close, pressed flat up

against him. Kissing my forehead, he holds the back of my head, then looks in my eyes. "You're a good girl being patient," he says, and it warms me to the tips of my toes. "We're going away. I've arranged for everything so we can go for a full week. We need a break, the two of us, and I can trust Nicolai to lead in my absence."

I grin. "Really? Are we going far?"

"Not this time. I don't want to go too far because Marissa is so close to having the baby."

I nod and smile. It's true. I hosted a baby shower here at the house just last week, and Stefan and Nicolai spent all last weekend sorting things out and hauling them over to their place.

"Now no more questions. It was hard enough to plan a surprise for you."

He leads me to where a car is waiting. Marissa stands with Nicolai a few yards off, her hand resting on her ample belly. They wave at us, and I wave back.

Since my mother died, the "found" family I have within the Bratva mean more to me than ever. I'm excited about Marissa and Nicolai's baby.

What does our future hold? He's older than I am. Does that mean he wants no more children? I wouldn't blame him, though I have to admit I'd love a child of my own.

Our relationship is so new. We have to discuss this and so many more things. But we will. And the knowledge gives me a deep, abiding sense of satisfaction. We have days and weeks and months and years together to get to know each other. To learn what makes the one another tick. To learn how to love each other more deeply, more profoundly.

And I'll revel in those days. If there's anything I've learned with the loss of my mother and the short trip to Russia, it's that things can change in the blink of an eye. No one knows what tomorrow brings, how quickly circumstances can change. It makes me grateful for every moment I have. Some long for the future, pinning their hopes and dreams on uncertainty and wishes. But me... I try to revel in the present. And right now, I'm going on a trip with the man I love.

He helps me into the car, though I don't need help. It's something he likes to do for me, so I let him. "Buckle up," he orders. I do, and he joins me, then he speaks briefly to the driver.

And we're off.

"Okay, so now I'll tell you," he says, taking my hand and giving me a little squeeze. "I've booked a week away at a luxury suite. Just the two of us. But we'll be right in downtown Atlanta, and Marissa mapped out the best photography galleries to visit."

I blink in surprise and my throat gets a little tight. I smile at him.

"Did she?"

"Yeah," he says, his own eyes shining when he sees me grin. "Tonight, we're going to a showing. Marc Adamus? I guess he's—"

"Oh, just one of the *most amazing* modern-day landscape photographers known to man," I sputter. "Oh my *God*, what that man does with light and setting—"

He chuckles. "Sound good, then? You know I'd rather stick toothpicks under my fingernails then go to an art show, but..." He brushes his thumb over the top of my hand. "If it makes you happy, it makes me happy."

I swallow hard. "It makes me happy," I whisper.

"I like that," he says softly. "So, first, we check into our hotel. Then tonight we'll get dinner and head to the gallery. Sound good?"

"Sounds *perfect*."

And it is.

We arrive at our hotel, and he gets our bags situated. I plop on the massive bed, and stare at the beautiful room. I've never seen anything like this before. The walls are silver, the carpet navy, the bed decorated in crisp white linen. A vase of vibrant red roses sits beside a bottle of champagne. Huge, crystal clear windows give us an amazing view of the city's highrises. The room is spacious and beautiful, but I only have eyes for the man who's prowling toward me with a hungry look in his eyes.

"I've got you alone," he says huskily.

"You get me alone every day," I tease.

"But not *this* way," he says. And he doesn't have to explain what he means. Here, there are no responsibilities or demands we need to meet. Here, we can revel in each other for a little while. He kneels beside me and takes my hand.

"Your hands are beautiful. Do you know that?"

I look at my very ordinary hands. "Well, no," I admit. "They look pretty damn ordinary to me."

"Ordinary," he scoffs. "You could hand model."

"Hand model? Sounds dirty."

He chuckles. "We could make it dirty." Then he sobers. "But there's only one thing that would make your hand even prettier."

I don't know what he's talking about, but I suspect, and my heart begins to race.

"Oh?" I ask in a quiet voice. I'm afraid if I speak too loudly, I'll somehow ruin this moment, and I want to savor it, just like I want to savor every moment with him. Every damn moment.

I go still when he reaches for his pocket and takes out a little black box.

"Stefan…"

I can't say anything more than his name. I'm all choked up and staring at the small cube in his hand. He opens the box and stares at it for a moment, before spinning it around to show me.

"This," he says, his own voice all choked. "What do you think, Taara?"

"About the box?" I ask on a whisper.

He grins and tugs a lock of my hair.

"Marry me, Taara? Will you?"

"Yes," I whisper. I can't imagine life with anyone other than him. I've loved him for so long, and never dreamed I would actually mean as much to him as he does me. And this seems so natural. So perfect and right.

"I love you," he says, sliding the beautiful diamond on my finger. Then he leans down and kisses me.

"And I love you."

I can't stop staring at the ring. There are so many things I still need to ask him, things we'll discuss and debate and get to the bottom of. Over time. Right now, this is utter perfection. Though a part of my heart left me when my mother died, I found a part of me I didn't know existed when I became Stefan's. And I love him. I love him so damn much it makes me ache.

Chapter 22

Stefan

WHEN I PUT the ring on her finger, and she looks up at me with those wide, eager eyes, I nearly lose my mind.

Taara Khan is mine.

I love her. I love her with every fiber of my being. I've done shit I'm not proud of, and we fought hard to get to where we are. But I'll spend every damn day for the rest of my life showing her how much she means to me.

"Christ, I love you, woman," I say to her, pulling her to me and kissing her so that her head drops back and she moans out loud.

"And I love you," she whispers.

My hands are at her top and I'm pulling the t-shirt off, and soon she's lying before me wearing nothing but a bra and her panties. I kiss her cheeks, her mouth, her forehead, her eyelids, the sweet spot on her neck that makes her ticklish, the top of each breast and the sweet, gentle slope of her belly.

Now that she's agreed to be mine, I have to claim her. I want to be in her.

I strip out of my own t-shirt and jeans and flip her over onto her belly. I feel such a sudden, overwhelming need to make her mine I can't wait for formalities or sweet seduction. I want to fuck this woman, and I want to do it now.

"On your knees," I order, giving her full, voluptuous ass a hard swat when she doesn't move quickly enough. "Spread those legs for daddy."

She grips the thick bedspread between her fingers, and the light catches the diamond on her finger. If she had any idea how much that thing was worth, she'd lose her mind, but she'll never know. She's worth it. She's worth that and so much fucking more.

Obediently she falls to her chest and spreads her legs. I tangle my fingers in her hair and yank her head back until she squeals and moans. I push the head of my cock through her slick folds and groan when I find her wet and ready.

"I love you, Taara," I say as I slam into her and she arches her back with a sweet, seductive moan.

"And I love you," she breathes.

I slap her ass and pound into her, and she braces herself and welcomes me. She's perfect. So fucking perfect. Brave and strong, self-giving and brilliant, and able to withstand me when I'm at my most ruthless. I'll never hurt her. Never again. But I won't hide who I am or what I do, and she loves me anyway.

She loves me anyway.

She moans while I thrust in and out, her pleasure building on mine until she screams her release. I'm on her heels, and with a grunt and final savage tug of her hair, I come. It's utter fucking perfection when she comes a second time, harder and longer this time.

"Christ, I love you," I tell her, rolling over and panting, sweaty and riding the high.

"Christ, I love you, too," she teases. "I have for a very long time, you know," she says, rolling over and laying her head on my chest.

"How long?" I ask.

"Long enough that it wasn't proper," she admits.

"Honey, this *still* isn't proper. You know that, right?"

She grins. "I do. And I kinda love it."

That makes me laugh, then sigh.

"Nothing really changes, you know," I tell her.

"Oh? How so?"

"I'm still going to be in charge as leader. I'm not turning away from the brotherhood now, not when we've forged so much together and I'm teaching Nicolai."

"Of course not," she says. "But actually, daddy..." She reaches for my hand and weaves her pretty fingers through my bigger, rougher ones. "*Everything's* changed." She smiles. "But for the better."

I think about it. She's right. I'm still the leader and we still have our friends and enemies. Now I don't face this alone. I face this with the most beautiful, loyal woman by my side.

The brotherhood will not die, and never will. But I've paid the king's ransom. And she was worth every damn penny.

EPILOGUE

One year later

"STEFAN."

Taara is standing in our living room, her hand on the piano. My entire home is different now because of her, and I love it. She's added her domestic touch to everything. She's gifted in that way, and this room is no exception. A gleaming black baby grand is the focal point of this room, complete with cream-colored walls and a comfortable sectional, her framed photographs both breathaking and eye-catching. My men love to drop in and visit with us, and Taara welcomes them all with open arms.

I never knew I needed her until I had her. Now that I do, my life feels complete in a way I never anticipated, as if she's the final piece to a puzzle.

But today, something's wrong. She's trembling, her back

to me, holding a piece of paper in one hand and some-thing I can't quite see in the other. I walk to her, my heartbeat accelerating.

Did she get into the grad school she applied for?

"What is it, baby?"

She turns to me and literally collapses on my chest, breaking into sobs.

"Taara, baby, *what?*"

First, she hands me the piece of paper, sobbing away on my chest, but I can't tell if these are sad or happy tears. I quickly scan the paper, my own eyes misting over when I read what's written.

Our application for adoption's been accepted. I knew it would be. I have friends in high places, and one phone call was all it took. Our lawyer assured me we'd be approved, but Taara didn't know that.

Two weeks after our quiet marriage ceremony on the front lawn of the compound, she came to me. She wanted to adopt a child, specifically one of the Afghani refugees. And how could I tell my wife no? I think it had something to do with her holding Nicolai and Marissa's new baby. She got this *gleam* in her eye...

I'm not a twenty-something year old anymore, but hell. I'm an experienced father. And I'll give our child the safest, most normal life he or she could imagine.

So I hold her to me and rock her in my arms. "Baby," I tell her. "This is amazing."

"But look," she sniffs, holding up her second hand. I look down, and when it finally dawns on me what I'm seeing, I'm not sure if I want to laugh or cry myself.

It's a white pregnancy test with two pink lines.

"Are you fucking kidding me?"

That makes her smile, and now *she's* laughing and crying at once, so I just hold her, because one of us losing their shit's good enough.

"So… we need to talk timing," I tell her.

"And school…"

"And a nanny…"

"No." She shakes her head and looks up at me. "*I'm* the one who will mother them."

Mother them. She's so cute.

"Yeah, baby," I tell her. "You will."

"I hope one of them is a girl," she whispers. "We'll name her Hesther."

I pull her to my chest and embrace her, suddenly overcome with inexplicable emotion.

"Yes," I tell her. "We will." I hold her to me, and give thanks for all that's happened. I made mistakes. Hell, we all have. But as the seasons of life come and go, an ever-changing landscape, new life comes in the spring. And with it, a new beginning.

From the Author:

Thank you so much for reading King's Ransom: A Dark Bratva Romance, the third stand-alone book in my Ruthless Doms series. I am so grateful for your support! Please read on for previews of my other books you may enjoy.

· · ·

Priceless: A Dark Bratva Romance (Ruthless Doms)

PREVIEWS

I look at the sea of faces in the cramped, humid high-school auditorium.

Cheerful. Youthful. Full of hope and promise and pride.

But I see past every one of them.

I'm not here to observe the masses getting their rolled-up diplomas and marching off to college, holding flowers from grandparents and parents and boyfriends, posting goddamned selfies all over social media. I've ignored every word the politicians and speakers said, more intent on the conversation around me than anything. I see every eye that looks at her. Everybody within arm's reach.

I know each exit in this school, and every few minutes run my thumb along the cold metal I have tucked into my pants and the knife in my boot.

Ever vigilant. Ever watchful. Because this is my job.

I don't give a shit about anyone else in this place.

The rest are faceless, nameless, my focus on the one girl

who stands out from the crowd because of her sheer, vibrant beauty. The belle of the goddamned ball. She's reckless and impulsive and brilliant.

My charge. My ward. The girl I've been commissioned to protect for four years.

The longest fucking years of my life.

Marissa Rykov.

Seventeen years old, just two days away from her eighteenth birthday. On the cusp of legal adulthood.

And the daughter of my father's best friend.

Off limits, *in every fucking sense of the word*.

I've been Marissa's bodyguard since she was thirteen years old. I've stayed in the background, attempting to give her the freedom a burgeoning teen needs, but honest to fucking God, screw that. I failed on that end. I could count every hair on her head. I could tell you the name, date of birth, location, and history of every single damn person she's interacted with, and every boyfriend knew *exactly* who I was. I got to know them, too, and each has a folder on file with detailed background checks. Slightly over the top for teen-aged kids, and the files were admittedly slim, but I have no regrets.

She was just a child when we met, innocent to the ways of The Bratva. Ignorant of the work her father did.

And now, as she prepares to go off to college, it's my job to keep protecting her.

I've kept myself aloof. Detached.

She's a *child.*

But as I watch her walk across that stage, her brilliant

278

smile lighting up the whole fucking Northern Hemisphere, my heart squeezes, and I swallow hard. Jesus, I'm proud of that girl. And I'd give fucking anything to keep that smile on her face.

I look away and school my features. I shouldn't have allowed my admiration to show even for a second. If anyone... *anyone* suspected how I feel about her...

My phone buzzes, and I ignore it at first, watching as Marissa walks down the stage on death-defying heels she should never have been allowed to wear. I swallow hard as her father embraces her and hands her flowers. She scans the auditorium, as if looking for someone, when her eyes meet mine.

I give her a small nod before I turn away and answer the phone.

"What is it?"

Laina, my younger sister, is on the line.

"Do not take your eyes off of her, Nicolai."

I'm instantly on guard. I swivel around to look back at Marissa, my pulse racing when I see her father at first, but I don't see her. She was here a second ago.

"What the fuck are you talking about?" I hiss into the phone as I push my way through the crowd to get to her.

"I overheard something I shouldn't have," Liana says, her voice shaking.

"Tell me." My voice comes out in a choked whisper.

Where the fuck is she?

I knock a lady's bag off her shoulder in my haste to get to

her. "Hey!" she says, but I plow on, ignoring the angry crowd I shove aside, making my way toward the front of the auditorium.

"I can't speak freely right now," she says. "I'll call you as soon as I can, but listen to me, *do not* let her out of your sight."

And then I see Marissa. Bending down to pick something up, then laughing as she adjusts the ridiculous square graduation cap on her head.

I exhale a breath I didn't know I held.

"You fucking tell me what's going on, Laina."

"I'll call you right back."

The phone goes dead. Cursing, I shove it in my pocket, keep my head down, and take my place beside Myron, her father. He shoots me a curious look.

I turn my focused gaze on Marissa. She's walking hand in hand with her motherfucking boyfriend now, and I clench my fist. I hate when he touches her and have had to endure night after night watching her sneak away to be with him. I give her a semblance of privacy. His background's clean, but Jesus what I wouldn't give to break his pretty boy nose for coming near her.

He has the fucking balls to shoot me an audacious glare. I glare back, narrowing my eyes on him. He knows I'm watching his every fucking move. The prick swallows hard and visibly pales.

Good.

My phone rings again. I answer on the first ring.

"Yeah."

"Listen to me." It's Laina. "I had to go where no one would hear me. I'm alone but I don't want anyone to overhear. Do you see Myron?"

"Yes," I say, my eyes reluctantly moving from Marissa to Myron.

"I went on a walk just now and overheard a talk between two of his men." Her voice is hushed, shaking. We deal with high stakes in the Bratva, and I know intuitively anything that would send Laina into a panic matters. "He made a deal, Nicolai."

The blood rushes in my ears so hard and fast it's hard to hear her. I know the kinds of deals she could be talking about.

"He's sold her," she says, her voice breaking. "He's put her up for auction. *One week.*"

"Who did?" I want utter clarity.

"Myron," she breathes into the phone. My hands clench into fists of rage so tightly my knuckles turn white. I could kill him, right here, I could beat his motherfucking body to within an inch of his life before I slit his fucking throat.

This can't be. Our brotherhood does not deal with human trafficking rings. There are no auctions with us.

What can she possibly be talking about?

"How do you know this?" I demand. This is no small task she's given me, no small accusation she makes.

"I heard it with my own ears," she says on a shaky whisper. "You have to take her. There's no other way."

Take her? What the fuck is she talking about?

"No," I whisper into the phone. "I can't do that. I'll come home and we—"

"Everything okay, Nicolai?" Myron stands a few feet away, his dark black eyes suddenly looking more menacing than I remember.

Is it my imagination? Or is he really guilty?

Laina would not lie.

"Fine," I tell him. It takes effort to keep my voice steady. "Are we off to the party?"

He's rented a large hall. Food will be catered and he's even hired a live band.

"Yes," he says, and then he reaches for Marissa. He strokes his hand along her hair with a wistful expression and kisses the top of her head. A fatherly gesture, but in light of what Laina's told me, his gesture makes my skin crawl.

"Nicolai," Laina pleads into the phone. "You have to believe me. She's being taken. Groomed. And put up for auction."

"Where?" I ask, rage boiling inside me at the very thought of anyone touching Marissa.

"I don't know," she whispers. "I have to go. *Get her out of there.*"

The phone goes dead.

I look wildly around the auditorium.

If Laina is wrong, my father will lose his mind, and I'll be punished as a Bratva traitor, facing painful, brutal torture and death.

If she's right...

I curse under my breath and follow them to the party.

READ MORE

Beyond Measure: A Dark Bratva Romance (Ruthless Doms)

Tomas

I scowl at the computer screen in front of me. As *pakhan,* the weight of everything falls onto my shoulders, and today is one day when I wish I could shrug it off.

A knock comes at my office door.

"Who is it?" I snap. I don't want to see or hear anything right now. I'm pissed off, and I haven't had time to compose myself. As the leader of the Boston Bratva, it's imperative that I maintain composure.

"Nicolai."

"Come in."

Nicolai can withstand my anger and rage. Over the past few months, he's become my most trusted advisor. My friend.

The door swings open and Nicolai enters, bowing his head politely to greet me.

"Brother."

I nod. "Welcome. Have a seat."

When I first met Nicolai, he wore the face of a much older man. Troubled and anguished, he was in the throes of fighting for his woman. The woman who now bears his name and his baby. But I've watched the worry lines around his eyes diminish, his smile become more ready. While every bit as fierce and determined to dutifully fill his role as ever, he's grown softer because of Marissa, more devoted to her.

"You look thrilled," he says, quirking a brow at me. Unlike my other men, who often quake in my presence, having been taught by my father before me that men in authority are to be feared and obeyed, Nicolai is more relaxed. He's earned the title of *brother* more readily than even my most trusted allies.

"Fucking pissed," I tell him, pushing up from my desk and heading to the sideboard. I pour myself a shot of vodka. It's eleven o'clock in the fucking morning, but it doesn't matter. I've been up all night. "Drink?"

He nods silently and takes the proffered shot glass. We raise our drinks and toss them back together. I take in a deep breath and place the glass back on the sideboard before I go back to my desk.

"Want to tell Uncle Nicolai your troubles?" he asks, his eyes twinkling.

I roll my eyes at him.

I made an unconventional decision when I inducted Nicolai into our brotherhood. The son of another *pakhan,* Nicolai came here under an alias, but I knew he had the integrity of a brother I wanted in my order. I offered him dual enrollment in both groups, under both the authority of his father and me, and he readily agreed. We've come to be good friends, and I would trust the man with my life.

"Uncle Nicolai," I snort, shaking my head. None of my other brothers take liberties like Nicolai does, but none are as trustworthy and loyal as him, so he gets away with giving me shit unlike anyone else. "It's fucking Aren Koslov."

Nicolai grimaces. "Fucking Aren Koslov," he mutters in commiseration. "What'd the bastard do now?" He shakes his head. "Give me one good reason to beat his ass and I'll take the next red-eye to San Diego."

He would, too. Nicolai inspires fear in our enemies and respect in our contemporaries. Aren falls into both categories.

"Owed me a fucking mint a month ago, and hasn't paid up," I tell him. I spin my monitor around to show him the number in red. "And you don't need me to tell you we need that money." As my most trusted advisor, Nicolai knows we're right on the cusp of securing the next alliance with the Spanish drug cartel. Our location in Boston, near the wharf and airport, puts us in the perfect position to manage imports, but the buy-in is fucking huge. We have the upfront money, but the payout from San Diego would put us in a moderately better financial position.

Nicolai leans back in his chair, rubbing his hand across his jawline.

"And you have meeting after meeting coming up with politicians, leaders, and the like."

I eye him warily. Where's he going with this?

"It's easy to say you need money. But that isn't what you need, brother."

I roll my eyes. "I suppose you're going to tell me what I need."

"Of course."

"Go on."

"You know what you need more than the money?" he asks. I'm growing impatient. He needs to come out with it already.

I give him a look that says *spill.*

"You need a wife," he says.

A wife?

I roll my eyes and shake my head. "Sometimes I think your father dropped you on your head as a child," I tell him. What bullshit. I look back at the computer screen, but Nicolai presses on.

"Tomas, listen to me," he says, insistent. "Money comes and goes, and you know that. Tomorrow you could seal a deal with the arms trade you've been working, and you know our investments have been paying off in spades. But a good wife is beyond measure, and Aren has a sister."

"You've been married, for what, two fucking days and you're giving me this shit?" I reply, but my mind is already spinning with what he's saying. I never dismiss Nicolai's suggestions without really weighing my options. Aren is one of the youngest brigadiers in America and has a reputation that precedes him everywhere he goes. He commands men under him, and I'm grateful he hasn't risen higher in power.

He grunts at me and narrows his eyes. "I've loved

Marissa for a lot longer than we've had rings on our fingers."

"I know it, brother," I tell him. "Just giving you shit. Go on."

"Aren's sister is single, lives with him on their compound. Young. I don't know much about her, and haven't seen a recent picture, but I met her years ago when I first came to America. And she was a beauty then. I imagine she's only grown more beautiful."

Seconds ago, this idea seemed preposterous, but now that I'm beginning to think about it, I'm warming to the idea.

"You think he'd let her go to pay off his debt?"

"With enough persuasion? Hell yeah. And a good leader needs a wife. You've seen it yourself. There's something to be said for having a woman to come home to. The most powerful men in the brotherhood are all married."

He's right. Just last week, I met with Demyan from Moscow and his wife Larissa. He brings her everywhere with him. The two are inseparable. And he's risen to be one of the most powerful men the Bratva has ever known.

"And face it, Tomas. You're not exactly in the position to meet a pretty girl at church."

I huff out a laugh. The men of the Bratva rarely obtain women by traditional means.

I lift my phone and dial Lev.

"Boss?"

"Get me a picture of Aren Kosolov's sister," I tell him.

Our resident hacker and computer genius, Lev works quickly and efficiently.

"Give me five minutes," he says.

"Done."

I hang up the phone and turn to Nicolai. "I want to see her first," I tell him.

"Of course."

"How's Marissa?"

He fills me in about home, his voice growing softer as he talks about Marissa, but I'm only half-listening to him. I'm thinking about the way a woman changes a man, and how he's changed because of her.

Do I need a wife?

The better question is, do I want Aren Kosolov's sister to be the one?

My phone buzzes, and Nicolai gestures for me to answer it. A text from Lev with a grainy picture pops up on the screen, followed by a text.

There are no recent pictures. This was from a few years ago, but it should give you a good idea.

Still, it's a full profile picture. I murmur appreciatively. Wavy, unruly chestnut hair pulled back at the nape of her neck, with fetching tendrils curling around her forehead. Haunting hazel colored eyes below dark brows. High cheekbones, her skin flushed pink, and full, pink lips. She's thin and graceful, though if I'm honest, a little too thin for me. The women I bed tend to be sturdier and curvy, able to withstand the way I like to fuck.

288

I don't want to have this conversation via text. I call him and he answers right away.

"Background?" I ask.

"Never went to college. Under her brother's watchful eye since her father died."

"Lovely," I mutter. He might not give her up easily.

"Temperament?" I ask, aware that I sound like I'm asking about adopting a puppy, but it fucking matters.

"Not sure, but she has no record on file at school or legally. Perfect record. Graduated top of her class in high school." He snorts. "Volunteers in a soup kitchen in San Diego and attends the Orthodox Church on the weekend."

Ah. A good girl. Points in her favor. Sometimes the good girls fall hard, and sometimes they're tougher to break, but they intrigue me.

"Boyfriend?"

"None."

"Name?"

"Caroline."

"Caroline?" I repeat. "That isn't a Russian name."

"Her mother was American."

I nod thoughtfully. Caroline Koslov.

She would take my name.

Caroline Dobrynin.

I drum my fingers on my desk, contemplating. I nod to Nicolai when I instruct Lev. "Get Aren on the phone."

The Bratva's Baby (Wicked Doms)

Kazimir

The wrought iron park bench I sit on is ice cold, but I hardly feel it. I'm too intent on waiting for the girl to arrive. The Americans think this weather is freezing, but I grew up in the bitter cold of northern Russia. The cold doesn't touch me. The ill-prepared people around me pull their coats tighter around their bodies and tighten their scarves around their necks. For a minute, I wonder if they're shielding themselves from me, and not the icy wind.

If they knew what I've done... what I'm capable of... what I'm planning to do... they'd do more than cover their necks with scarves.

I scowl into the wind. I hate cowardice.

But this girl... this girl I've been commissioned to take as mine. Despite outward appearances, she's no coward. And that intrigues me.

Sadie Ann Warren. Twenty-one years old. Fine brown hair, plain and mousy but fetching in the way it hangs in haphazard waves around her round face. Light brown eyes, pink cheeks, and full lips.

I wonder what she looks like when she cries. When she smiles. I've never seen her smile.

She's five-foot-one and curvy, though you wouldn't know it from the way she dresses in thick, bulky, black and gray muted clothing. I know her dress size, her shoe size, her bra size, and I've already ordered the type of clothing she'll wear for me. I smile to myself, and a woman passing by catches the smile. It must look predatory, for her step quickens.

Sadie's nondescript appearance makes her easily meld into the masses as a nobody, which is perhaps exactly what she wants.

She has no friends. No relatives. And she has no idea that she's worth millions.

Her boss, the ancient and somewhat senile head librarian of the small-town library where she works won't even realize she hasn't shown up for work for several days. My men will make sure her boss is well distracted yet unharmed. Sadie's abduction, unlike the ones I've orchestrated in the past, will be an easy one. If trouble arises eventually, we'll fake her death.

It's almost as if it was meant to be. No one will know she's gone. No one will miss her. She's the perfect target.

I sip my bitter, steaming black coffee and watch as she makes her way up to the entrance of the library. It's eight-thirty a.m. precisely, as it is every other day she goes to work. She arrives half an hour early, prepares for the day, then opens the doors at nine. Sadie is predictable and routinized, and I like that. The trademark of a woman who responds well to structure and expecta-tions. She'll easily conform to my standards... eventually.

To my left, a small cluster of girls giggles but quiets when they draw closer to me. They're college-aged, or so. I normally like women much younger than I am. They're more easily influenced, less jaded to the ways of men. These women, though, are barely women. Compared to Sadie's maturity, they're barely more than girls. I look away, but can feel their eyes taking me in, as if they think I'm stupid enough to not know they're star-ing. I'm wearing a tan work jacket, worn jeans, and boots, the ones I let stay scuffed and marked as if I'm a construction worker taking a break. With my large stature, I attract attention of the female variety wherever I go. It's better I look like a worker, an easy role to assume. No one would ever suspect what my real work entails.

The girls pass me and it grates on my nerves how they resume their giggling. Brats. Their fathers shouldn't let them out of the house dressed the way they are, espe-cially with the likes of me and my brothers prowling the streets. It's freezing cold and yet they're dressed in thin skirts, their legs bare, open jackets revealing cleavage and tight little nipples showing straight through the thin fabric of their slutty tops. My palm itches to spank some sense into their little asses. I flex my hand.

It's been way, way too long since I've had a woman to punish.

Control.

Master.

These girls are too young and silly for a man like me.

Sadie is perfect.

My cock hardens with anticipation, and I shift on my seat.

I know everything about her. She pays her meager bills on time, and despite her paltry wage, contributes to the local food pantry with items bought with coupons she clips and sale items she purchases. Money will never be a concern for her again, but I like that she's fastidious. She reads books during every free moment of time she has, some non-fiction, but most historical romance books. That amuses me about her. She dresses like an amateur nun, but her heroines dress in swaths of silk and jewels. She carries a hard-covered book with her in the bag she holds by her side, and guards it with her life. During her break time, before bed, and when she first wakes up in the morning, she writes in it. I don't know yet what she writes, but I will. She does something with needles and yarn, knitting or something. I enjoy watching her weave fabric with the vibrant threads.

She fidgets when she's near a man, especially attractive, powerful men. Men like me.

I've never seen her pick up a cell phone or talk to a friend. She's a loner in every sense of the word.

I went over the plan again this morning with Dimitri.

Capture the girl.

Marry her.

Take her inheritance.

Get rid of her.

I swallow another sip of coffee and watch Sadie through the sliding glass doors of the library. Today she's wearing an ankle-length navy skirt that hits the tops of her shoes, and she's wrapped in a bulky gray cardigan the color of dirty dishwater. I imagine stripping the clothes off of her and revealing her creamy, bare, unblemished skin. My dick gets hard when I imagine marking her pretty pale skin. Teeth marks. Rope marks. Reddened skin and puckered flesh, christened with hot wax and my palm. I'll punish her for the sin of hiding a body like hers. She won't be allowed to with me.

She's so little. So virginal. An unsullied canvas.

"Enjoy your last taste of freedom, little girl," I whisper to myself before I finish my coffee. I push myself to my feet and cross the street.

It's time she met her future master.

READ MORE

USA Today bestselling author Jane Henry pens stern but loving alpha heroes, feisty heroines, and emotion-driven happily-ever-afters. She writes what she loves to read: kink with a tender touch. Jane is a hopeless romantic who lives on the East Coast with a houseful of children and her very own Prince Charming.

What to read next? Here are some other titles by Jane you may enjoy. And don't forget to sign-up for my newsletter!

CONTEMPORARY ROMANCE

Dark romance

Island Captive: A Dark Romance

Ruthless Doms

Priceless

Beyond Measure

Wicked Doms

The Bratva's Baby

The Bratva's Bride

The Bratva's Captive

Undercover Doms standalones

Criminal by Jane Henry and Loki Renard

Hard Time by Jane Henry and Loki Renard

NYC Doms standalones

Deliverance

Safeguard

Conviction

Salvation

Schooled

Opposition

Hustler

The Billionaire Daddies

Beauty's Daddy: A Beauty and the Beast Adult Fairy Tale

Mafia Daddy: A Cinderella Adult Fairy Tale

Dungeon Daddy: A Rapunzel Adult Fairy Tale

The Billionaire Daddies boxset

The Boston Doms

My Dom (Boston Doms Book 1)

His Submissive (Boston Doms Book 2)

Her Protector (Boston Doms Book 3)

His Babygirl (Boston Doms Book 4)

His Lady (Boston Doms Book 5)

Her Hero (Boston Doms Book 6)

My Redemption (Boston Doms Book 7)

And more! Check out my Amazon author page.

You can find Jane here!

The Club (Facebook reader group)

Website

Amazon author page

Goodreads

Author Facebook page

Instagram

Made in the USA
Columbia, SC
21 July 2020

14413761R00167